HELLCROSSED

(RAVEN CURSED BOOK 5)

MCKENZIE HUNTER

This is a work of fiction. Names, characters, businesses, places, events, and incidents are either the products of the author's imagination or used in a fictitious manner. Any resemblance to actual persons, living or dead, or actual events is purely coincidental.

McKenzie Hunter

Hellcrossed

McKenzieHunter@McKenzieHunter.com

Cover Artist: Orina Kafe

———

For notifications about new releases, *exclusive* contests and giveaways, and cover reveals, please sign up for my mailing list.

ISBN: 978-1-946457-22-6

ACKNOWLEDGMENTS

"Books are good company, in sad times and happy times, for books are people— people who have managed to stay alive by hiding between the covers of a book." — E.B. White

Each time I complete writing a book in a series, I am reminded that there is an audience ready to read my story. I am forever grateful to have readers invested in Erin's journey. Thank you.

I would also like to extend my appreciation and thanks to Elizabeth Bracker, Márcia Silva, Robyn Mather, Sherrie Simpson Clark, Stacey Mann, and my editors Meredith Tennant and Therin Knite for their help with Erin's adventure.

CHAPTER 1

*W*armth licked at my skin, and the stringent spiced peppery scent swept over me. I was on my hands and knees, the same position I was in when I was clawing for purchase, trying like hell to keep Dareus from sending me to the demon realm. My fingers throbbed, a few nails torn.

A soft melon glow ebbed in from the open windows, providing enough light for me to see that I was in a house, in a bedroom. Whose house? Pulling the blade from my shoe, I felt grateful but too panicked to gloat that it hadn't been confiscated in the search before entering the club. My heart raced; I took slow, controlled breaths in an attempt to steel myself and relax. My palms were sweaty, making it difficult to hold my blade as I stood and took inventory of the bedroom. I swiped my hand across the air, closing the open door. My magic worked! It didn't relieve the ball of tension and anxiety in my stomach, but knowing I had magic eased my fear a smidge.

The room was large and minimally furnished. Four-poster bed, armoire, single nightstand with several books stacked on it. Finding the light switch, I turned it on. Plain beige walls. No pictures, decorations, or any evidence that this room was enjoyed for any other purpose than sleeping. And maybe studying, too. Keeping my blade in my hand, I split my attention between the door and the books on the nightstand. Flipping through the pages revealed drawings of sigils and what looked like spells in an unfamiliar language. Maybe like the elves, demons had their own language.

Moving to the armoire, I discovered a drawer full of men's clothing, and more books. A talisman, a book with runes on it, tannin, salt, fennel, an athame, and a knife with symbols carved into the blade instead of the handle. Curious as to what ceremonial ritual the knife and athame were used for, I picked up the knife because it was larger than the small one I'd gotten out of my shoe. Then I moved through the house. It was a small place, just two bedrooms, modest kitchen, living room, and den that had been converted to a library. Rich wood furniture throughout the home was the only thing that added personality and a hint of warmth to the house. Once I established I was alone, I was able to search more thoroughly.

Immediately, I returned to the library. On the desk next to a stack of books, in large sharp loops, my name was scribbled across a piece of paper. Elven Touched was noted under my name. It had been written with so much pressure, the paper was ripped in places.

I was positive I was in Dareus's home. Where else would that asshole send me? Taking a seat at the desk, I looked through the books. They were all in the unfamiliar language. No help to me.

Moving to the bookcase, I carefully reviewed each book, hoping to find anything in Latin or English that I could understand. There were several in English. The books I wasn't familiar with or didn't already own were my priority.

Plopping down onto the desk chair, I sleeked back the fly-aways from my ponytail and restyled my hair into a bun.

Then I went through the books, reading each spell carefully, hoping to glean something of use. Nothing.

My confidence in my ability to weave a spell together was nil. Dareus gave me the demon mark, but Elizabeth invoked the spell to send me here. I knew the spell had two parts, or else it could be done by anyone, and Elizabeth had wanted the pleasure of sending me to the demon realm.

I stood and paced the room, tracking back and forth, going over the events of that night. My mother had made a deal with Dareus, probably to kill me to amplify her magic so she could create another army. In return, she'd give him access to an elf, who would make him corporeal. The witch body Dareus was using couldn't hold his magic. The deal was supposed to be a neat and tidy bow, constructed by murder and malice.

But learning that my mother couldn't deliver him an elf, Dareus betrayed Malific and allied with Elizabeth. His betrayal had to have stung. That was the only thing that brought me solace. Was the betrayal worth it? She'd make him pay for it. Macabre violence was as much a part of her being as her limbs. She didn't seem to be able to function without it. Or rather she refused to function without it. Violence was as vital to her as air.

Elizabeth, my morally misguided aunt. The only thing keeping her alive was the oath my mother was forced into entering in order to get to me. The oath protected her, Nolan, and the elves. I, however, was excluded from that protection.

Hopelessness had taken up residency. And I was spiraling, letting it overtake me. There had to be something I could do. I was elf and god, and there was absolutely no way I'd be defeated by a demon and a self-righteous elf/fae hybrid.

Reality set in. That was a lot of magic I had to contend with. Then desolation crept in in the longer I paced. A sharp pain shot through me, leaving a husk-like emptiness, at the thought of Mephisto trying to find me. We'd had so little time together. Never given the chance to explore what could have become of us. I shook off the feeling; it was only adding to my despair.

Maddie was probably tearing through the city trying to find out what happened. Did she see what happened? Did they know Elizabeth was involved, or would they only link it to Malific? There were so many unanswered questions.

Waiting for them to help wasn't an option. I needed to find a way out.

The demon mark taunted me along with Elizabeth's parting words. I had to be summoned.

"Nolan will never forgive you for this," I had said in return.

And her response? "He'll never know. You got what you wanted, to be unbound from Malific. I doubt he'd expect you would want any more from him. I've served my purpose to you. Now you'll serve yours to us. Goodbye, Erin."

Her goading about me being arrogant enough to think I could learn to be summoned in order to return... No, I wasn't that arrogant, I was that pissed. Hate and revenge are horrible emotions, but they burned out the despair and were now an inferno rampaging through me.

How does a person come out the other side after matricide? Good question. What becomes of a person after killing her mother *and* aunt? I was going to find out.

The Veil. Maybe I could get back home by way of the Veil. Standing in the middle of the library, I tried to envision it, recalling the first time I went there, unintentionally, after borrowing Mephisto's magic. Stilled in the room, I recounted the times I'd stood in front of Mephisto, his magic pulsing through my body and me being introduced to a new world. One with winged supernaturals, fae, shifters, and magic wielders far more powerful than anything we'd experienced that led to power struggles in the Veil we hadn't experienced in our world.

I took a deep breath and tried to see the diaphanous wall that separated the worlds. I concentrated harder when nothing revealed itself, took breaks to meditate, center myself, improve my focus. I had to do this. Seven attempts left me exhausted. I waited between each one to see if there was a delay. There wasn't. Fatigue was getting the best of me. I needed sleep. Food and sleep. Did demons eat? I pondered, making my way to the kitchen.

If he had a kitchen, he had to eat. Vampires didn't need food, although all the ones I encountered had a kitchen for guests. Dark thoughts of what the demons considered food kept creeping into my thoughts.

To my relief there was food, and it wasn't too offensive. There was a container of pressed meat that looked suspicious and smelled even worse. Some type of salad that gave off strong smells of mustard and pickles. I was hungry enough not to be picky and was about to give it a try, when I found a few eggs, nectarines, and bread.

The egg was larger than the ones in our world and the shell was gray, but it was food and I needed to eat.

I made an egg sandwich, ate it and the nectarine and the canned lentil soup I found in the pantry. There was meat in the freezer and plenty of canned food and rice. As I ate, I wondered if I would be alone in the house for long. Did Dareus live with someone? Would I be accosted while I slept? Everything that had taken place over the last few days was making me overly cautious and paranoid.

Before going to sleep, I shoved the armoire in front of the door. Moving it scratched up the hardwood floors. Admittedly, I hadn't been careful. I looked at the large gouges with satisfaction. The pettiness in me found it comforting enough to find sleep more easily than anticipated.

CHAPTER 2

I awoke to the muted greenish yellow that seemed to be the demon realm's sun. A reminder that I wasn't at home in my bed. The mattress, which was just a mini-step from being as hard as the floor, was another reminder. I searched the room for an extra toothbrush and toiletries. No toothbrush. Brushed my teeth with my finger.

Showering, I washed my hair with the shampoo/conditioner combo I found in one of the drawers in the bathroom cabinets and used the shower gel clearly made by someone who'd never been anywhere near a mountain spring. I didn't feel clean—not the way I wanted. It felt like a film of dark, dank magic sheathed me. It was in the air, remnants of magic that had been performed, probably from answering summons. Which I needed to learn to do, if I wanted to get home. Without knowing demon language, I wasn't sure I could learn to do it.

My panties had dried rather quickly, something I really didn't want to wait on but was forced to after my failed attempts to clothe myself using magic. I rummaged through Dareus's stuff and found a shirt. It was too large, but I cuffed it at the sleeves and tied it at the waist. I considered using his boxers to fashion some shorts but didn't want anything that had been near his demon giblets so close to me. I wasn't that desperate. Yet. The sweatpants I found couldn't be cinched enough to keep from sliding a little whenever I walked, but they'd have to do.

After trying to make sense of the books on the nightstand and reviewing the spell books with fresh eyes, I realized I had to go out in the realm. I had no idea what to look for. A friendly demon. A well-intentioned one. I was likelier to find a friendly one, and his help would come at a cost. I was desperate enough to pay it.

In my makeshift attire, I didn't look like anyone someone would stop and talk to. I looked bad. I usually didn't care about things like that. Yes, my self-awareness was astute enough to recognize that I was procrastinating. I was afraid to go out into this unknown world. It wasn't like going to the Veil, where I had someone on the other side awaiting my return.

Taking in the unkept grass that came up past my ankles, some of it a greenish-brown color, the crowd of trees that obscured the houses behind them, and the stretch of land between the next home, it was debatable whether to find comfort in that. Did I want people aware of my presence in the demon realm?

Instead of going out as a human, I decided a feline would be more discreet. Double-checking the back door to make sure that it was unlocked, I shed my clothes, placing them near the door and setting books on top to prevent them being blown away by the winds that were inconsistent and sporadically high. As if they were coming from both directions, east and west, fighting for dominance. I assumed the erratic winds were indirectly related to magic and something occurring in the realm.

I made my attempt to Wynd, aware that I'd be forced into a cat form. I really wished that the Wynding attempt would lead to me actually doing it, but being a cat here would have its advantages. I could navigate relatively unnoticed. Although as a Maine Coon, it was a little harder to escape notice.

In my feline form, I moved through the streets easier and surer footed. The wind brushed against my fur along with an acrid smell. No one could see my disgust as I passed demons in the forms they used in their realm. I had suspected what we saw was different than what they presented. No one would make a deal with a creature with dark clay, obsidian black, or putrid green leathery skin. And horns. Some horns with spikes and others large and curled in elaborate twists. I had only seen beautifully colored feathered wings that expanded to form a glorious tapestry of color. When demons became tired of walking, they expanded their wings to reveal stretched skin and membrane similar to a bat, complete with an unappealing patchwork of veinlike lines.

Ignore it all, Erin, I directed myself. *I'm looking for a friendly-looking demon.* Which definitely didn't mean they would be a good demon or amenable to helping. Mephisto and the Huntsmen were handsome but ruthless. So were Landon and Asher. Malific could be described as a regal beauty and yet relished in violence the way sommeliers savored wine.

Padding down the street, I wove my way through the neighborhood, each home so far apart that being considered neighbors was a stretch. The homes near Dareus's were dark and there didn't seem to be much activity from the residents. Cautious as I moved through the realm, the home sizes increased. Although the landscape wouldn't be considered vibrant, the dull greens and browns diminished and normal verdant colors appeared, which eased some of my anxiety about being in the unknown place. The homes closer together offered me more cover. Being careful to go unnoticed by the demons in houses where, unlike the homes near

Dareus, the curtains were drawn, increasing the likelihood of me being seen, I slithered around the buildings until concrete and grass gave way to cobblestone as I neared a marketplace.

Quickly padding through the marketplace, I attempted to be unobtrusive. In contrast to the neutral-colored homes, the marketplace was vibrant, each of the shops making an effort to draw attention. Acutely alert of my surroundings, I watched the demons move to and from the few tables outside the stores and buildings. The marketplace was a mixture between a strip mall and flea market. Signage for butchers, specialty shops, and occult stores. The harsh smells wafting from one of the shops singed my nose. It was probably the reason it was the only one with its store door closed. I was on the downdraft when someone opened it. Moving closer, I noticed it was another occult store, one that I was sure participated in the darker elements of demon magic. The very idea of a darker version of demon magic was concerning.

At the end of the block were tables laden with an assortment of wares. I slowed at one table that had nothing but a board with names on them, city location, and what looked like an elaborate rating system. I paused midstride at the sight of Wendy's name, the nefarious, greedy, and powerful witch from the Lunar Marked coven. I didn't want to look conspicuous, taking too long to stare as if I could make sense of the information while in cat form. There were other animals: dogs, rabbits; I'd seen a snake slithering about. No shortage of pigeons or rats. That seemed about right. There were cats too, but none that looked like me—so I stood out. I scuttled along, pausing occasionally when I saw demons interacting.

A group of demons were talking under an awning. I ducked into the alley space between it and the building next to it. Enough light was blocked that I could stay in the shadows and listen to the exchange. English. They spoke in English. Their lovely melodic voices annoyed me the way Dareus's did. The deception of it was off-putting. At least the appealing human form wasn't a stark contrast like their realm form.

Gossip. Nice. And it sounded like they were discussing Dareus. "He told me he had a way out. Had a body that he was almost guaranteed."

"A witch, I was told. One that had a debt owed to him. He was going to get his body."

"Really," said another, fascinated. His lips pulled from his misshapen mouth to form a devious smile. Nothing about it seemed friendly. A maw like that coming at me would instill fear.

The chatter continued, Dareus's escape the main topic. The wistfulness in their voices was undeniable. They appeared fascinated by his ability to negotiate a murder and get a body. The most horrific thing I heard was the whispered suggestion that he might find a way to release them from the demon realm. That was the last thing we needed.

Not only did I need to get out of the realm, if Dareus was sincere about his plans to release demons from their realm, he had to be stopped. Recalling the dark smirk of satisfaction on his face, returning him to the realm was no longer the first thing on my list. Getting rid of him was.

My thoughts were rampant as I trotted back to the house. They spoke English, so there had to be a key to their books. I just had to figure it out. My magic working and the potential for finding a key to the spell books in Dareus's home gave me cause for optimism. Pieces of the spell Elizabeth used came to me. I didn't understand the language—definitely Elven, although I wasn't sure of the words. But it was something.

Thoughts of the Black Crest grimoire flashed in my head. Was it the only one? Could there be something similar here? If so, where would he have hidden it? I had to go through his books again. My movements had quickened to a run as I neared the house, when I was snatched up. A warm leathery body pressed me against it. The stench of sulfur and pepper flooded my nose.

"You don't belong here, do you?" said a gravely, low, refined voice. I wiggled and squirmed while a collar was secured around my neck. It was tight, the pressure of the leather pressing firmly into me. The demon was unaffected by my claws slicing into its skin. My assailant bundled me into a fluffy ball and carried me away from Dareus's home, keeping a firm hold on me as I twisted, contorted, and struggled. It wasn't until I was in the confines of a house that I was released into a living area. A sofa, table, and bookcases lined the wall farthest from the door. A worn writing desk was in the place where most people would have another chair, a place for guests to sit.

My capturer stood in front of me, leathery wings expanded from his carbonite skin. Wide bridged nose, wide expressive eyes framed by thick brows. A ram's horn stretched from the top of his head. The body was human, or as human as one could get with leathery skin. Shirtless, slacks covering the lower part of his body...feet that were a disturbing combination of hooves on human-like feet. His hands shared the same characteristics. Long nails with a slight curve that gave him the dexterity to quickly and efficiently put the collar on me. No wonder demons presented their summoners and potential deal requesters with their palatable human façade, because no one would make a deal with these creatures. Each step he made in my direction, I made one backward. He grinned, exposing jagged sharp teeth.

"I am Asial," he introduced himself in a low, polished voice that was in stark contrast with the creature before me. I didn't think that cats could frown, but my face must have revealed something because his eyes narrowed. His smile melted into a scowl as he gave me a small nod.

Within a blink, he was a man, close to his previous six-four medium build. His carbonite leathered skin now a wintry dusk color. Broad upturned nose. Big gamine eyes that made him look innocuous. It was an appealing look, not quite handsome but a substantial difference from his demon form. His mild appearance didn't make him seem like a threat—and that was the point.

"And you are?" he asked, after making his transformation in less time than shifters took to don their animal form. They did it shockingly quick.

"You can't speak in this form," he noted with a frown. I just stared at him then meowed. I was a cat and he wouldn't be shown otherwise.

His bark of laughter had a low musical sound that came from him with ease. He did it often, as indicated by the creases along his eyes that were obscured when in his demon form.

"I know you're not a cat," he said with sharp bemusement. *Meow. Meow. Freaking Meow. Prove it.*

He shrugged. "You can't change with that collar on, you'll strangle yourself."

He plopped onto the sofa and regarded me for several tense moments. "How did you get here, witch?" He grinned, displaying straight, slightly yellowed teeth often seen with heavy coffee consumption. Demons' attention to detail was uncanny and disconcerting.

"Dareus is gone, you are here. That can't be coincidence… but how did he make the trade?"

"Meow."

He chuckled and gave me a wry smile. He wasn't fooled but I left the burden to him to prove I wasn't just a cat. As he continued to study me, I took inventory of the room, looking for an escape. The windows were small, round, and unusually high. I could get through them in my cat and human body. There was no furniture close to them to leap onto or climb. In human form, I would need a few inches to boost me to reaching distance. Cat form required something to leap from and there wasn't much of a ledge for purchase.

"Oh, kitty, I see you looking for a way to escape. You're going to make it harder than it needs to be."

Moving with an unexpected swift grace, he tried to grab me. I ran, sprinting into another room with him in quick pursuit. I was hoping he'd follow me into it where I could quickly change and hopefully lock him in. What spells did I have to lock the door? But I couldn't change with the damn collar around my neck. I clawed at it, trying to slice through the material. I suspected it was a quick release but with the release on the back of my neck, it couldn't be reached, and it was doubtful I could manipulate it with paws. My claws grated against something underneath the leather. A chain.

"Witch, you are going to make it hard on yourself, aren't you?" he called out after I made my way to the kitchen. On the counter, I was met with the same obstacle of high small windows with minimal ledge. But there was a door. Should I risk changing, hoping if I changed fast enough, the sheer force of the quick change would break through the chain?

Arms crossed over his chest, the demon looked amused at my dilemma. I was about to launch at him and introduce him to a kitty claw hug when he darted out of the kitchen and returned with a cage large enough for a human to be uncomfortably contorted into it.

"Stubborn, stubborn witch," he chided. The magic he slammed into me felt like a taser when it pelted into my stomach mid-lunge as I leapt at him, claws first. I crashed to the ground. He wrangled me into an unbreakable hold and tossed me into the cage.

Slipping his hand through the slim bars, he grabbed for me. I wiggled out of his hold, not wanting him near me.

"Will you hold still for me to remove the collar, or shall I use force?" There was a twinkle in his eyes that made me think he'd prefer the force. He wanted me submissive. I had a hard time being amenable, let alone submissive. Body still aching from his display of magic, I bowed my head. The act made bile creep up my throat, but this was about survival and getting back to my world. "Change," he ordered.

I meowed.

His lips lifted into a smile. "Kittens meow to let their mother know they are cold or hungry. Cats don't meow to other cats. They do it for attention from adults to get what they want. Your meows have no effect on me. You *will* do what *I* want. Not the other way around. Now change," he demanded.

I wasn't about to change for Mr. Cat-Wiki without clothing.

Whether he was good at reading animals or my human expression showed through my feline face, he smiled. It sent chills through me. "A modest human girl."

Woman, asshat. Modest I wasn't, but I wanted clothing, a barrier between injury and the peace of mind that would allow me to think. Moments later he shoved a shirt through the bars.

He waited for me to change, and I waited for him to give me privacy, leaving us at an impasse.

He huffed, slid past the cage, and exited. The change to human was uncomfortable, as was the cramped cage that only allowed space for me to sit with my legs pulled to my chest.

"Well, well, well. How did you—" He stopped abruptly, his eyes landing on my demon mark. He moved his jaw from side to side, a weird movement as if he was chewing on his thoughts.

"That sneak," he ground out. "Always with a magic trick under his sleeves and never one to share. They're foolish if they believe he's looking for a way to break the barrier between us and the demon realm," he said bitterly. Very bitterly. This level of bitterness led to thirst for vengeance. Maybe I could use that.

His pronouncement gave me some relief. I hoped Dareus was that selfish.

"What do you mean?" I asked, my voice hoarse. I didn't realize how thirsty I was. He sensed it. Going to the sink, he brought back a small cup of water and filled it several times until my thirst was quenched.

He showed me a similar marking on him. "It is what keeps us tethered to this realm. We all have them."

"He has a body," I told him. "That doesn't remove the mark?"

He shook his head. "Technically no. When we are being hosted, the mark is suppressed by being in the host. If we get a body, then the mark stays with their shade, once again suppressing it. In the unlikely event something happens to the person's shade, it will force the demon back. He managed to transfer it to you. How did he do such a thing?"

This was getting worse. To leave here, would I have to transfer it to someone else? Or maybe because I wasn't a demon, I wouldn't have to. I decided against asking him for confirmation until I knew he could or would help me.

"How did he do it?" Another musing because he was looking past me in speculation. I quickly squashed the idea of telling him I remembered some of the spell, because I couldn't get out of my mind that he had a human-size cage. What type of sociopath had that?

Might as well find out. "Why do you have a human-size cage?"

He canted his head, regarding the cage as if it was his first time seeing it. *You put me in this damn thing, so clearly, it's not your first time seeing it.*

"Although we've had our share of witches here—well, two

to be exact—I've never been able to cage one." *Great. He wanted to cage a witch, that's not troubling.* "They don't last very long. Once their magic is used up here, they tend to wither away. Fragile things you are."

"Magic used up? What do you mean?"

His smile widened. There was a dark cruelty to him that I needed to keep wary of. "Witches aren't meant to be here, nor your ineffectual peculiar diminutive magic. So it seems like you store some in you, and once it's gone, it's gone."

Crap. Crap. Crap. How much magic had I used unnecessarily over the past day? But I wasn't a witch. Maybe the same rules didn't apply to me. I made a request to the fates it didn't because I was going to need my magic to get out of this mess.

"Why were the witches here? How did it happen?"

"Never found out how the first one got here. She saw us in our form, headed for our woods and, well, the animals got to her." His eyes flicked to me. He wanted a reaction. Fear. I denied him it, schooling a look of impassivity on my face. He tapped on the cage. "That's what this cage is for. I like to hunt —fresh meat is the best." His mouth made a weird movement and when he smiled, he revealed his weird jagged teeth.

I didn't want to think about the sort of wild animals that existed in the demon realm.

"The other witch?"

His eyes rolled. "A feisty one with a vendetta. Her appearance was clearly by accident. Apparently, she couldn't stop her coven from calling on demons, so she tried to find a spell to prevent us from being summoned. Don't know how she did it and was unable to get that information out of her. A powerful witch, it took weeks for her to exhaust her magic. She was all spitfire and retribution. Even when sold at the marketplace, she cursed our existence." The memory brought a smile to his face. "It drove the price up. After all, her submission would be hard earned. Fun for the right person." An easy smile moved over his face. I hated him.

"Did you have fun?" I asked through clenched teeth.

"No, I was outbid. But she didn't last long. Her owner"—I couldn't hide my disgust no matter how I tried—"found that she was more trouble than she was worth. She couldn't be resold, so she was discarded." The flippant way he discussed the murder of a witch caused my fist to ball. That pleased him. He enjoyed breaking people. That strengthened my resolve. He'd break before I did.

He crouched down. "So, my feisty little witch, what should I do with you?" He tapped on his chin in thought. "Marketplace?" He looked over me. "I think you'd get me a good price." More tapping on his squared chin that I wanted to pummel until it caved in.

"You're full of it," I blistered out, my tone steely and cold. He would not get fear from me.

I did a quick assessment of everything I'd learned from him, and my experience dealing with the variations of his type. Same people, just different species. "You're not all about talking but action. If you wanted to sell me at the market-place, you wouldn't be contemplating it. I'd be standing up there being bid on. If you wanted to hurt me, I'm damn sure I'd be hurt. And you seem pretty goddamn envious that shifty-ass Dareus found a way out. That asshole put me here with the help of my aunt."

I had piqued his interest to the point he was leaning forward as if at a movie waiting for the action to begin. My heart fluttered with doubt. The next admission could save me or ensure my death.

"She's an elf. A *powerful* elf." If he could determine a lie, there was none present in my comment. "I don't think Dareus knew how to transfer the demon mark. I believe my aunt showed him how."

I didn't have confirmation of that, but he didn't know

that, and me being the link to him getting out, transferring his mark to someone, would ensure that he needed me. My perceived value would force his assistance and keep me alive.

"But he doesn't need a body. She has the ability to make you all corporeal. Your magic wouldn't be diminished by being in a host. He's alive, in his human-shape body, magically unrestricted."

Hate and envy flicked in his eyes and moved into his expression. The emotions tensed his body. These were emotions I could work with.

Finally, deviance curled his lips. He was interested. No, he was covetous. He'd do anything to have what Dareus had, and that was the craving I needed.

"Not a witch," he said, interest heavy in his eyes.

"Not a witch," I repeated. The god part and the human part I left out. It was doubtful either one held interest for him because it was elven magic could make him corporeal in my world, allowing him to live without the use of another body.

The calculating look only confirmed it. "You can get me out of here?" he asked.

"I can," I lied. Wasn't really a lie, just an incredible play on the truth. Creative license with it. "I can make you corporeal. I can't do it here. Help me get out of here and I'll force my aunt to make you corporeal, or I'll figure out a way to do it myself. My magic can do it."

His eyes narrowed with suspicion.

"Are you willing to make a demon's oath to that promise?"

Of course it wouldn't be that easy. What about a pinky swear? Make the agreement now and worry about finagling out of it later, I told myself.

I nodded. "But only after we have confirmed I can get out of here."

"Of course." Pulling the key out of his pants, he started to

18

unlock the cage but stopped. Baring his jagged, flesh-ripping teeth, he snarled, "Don't make me regret trusting you, not-a-witch."

What was his weird obsession with witches? Just call me a freaking elf. "Erin," I provided. "I'm Erin."

His expression didn't change with the introduction. In fact, it seemed to make him surlier. Cold, calculating eyes bored into me. "Don't make me regret trusting you, *Erin*."

"Look, I regularly fight with the Alpha of the local pack, I've had gods try to kill me, the last time I worked with the vampire who controls our city I gave him the finger, and I've beaten a murder rap. I don't cower easily, so don't threaten me. I assure you, there are no words to express how much I want to exact revenge on Dareus, and if making a deal with you is how I do it, I'm the ally you want."

His eyes raked over me. The dagger teeth melted away to his human ones and an enthusiastic smile replaced his glower. Pettiness, envy, and thirst for revenge were emotions you could always count on to make strange bedfellows.

"Are you hungry?" he asked, unlocking the cage and stepping aside to let me out. Stretching my legs, I considered everything he told me earlier about liking fresh meat and the animals in the demon world he ate and decided against it. Not hungry enough.

"Let's figure out how to get *me* out of here—*us*, out of here."

CHAPTER 3

*I*f I was under any illusion that Asial could be kind or that there wasn't something dark about this demon, they vanished when he provided me with clothing. Three shirts that could have been a smidge larger, three pairs of joggers, and underwear. A fiendish smirk lifted the corners of his human lips when he offered me a dark green puff-sleeved shirt with a coven's crest stitched in it. Some witches did that as a reminder of their commitment to their coven, to keep them grounded. If they were performing complicated magic, some believed having their coven crest was a source of strength. Most had it in the form of a bracelet or charm. Cory had dismissed it as nothing more than superstition. This offering was rooted in Asial's malevolence. A reminder of a witch who was here before me. A thinly veiled threat.

Without giving him the response of fear that he wanted, I took the clothing back to Dareus's, confident that Dareus wasn't coming back and that he lived alone. If he didn't live alone, I'd rather hedge my bets against an unknown stranger than Asial.

"Have you given anyone your demon name so they can

summon you?" I asked, a comfortable distance from Asial. Despite him keeping his human-like form, I knew what he looked like and had an idea of the menace he was capable of. I sat at the writing table. It hadn't escaped me the skeevy way he kept looking at me in the too-small clothes.

He nodded, leaning back on the sofa.

"Plenty." He made a face. "I don't think you understand how infrequently we are called upon," he admitted.

We definitely had a different definition of what was considered infrequently. Dealing with demons made a magic wielder a dark practitioner, but I'd recently discovered that there was a caveat. More witches dealt with demons than I'd suspected, yet none of them considered themselves dark practitioners but rather explorers of magic, or magically resourceful dabblers in diablerie, or other innocuous descriptors. Attributing only death and blood loss the darker elements.

"How often are you summoned?"

"Maybe twice a month. But I'm not sure if you'd be able to respond with me."

Twice a month. I could be here for months.

"General summons might be the best route." He frowned. "Those are very hard to answer. There are hundreds of us vying for that spot, trying to answer. My response time is fast but there are others who manage to beat me." His brows inched closer. "Do you know how to respond to a summons?"

That was the issue. Elizabeth had berated me for being arrogant enough to believe I could. It wasn't arrogance, it was hope. Without anyone knowing where I was, I couldn't even stay optimistic that they would know how to find me.

I shook my head.

"Feeling the summons isn't the hard part. It's the answering that becomes difficult."

He moved closer. His lips twisted. He opened and closed

21

his mouth several times. I suspected he was searching for the right way to describe how it felt.

"It's a squeeze, maybe a clench. If you are being summoned, the location is revealed to you once you answer it—the summoner has an undeniable denotation. You'll know."

"But sometimes you won't answer." I remembered how Mephisto's summons went unanswered. Thinking of him brought a small ache in my chest. It was an ongoing task not to think about him, my family and friends. The last thing I needed to do was work off emotions or spiral from it. Mephisto. It was just the beginning of whatever was happening between us and never before had I been so curious as to how the relationship would progress. Craving someone so much couldn't be good, yet I did. Having denied it for so long, it was freeing to give in to it.

"If the magic feels peculiar or is an unknown, we don't. It's best not to put yourself in unfamiliar situations." I didn't press for more information. I didn't know if they knew of gods and decided not to answer their summons or had a self-protective aversion to the unknown.

Asial stood, shedding his human form and walking the length of the room tapping his claw against his chin. "I think it would be best if we establish if you can answer a summons with me."

"How do I do that?" I asked.

His face contorted in derision before tsking me. His clawed hand waggled at me. "First things first. The oath. If you are able to answer summons, we are partially there."

It wasn't as if he'd forget. I had agreed to it, but seeing him produce the paper out of the ether and hand it to me was a testament to how eager he was to get out of the realm. Taking the paper, I read over the ironclad agreement that didn't offer room for interpretation, maneuverings to break it on a technicality, or exceptions. The oath even prohibited transferring the oath, something I hadn't considered. It bound me to a person, not a name—something I had considered. When I got to the part that bound me to serve as a host if he wasn't made corporeal within thirty days of me leaving that realm, he pointed his claw in my direction. "No part of it is negotiable," he said. His tone was taut with determination. Stone-cold eyes held mine.

Sucking in a ragged breath, I reviewed the oath again and went through all the options I had. Could I figure out how to answer summons on my own? Did I really want to deal with the consequences of reneging on an agreement and making him an enemy? Looking in his direction, I met his eyes and saw the pitiless maliciousness that lurked in them.

"I wouldn't expect it to be any other way." I gave him a weak smile. "I need a pen."

Giving me a long measuring look, a dark amused smile tugged at his lips. "You are a wily one, aren't you?" He moved closer to me, snatched my hand, and slowly and with obvious pleasure, showed me how sharp his claws were, sliding one across my index finger and slicing open the skin.

"Sign it," he demanded, flint cold eyes searing into me.

Despite knowing I didn't have any options, I still hesitated. Signing my name to it, I felt the blood binding of the oath cocoon around me and the gossamer link of the bond.

With a broad smile, he took it from me, taking several steps back as if he expected me to snatch it away. His lips moved as he invoked a spell, causing the oath to vanish.

Pacing the room in thought, he stopped periodically to ask me to tell him everything that occurred prior to me being banished.

He frowned at the mark. "You will be answering summons with me. We will travel together. When I answer a summons, you'll maintain your body because you aren't a demon," he surmised. "Once we are summoned, you need to convince the summoner to break the circle and let you out."

"If they break the circle, it will let you out in the process," I offered.

He nodded once. "That would be quite advantageous for both of us. And if it is someone who has hosted me before, there will be a connection and..." He let the remainder of the sentence linger. Apparently, he found suggesting murder far more distasteful than facilitating it.

If only the people who hosted a demon knew that the link they established with the demon was more dangerous than any potential damage their body could suffer from misuse by the demon. They made themselves vulnerable and a potential temporary host until they found a way to become corporeal. And the only thing preventing it was the demon finding someone willing to murder on their behalf.

"I'm not killing anyone."

"It would be an act of good faith. A temporary body until mine is corporeal."

"That's not part of the deal."

He growled his displeasure and with a look of contempt.

Slipping into his human form, he plunked onto the sofa. "Now it's just a waiting game," he told me, patting the area next to him.

The wait wasn't long, just twenty minutes. The only thing I had to guide me was him growling out a word I didn't understand and roughly grabbing my hands, his soot-laced magic spinning around me, connecting me to the power word. After being ripped from the sofa, his frenetic magic crackled around me. I was out of the realm and locked within the circle.

It took a few moments for my vision to clear and my mind to settle. Excitement had me inching too close to the confines of the demon circle, but an electric charge of pain shot into me, rebounding me back. The circle didn't look like others I'd seen. The person who summoned us had taken extra precautions. Taking in his ivory-colored skin, shaggy, dark copper-colored hair, and ink crawling over his arms and a few tattoos lacing around his fingers, my recognition came before his: Trace, the witch who attempted to give me to Dareus in exchange for the Black Crest grimoire. Mephisto had threatened him but not before I'd made my displeasure with him known.

At least he'd learned from our first encounter to make his demon circles stronger. He was now overly cautious and scrutinizing the appearance of what he probably considered two demons showing up. It was obvious that he didn't consider this situation fortuitous. Frowning, he shook his head and waved a dismissive hand in our direction.

"No," I pleaded, attempting to step closer to the circle's edge, only to be thrashed back by the circle's magic. Experiencing the same gut-wrenching feeling of struggling for nonexistent purchase. Desperately trying to stay anchored and failing.

The hours ticked by and we encountered a number of failures, not for the lack of being summoned. We weren't fast enough. There were far more people interacting with demons than I would have ever suspected. It made me simultaneously hopeful and discomforted by the number of witches who'd never claim they were dark magic practitioners but definitely were.

By the time I encountered their weird-colored nightfall, I'd had my share of being around Asial, and there hadn't been a summons for several hours.

"I'll be back tomorrow," I said in a tired, defeated voice. It had been a crap day and I was spiraling into despair.

CHAPTER 4

Over the span of a week, we answered six summons and each one withdrew their summons at the sight of seeing two. Apprehension pulled quizzical looks to their faces. To one of them, I was able to explain I wasn't a demon. The unyielding sneer of disbelief was quickly followed by sending us back. I was never given a chance to offer an explanation. Summoning one demon and getting what looked to be two was proving to be a bigger problem than I thought.

Being around Asial so much provided me with details about demons that I could happily live a lifetime not knowing. They needed to eat, but their meat wasn't like ours. They consumed a variety of eggs, but there wasn't any way to pretend the speckled orange-and-black shell the size of an ostrich egg came from a chicken. The cheeses…well, I just continued to pretend it was from cow milk although nothing about the texture or the smell would support that. And I hadn't been hungry or convincing enough to my palate to eat the creature Asial had prepared. The variations of berries that existed in the demon realm was surprising. I was subsisting on familiar fruit more than anything.

"I think I need to answer summons alone," I told him as we stood outside. I was making a concerted effort to ignore whatever lurked in the forest. It wasn't just the sounds that came from the woodland, or the red eyes of whatever creature skulked in the tall grass that was more akin to a jungle than a forest. The unusual lack of light was always creepy, but going outside was the only alternative if I wanted a change of scenery. Asial had an aversion to being at Dareus's home; the hate ran deep. My demon ally had made it quite clear that keeping my presence in the realm hidden would be to my advantage. I didn't consider him trustworthy, but based on the fate of the others who had entered the realm, I took his advice.

With narrowed cool eyes, he closed the few inches between us, examining me with a suspicious speculation. He was always watching as if he couldn't trust me. He wasn't wrong. There was something cruel and unsettling about him, and I had agreed to release him in our realm, and I didn't want to. *Focus, Erin. That is a problem for another day. It was your only option.*

"What are you trying to pull, Erin?"

Backing away, I shook my head. "Nothing." I remained on high alert anytime we neared the forest, fully aware I was prey to the creatures in it. Based on the meats and stews Asial always had available, the animals were prey to him.

"You need me to notify you when there's a summons."

I let him believe that. I'd learned that summons caused an atmospheric change. The peculiar dominating winds that I'd noticed only occurred right before Asial informed me there was a summons. First time might have been a coincidence, the fourth time, it was safe to assume it was a pattern. Along with the distinctive spicy smell that inundated that air, I was confident I could determine when a demon was summoned. The scent wasn't something the demon had noted, nor the change in the air. He'd not made the association. But it was about survival for me, so I noticed everything. Especially how effortlessly the demons held their alternative form and slipped in and out of it with the ease of removing a shirt. He'd now donned his demon form and the razor-sharp claws.

"If I don't go with you, then you will be pulling from your finite well of magic," he countered.

I knew that and didn't want to exhaust it and be here without magic, which was why even with the knowledge of knowing when a demon was summoned, I hadn't tried it alone.

"Is there any way I can answer a summons for you?" He'd only answered one in the time I'd been with him. He shook his head. There had to be an easier way. "In the marketplace, there was a list of names and locations. What was that for?"

A sly smile skipped over his lips. "Just information."

"What type of information?"

Giving me an assessing look, his odd demon mouth twisted in consideration. "Different things. Those with weak circles. Potentials," he offered cryptically.

"Potentials for what?" He shrugged a response, and I was confident he meant potential hosts or people they thought would help them find a body.

"Then we don't have any options other than me going at it alone," I concluded.

His sharp, narrow-eyed look remained on me as he backed away and went to the house, returning with a notepad with a word scribbled on it.

"Here." He shoved the paper at me. "Say this."

"Ocolesi." He corrected me until I said it correctly.

"What does this mean?"

"It will allow you to answer a summons."

I wanted to learn more about the demon language, but Asial didn't seem to want to help me with that.

"The meaning," I repeated.

"Just say it," he said through gritted teeth. "This will allow you to answer a summons. You must be quick," he explained.

He shot me a dark look that silenced further questions. We waited, his bemused eyes monitoring the activities of the creatures who populated the area behind me. I palmed the small knife that I'd removed from the shoes I had on when I entered the realm. It was to ward off any attacks from the forest creatures, but the more pernicious his looks became, the more I wondered if he'd be on the receiving end of the small but dangerous blade.

"Now!" he blurted. I didn't react immediately and hoped the wasted time hadn't cost me.

Despite using my magic to answer the summons, there was something dank to it. Filtered through the demon realm made it seem off-putting. I wondered if it was something that the summoner would notice. Would it work to my advantage or disadvantage?

The man on the other side ran his hand through his violet-colored hair. Bright body art ran along the outside of his arm. Stud nose ring. Piercing amber eyes studied me with wariness. Pale, wheat-colored skin held a flush to it. Fear. Maybe shame. There was hesitation as he inched closer to the circle.

"I was expecting something different," he admitted. He was a first-time summoner. This could be a good or bad thing.

"I need your help," I blurted a little too aggressively because he backed away several feet. "I'm not a demon," I explained.

His lips beveled into a frown of disbelief. As if he was expecting deception and I hadn't disappointed.

"You're not a demon, but you came when I summoned one?" His response was smug and his expression full of doubt.

"I know it's hard to believe, but someone exiled me to the

demon realm." A spark of fear moved over his face, then disappeared. It had to be harrowing to know that was possible.

"I know it seems unlikely. I get it. My name is Erin Jenson. If you contact Madison Calloway, she's the Runes and Recovery of STF, or Cory Keats, they'll tell you I've been missing for a little over a week."

He took more hesitant steps away and reading his expression became harder. It was blank for a moment before he twisted his lips to the side. He shook his head. Of course he'd be hesitant to find someone for me, because then he'd have to admit to dealing with demons and darker magic.

"They won't tell that you summoned a demon, I swear to you." My promise meant nothing to him, because as far as he was concerned, I was a demon attempting to trick him.

I considered showing him my mark, but how would that convince him, since demons all had them? He probably wasn't even aware they had them. "What do you need to convince you?" My mind was a frantic whir. Who would he trust? "You're a mage?" I guessed, glancing at the symbol for their god, Prae.

I was losing him. "What's your name?" I asked, desperation thick in my voice.

"I'm not going to give you that," he snapped.

"A demon can't do anything with a name," I told him in a tight voice as I attempted to keep the frustration out of my voice. My fear and distress probably made me look rabid. "Asher," I blurted. Maybe he'd feel more comfortable telling a magic non-wielder. Everyone knew the Alpha; he made a point of it. "The shifters' Alpha. Will you contact him?"

"You want me to contact the Alpha of the Northwest Pack and tell him what?"

"That I'm in the demon realm. He'll let people know."

He frowned. "Maybe you're telling the truth, but I don't want to get involved."

His mouth opened. He was about to send me back. A raw feeling of helplessness had me launching at the circle, only to be rebounded back. "Break the circle. I'm not a demon. Break the fucking circle," I demanded. "Please don't—"

Asial shared in my disappointment as I slumped to the ground where I'd started and blinked back tears. Each failure meant he wouldn't leave the realm, either.

I won't be defeated. How could I convince them of who I was? Who did I know who would instill confidence in the summoner?

CHAPTER 5

$\mathcal{I}$ had been in the demon realm for two months. My efficiency at answering summons had improved. Over the last three days I had answered four. My ability to answer summons without Asial prompted me stay outside the majority of the time, allowing myself two to three hours a day to be available for summons. The lack of sleep was affecting my tolerance and patience, which I needed, along with the astute gift of persuasion to get out of the realm.

"Do you have a phylaca urn?" I blurted to the summoner. None of the scripts I created to use on the summoners had worked. No one was willing to contact Madison, Cory, or even Asher. I even evoked Mephisto's name, but he wasn't as known in the crowd who were summoning demons unless they were several shades of shady with an impressive bank account to match. The magical elite were his crowd.

Never trust a demon was the belief that most carried. I answered a summons; they were convinced I was a demon trying to trick them. They all regarded me with wary suspicion.

"What?" asked the wiry Latin woman in front of me. Definitely a witch. A powerful one with a curt disposition.

"I'm not a demon, but if you don't trust me, put the phylaca urn near the circle and open it and use it to capture me," I implored. Asial was confident I would be corporeal because that's the way I started.

Her brows drew together. I was giving her homework? Not likely.

"I have one and I'll give it to you," I told her. She hadn't reared back like the others, which made me optimistic. "In my apartment, there's one. You can have it. Once you realize I'm not a demon, it's yours. They sell for a lot of money."

"So you can't get me a Denuck," she asked, interest in this situation, in me, seeping from her expression.

"No, I can't get you that. I'm not a demon and why the hell are you trying to get hold of the dark spells found in them? Are you trying to animate people, animals, things?" I asked. *Don't chastise her. Don't judge, Erin. You need her.*

Her lips tightened into a thin rigid line.

"I can try to help you, but I need you to let me out. Break the circle."

"I should have the phylaca urn first, right?"

I nodded.

"And the Denuck?"

"I can try. If you tell me what you need it for, I'll do what I can to help you. You'll get what you want, which I assume is any spell in that grimoire, and a phylaca urn, and you won't have to make a deal with a demon. The urn can be sold for close to ten grand."

I shuddered at what I'd paid Maddox, the dragon shifter, for it, to use against Dareus.

"So I will have to find a way into your *apartment.*" She scoffed. "Obtain the phylaca urn. Then release you from the circle and hope that you can help me with the Denuck?" Derision and incredulity had pulled a rigid grimace to her face.

"You're going to be compensated for it."

"How will I get into your apartment?"

"My sister has a key," I blurted. "Maddison Calloway."

As soon as I said the name, I watched the witch turn the name over in her mind, trying to figure out where she'd heard it. My failure was painful as the realization of who Madison of the STF was showed on her face. I'd asked a witch to get a key from Madison, after summoning me to request a highly illegal Denuck grimoire, to allow her to probably do an equally illegal animating spell.

I wasn't given a chance to make an appeal before she whispered the spell to send me back.

Lying back on the rough grass, anger, thirst for revenge, and despair warred in me. The only comfort I found was the violence I planned to exact on Elizabeth and Malific. Depraved cautionary tales would be told about me. People would part when they saw me, fearful of my wrath. I didn't care that these were the fever dreams of a psychopath. I wanted vengeance. I deserved it.

Crescent-shape indentations marked my palms from clenching my fists. My breaths were ragged and shallow as I inhaled the acrid air. I tried to cling to a tendril of hope, but it was fading fast. This could not be where I spent my final days. It just couldn't be.

"I thought you'd be gone by now, working on a plan to renege on your oath."

I sat up to see Asial in his demon from. The accusatory scowl never really left his face. It dampened but was never absent.

"The oath is binding," I reminded him. I hated the weak, desolate sound of my voice. It even gave him pause.

"I want out, Erin. You're not giving up, are you?" He narrowed his eyes on me as if he saw his chances of escaping the realm being whittled down with my confidence.

Shaking my head in response was all that I could muster.

"Ah, that's why we've seen you so infrequently," said a

voice behind me. It was deep, with a rough timbre, but not unpleasant by any means. I was sure the owner was the opposite. Discreetly, I palmed the athame I'd borrowed from Dareus's room, then stood and turned around.

Asial was tall. This demon was massive, both in a bulkier powerful build, and a height that had Asial by over a foot. His leathery skin was a putrid green. Ridges above his brow seemed sharp enough to cut, giving him an alternative to skewering a person if by some chance the horns didn't impale you. I desperately wanted to see his more palatable human form because his demon one made every alarm ring and urge me to run.

The violence that existed between the two was palpable. Asial regarded him for only a moment before focusing on the unleashed red-eyed animal at his side. Thick fur and its massive size reminded me of a Tibetan mastiff. But that was where the similarities ended. It bared razor-sharp teeth. A spike, which was a distorted version of a horn, protruded from the middle of his head. Back and forth whipped a long leathery tail that could easily be used as a whip and, depending on the control of it, to subdue someone.

"Sariez," Asial bit out through clenched teeth. "This is not your property. Leave."

Sariez frowned. "It's not yours, either, and based on the contentious relationship you had with Dareus, you'd never step foot near his property, nor would he want to find you on it. So"—his eyes snapped to me—"I assume he's not coming back." The new arrival inched in my direction. I gripped the athame tighter, unsure how much force it would take to penetrate the thick layers of skin and even if it felt pain the way our skin did. It had to. I hoped like hell it did.

"I believe it's because of our new guest," he cooed. The demon dog padded by his side. I inched back, keeping my weapon at my side, ready to strike if necessary.

"Mine," Asial hissed. I wasn't happy where this was going.

"Yours?" Sariez quipped with dark amusement. There was something insidious and suggestive in his words. "You never gave anyone a chance to claim her. No bidding? How selfish of you."

My stomach became queasy. Could he force Asial's hand and make him do it? Was that part of their law, a social norm, or a tacit agreement among the demons?

"Go away," Asial bit out through clenched teeth.

"Hmm. I heard what you said to her." He stalked too close. Just inches away. I prepared to defend myself as he canted his head and scrutinized me. "How will you help him out of here?"

Refusing to cower at his imposing presence, no matter how much it elicited such a response, I squared my shoulders and stood taller. He reached out to touch or grab me, but Asial's body collided with him, his claws slashing into Sariez's neck. Deep blackish-red fluid oozed from it. They could bleed, but the level of force needed to cause it was concerning. I watched the dog, whose red eyes homed in on me.

As the violence unfolded, I had no idea who was winning. Sariez had secured some distance between them. He charged at Asial, impaling him with his horns. Asial pounded his fists into Sariez's back and rained more powerful blows into his side. Between Sariez's attempts to dodge the hits, Asial managed to pull away from the horns, his wings spanning out, and he weakly winnowed into the air with great effort. They were both injured, but I couldn't determine if the wounds were fatal.

Asial's death would void my oath with him, but if I couldn't find a way to get out of the demon realm and Sariez survived, could I strike the same deal with him or would he sell me at the market? My heart was hammering so violently that I nearly missed the change in the atmosphere and the accompanying scent of the summons. I whispered the power word and swept away just as the demon dog's tail whipped in my direction.

CHAPTER 6

*R*ealizing that I had managed to answer the demon
summons and avert the attack by the demon dog
had me sagging into a sigh of relief. Then I nearly let out a
squeal of joy when I saw Wendy on the other side of the
circle. Confusion ignited on the avaricious witch's face. She'd
summoned a demon and got me instead.

"What?" Her brows knitted together. "How did you get
here?"

"It's a long story. I need you to remove the circle. Let me
pass." Instead of moving closer, she stepped back. "Wendy,
please," I tacked on weakly. "Please. I really need you to do
this. It's a long story and I can explain it later. But I need to
get out of this circle. It's a matter of life and death." I needed
this so much I wasn't above dropping to my knees in
supplication.

She eased closer, still scrutinizing me with skepticism.
My heart pounded. Over two months, and one slide of
Wendy's foot over the circle and it could possibly be over.
The constant disappointment had left me drained and I
wasn't sure how I'd survive another.

She hesitated. "Are you a demon?"

"No, I was cast here by another demon. I have the marking like theirs but I'm not one."

She stared at the floor, clearly in thought. "Won't you be incorporeal when you cross over?" she asked. She didn't care about that; she just didn't want me to try to use her body as a host.

"Even if I was, you'd have to agree to do a *Gavale Bradish* atropism, to offer your body as host."

Being incorporeal was something I feared as well, but I wasn't a demon; I just bore the mark. If a witch could move from our world to the demon realm, it had to work in reverse.

I admit, fatigue, hopelessness, and desperation had taken its toll. I was folding into myself, without the strength to even take the harsh rebound of being in the circle.

Calculation flitted across her expression and dwelled in her eyes. "What are you, Erin?" she asked, just mere centimeters from the binding circle she refused to break.

"Will you keep the information between us?"

She gave a noncommittal nod. She didn't have an obligation to secrecy. My only hope was the leverage it provided would encourage her to do so. Perhaps it was time to reveal myself.

"A demi-elf or demigod. Everyone seems to have their individual preference as to my designation."

Her eyes widened and for a brief moment, I got the odd impression she was going to bow or show some signs of reverence. Excitement brightened her usually puckered expression. "I knew you weren't a mage. I knew it!" Her feet slipped over the barrier, breaking the circle.

Falling face forward, exhaustion and raw diablerie magic took over. The world whirled around me.

"Thank you," I breathed out before darkness took over.

"Erin." Cory's voice was a ragged whisper, tearing through the darkness. I cracked my eyes a little and could see his shadowy face through my lashes. He came into focus when I widened my eyes.

"You're here." His voice broke as he pulled me to him. His hug was bone-crushingly tight but welcome. So very welcome.

"Why am I on the floor?" I asked, looking around the unfamiliar room. Wendy was standing at the door.

"That's where you landed and I didn't want to touch you. After you passed out, your arm turned a burnished orange and black soot rose from your body. I didn't want to be exposed to whatever it was, so I left the room," she admitted, glancing at Cory, perhaps to check for any adverse reaction to being so close to me.

No one is going to accuse you of being a hero, are they?

I glanced down at my arm. The demon mark was gone. That explained the burnished glow. I wasn't sure if it would return to Dareus, alerting him to my escape and letting him know I'd be coming for him. It was very satisfying to think he might be a little afraid, maybe even panicking. Unfortunately, in place of the mark was a thin, interlocking, charcoal-colored ring around my wrist. My oath to Asial. He'd survived his encounter with the other demon.

Cory raised his eyebrows at the oath mark. I gave him a weak smile. "I'll explain later." From my expression, he had to gather that it wasn't something I wanted to discuss around Wendy.

"Ready to go to the car?" Cory asked, extending his hand and hauling me up to stand. I was wobbly from nutritional deficiency and limited sleep. For the last couple of months, I had been fueled only by tenacity, determination, anger, and thirst for revenge. A person can only thrive on it so long, and I had met my limit.

He slipped his arm around my waist.

"Want me to carry you?" he whispered.

"A thousand nos. Just give me a few moments."

"I've missed you," he admitted.

My stomach grumbled and my eyes were heavy, but I made it to the door where Wendy stood, still keeping a cautious distance from me.

"I hope you'll remember this," she said. Translation: She'd definitely expect a favor in return.

"Of course." I'd ignore the fact that Wendy seemed to deal with demons often. At what point was she considered a dark practitioner?

"Where do you want me to take you? You can stay with me. I only have the one bed, but it's yours if you want. I can't imagine you want to stay alone. Or Madison's? She's at work, but I'll—" He frowned. "Your purse and phone were found at the club, so you don't have keys, do you?"

I shook my head. "No phone or keys or ID. I presume I don't have a home to go to. I haven't paid my rent in over two months."

Cory grinned. "No, you definitely have a home. I went to pay it and apparently you had an abundance of people vying to keep you housed. The business office seemed quite amused by it. Mephisto beat me, Madison, and Asher to it. You're fine for the year."

Damn. I couldn't imagine how it had to feel for them, giving in to the idea I might be gone for a whole year.

CHAPTER 7

During the drive home, Cory managed to withhold his questions but was unable to resist several furtive concerned glances. Madison was skilled at containing her emotions, giving a look of stoicism as the world burned. An ability I was sure she put to great use during my absence. Seeing me caused it to fall away. Her lips parted, but the words didn't come as she took a shaky breath and made an attempt to greet me. A withering rasp left her before she launched at me to give me a hug, her body leaning into me. I could feel the toll my absence had taken on her.

"You made it back," she said, shifting but refusing to fully take her hands off me.

"Not without consequences," I admitted, causing a flash of worry in her eyes.

"Are you hurt?" she asked, taking appraisal of me before running her hands over my shoulders and arm, followed by a cursory look at my lower extremities.

I shook my head, but she stepped away and frowned at my appearance. I had lost weight, hadn't cared for my hair the way I should have, and the products in the demon realm and the soot-like magic that lingered made me feel grimy, even though I didn't think I looked that way.

"You're okay?" she asked. The affirmation came but not very convincingly. Something made her leave it at that. Maybe not wanting me to relive it before I had a chance to surround myself in familiarity. Opening the door of my apartment, with Cory and Madison behind me, the magnitude of everything hit me. I was home. A cleaner, lemon-scented, fluffed-pillow, everything neatly placed version of my home. Looking over my shoulder, I couldn't tell who had buried their frustrations in cleaning my apartment. I simply offered a thank you.

I was more appreciative of them not bombarding me with questions. Based on how I'd returned, I was sure they had an idea of where I'd been.

My emotions bounced between the delight and relief of being home and the overwhelming fear of what awaited me now that I had returned. Madison slipped my phone, which had somehow managed to survive, into my hand. Unlocking it, I glanced at the notifications.

"Don't call our parents," Madison advised, knowing that a significant number of the notifications were missed calls and messages from them.

"Why not?"

Eyes cast to the floor, her shoulders sagged in a sigh. She ran her fingers through the coils of hair where her natural copper color was inching out from the dark color she'd dyed it.

"I didn't want them to worry, so I told them you were on a job and communication with you was limited." Her lips tightened. We never lied to our parents. Not blatant lies. We definitely peddled in omissions, redirection, and provided information on an as-needed basis.

Nodding, I gave her a pensive smile of understanding,

fully aware of what she'd gone through over the last two months dealing with our parents and searching for me.

The silence was thickened by curiosity, but I needed a moment. Reluctantly, they nodded their understanding when I told them I needed a shower. Not just to wash away the remnants of the demon realm but also to process all that had transpired before having to retell it.

"Food?" Cory asked.

"Pizza."

In my bedroom, I looked at the vast number of notifications on my phone. I had calls and messages from Asher and Landon, messages for jobs, more than half of the calls were from my parents and my secondary parents, but nothing from Nolan. Why not? I called him first. It went straight to the automatic response provided when a person hadn't set up a personalized response. My next call was to Mephisto.

"Erin." His voice was rough and anxious.

"Hi." It was all I could manage as I slumped against the closed bedroom door.

"Where are you?" he rushed out. There was rustling in the background that sounded like he was putting on his jacket, making his way through the house.

"Home. I'm safe. Here with Cory and Madison."

There was a short silence. "Do you need time?"

I did. I wanted time with Cory and Madison, but I wanted him here when I was going over the events in the realm. I only wanted to relive that once. "I'd like you to be here...I don't...I'll tell everyone at once," I managed.

"Of course." We should have disconnected, but neither one of us seemed capable of doing so. The silence, his silence, filled a void I wasn't aware existed. "I'll see you soon." Then we disconnected.

Before heading to the shower, I debated whether to send a message or call Asher. I settled on messaging him, leaving me with the advantage. No comments from him about the changes in my breathing or noting what he gathered from the modulation or lilt in my voice.

"I'm home," I messaged.

"Home?" The response was immediate. Then another message quickly followed. "Is that all you plan to tell me?"

"No. We'll talk later."

"Later today?"

"No. Later. Tomorrow, maybe. It's complicated and I have a lot of fires to put out."

"I'm a fire station," he shot back. Of course he felt the need to send fire and wolf emojis. Like anyone would ever forget he was a shifter and the Alpha. Asher was going to be Asher.

"Don't need a fire station. Just a lot of magic that I don't have. Talk later. Okay?"

His response took longer. I could see him typing, then not. Then typing again. Then nothing. Finally, I received an okay.

Clean felt good. In the demon realm, my determination to answer as many summons as possible ensured that my showers were so quick, I'd never feel as clean as I did after the leisurely ones I took at home. Not to mention the sooty film of demon magic that clung to my skin and never seemed to leave me even after showering. Here, the lingering floral scent of my shampoo and the vanilla shower cream inundated my bathroom and my senses. Home. It felt like home.

Cinching the towel tighter around me, I invited the person knocking at my door in. Mephisto peeked in, his smile pensive and wary.

"Hi." There was a rough edge to his voice. His appearance —granite shirt and slacks—was at odds with the wariness in his eyes. A light shadow of a beard was starting to show, and his hair was a little longer. Loose waves furled at his forehead and ears.

Maybe it was because I missed it, or I'd become used to

that imperceptible movement, but he was at my door one moment and directly in front of me the next, placing a kiss on my forehead.

"Thank you, cousin M. I've missed you, too. What are you bringing to the next family reunion, perhaps coleslaw?" I teased. His lips covered mine in a gentle, tender kiss.

"My demigoddess," he whispered, ending the kiss. Burying his face in my neck, he cupped my body closer to him. Eventually pulling away, his finger trailed over the edges of my jawline, sweeping to my neck, my exposed shoulder, and along the curves. His exploration ended with a feather touch over my brow before pressing a gentle kiss to it. The warmth of his body and touch chased away the chill of the room.

I leaned into him, melting into the warmth of his embrace. He breathed in my hair and whispered, "I'm sorry." Desperation and pain wrought in his voice as if he needed to be absolved.

Pulling away, I looked into his depthless dark eyes. "For what?"

"For not finding you. I had no idea where you were. I never would have guessed the demon realm."

I assumed Madison and Cory had shared what they knew. Mephisto wore the assumed failure in the grim frown that I'd seen on Cory and Madison. The self-flagellation, guilt, and feeling of failure were being directed at the wrong people. Elizabeth and Malific bore the responsibility, although they'd never feel or show any remorse for their hand in it.

"There's nothing to be sorry for," I told him, slipping a hand over his. "This is not your burden to bear." I could say it a hundred more times and he'd never believe it. The weight of his perceived failure was palpable. "I should get dressed," I said.

"Mhmm," he said, but neither of us moved.

"My clothes are over there." I pointed to the dresser. His

hand dropped from me, taking with him the heat from his touch.

"You don't have to leave," I objected when he started for the door. Giving him a reassuring smile, I added, "I just need to get clothes."

I dressed while he watched me with the same careful inspection I'd gotten earlier from Cory and Madison. Something that needed to stop.

Fatigue was setting in hard and staying awake was becoming increasingly difficult. I managed to do so while ignoring Cory's looks of judgment as I scarfed down slice after slice of pizza and recounted the entire sordid details of Elizabeth's betrayal and her deal with Dareus. I detailed every minute discovery and occurrence of my time in the demon realm: the number of people who were summoning demons, even the two witches who had made their way to the realm, my oath with Asial and his fight with Sariez, the books, spells, and every tiny thing I hoped could be of use in the future. Cory was left tense and repulsed by so many witches practicing dark magic. Madison took measure of the information, formulating the steps the Supernatural Task Force needed to take to rein things in.

I kept checking my phone for a text from Nolan or perhaps a missed call despite having the ringer on. No calls from Nolan, but a missed one from Landon that I had no intention of returning anytime soon.

Madison was seated in the chair across from me, where I sat next to Mephisto, who hadn't given me a lot of space since leaving my bedroom. It was as if everyone expected me to be pulled from that spot. It wasn't just the constant attention from Mephisto or the frequent thoughtful looks from Cory and Madison; I was aware of the stilted exchanges between Madison and Mephisto. Whenever she spoke to ask me for clarification or even questioned Mephisto, his jaw clenched. It was so nearly imperceptible I questioned whether I was reading too much into it. Could I be imagining the intangible cloud they both seemed to be wading through?

No, it was definitely there. Cory's assessing gaze as they interacted confirmed it.

"The person who wanted the Denuck, do you have any idea who it was?" Madison asked.

I shook my head. "If I saw her again, I'd know. But there are a lot of witches who stay under my notice." I described her to Cory.

"I don't know her." He looked at Madison. "I'll look into it." There was a condition that lingered in the tail end of his response. "Do you think it's something that needs to be pursued now?"

She shrugged. "It's been ignored so long, the grays of magic are getting darker, and witches"—her gaze flicked to me, a reminder that it wasn't just witches—"and mages seem to be pushing the boundaries. If we don't do anything, I fear that humans will. We now have a demon living among us. He's been inactive so we had no idea until now. He had Harrison's body and now he has his own. But I haven't seen him with it. I should have suspected that there was more when Harrison's body was discovered."

Giving me a weak smile, she said, "It was left in River's backyard. The investigation is ongoing. Of course, River has inserted himself into the investigation." I wasn't sure who'd left the body. Elizabeth, as a backup if I managed to escape the demon realm? Me imprisoned for murder would still keep her promise to Nolan and I would continue to serve my purpose of being the reason for her magical suppression. Malific, for no other reason but to make my life more hellish? Dareus, for any number of reasons such as retaliation or redirection?

River was probably searching tirelessly to find evidence that would implicate me in Harrison's murder, continuing his single-focused mission to see me behind bars after Madison worked out a plea deal where I spent time in the Stygian instead of prison. The officer with political ambitions was determined to see me serve time. And someone placing Harrison's body at his home was a taunt he couldn't ignore. If he discovered any evidence, there wasn't any doubt I'd find him at my door. Until then, River and his vendetta would have to be a problem for another day.

"I don't think Dareus is as inactive as we believe. He's being hidden," Mephisto added, "I suspect with the same magic that has allowed Elizabeth to stay undetected. I don't think for one minute she's not around, monitoring the aftermath of her work."

The mention of Dareus and Elizabeth brought to the forefront the massive elephants in the room: my oath with Asial and Elizabeth's possession of the Laes.

"Elizabeth has the Laes," I reminded him.

Mephisto inhaled a ragged breath. When he released it, the stoicism he showed had been hard earned. "I know." Never before had so few words said so much. The topic wasn't something that he wanted to discuss. Whether indefinitely, or in the presence of Cory and Madison, I didn't know.

"Have you contacted Nolan?" Madison asked. "If Elizabeth made Dareus corporeal, maybe he can help you with Asial."

"I've called," I admitted with a tinge of disappointment and fighting the urge to contact him again. Conversation dwindled to banalities when options seemed nonexistent. With the looming thirty-day window, our mood became bleak. When Cory and Madison decided to leave, I touched Mephisto's hand, signaling for him to stay.

Madison reminded me she'd be by at two the next day to pick me up. My car hadn't been replaced when Malific destroyed it during a fit of rage after showing a modicum of restraint and not killing me. Cory's and Madison's reluctance to release me from their farewell hugs made me appreciative of the affection but committed to this not becoming the new normal. It wasn't just affection, it was fear. We shared an emotional unrest and I despised it.

Out of the demon realm, I thought my hate would fade, smooth out some, but it was vehement. A firestorm that couldn't be quelled.

"Elizabeth has the Laes," I repeated, leaning back against the closed door.

"I know." Mephisto frowned. "She's approached us with a proposal." His tone had sharpened to a knife's edge with barely suppressed anger. He took a deep breath and attempted to rein in his emotions.

"Four days after your disappearance she sent a text message. I suggested we discuss things in person, but she declined. She knew that if we were face to face, her absurd proposal wouldn't be met in kind," he said.

"What was the proposal?"

He grimaced and linked his fingers with mine. "Destroying it and releasing us from our restriction, with the condition that we remain in the Veil."

"Indefinitely," I guessed.

He nodded. "An oath."

Although I was happy with his choice to stay, I knew the decision placed an additional strain on the existing one between him and the Huntsmen. One that I was the root cause of. This cemented their apprehension and caution around me. They'd determined that I was Mephisto's weakness and they wanted to protect him. And, probably more importantly, to shield themselves from the harm of having me in their lives. They were stuck here because of me. Over fifty years they'd been trying to find a way back into the Veil, and it was whisked away by Mephisto because he didn't want to commit to only living in the Veil.

As if he could read my thoughts, he gave me a weak smile. "Erin, I didn't make that decision for them. I told them to do what they felt was best for them and to leave me behind. They decided to stay." He said it with palpable relief. It would have been difficult being here without them.

"Kai?" I asked through a suppressed yawn. Kai struggled constantly and it seemed like he was at his breaking point.

"He would not take the offer without us." There was more but Mephisto didn't share. Despite how difficult it was not knowing every facet of his life, I knew that I'd never truly understand the nuances of their fraternal bond.

He tilted my chin up and kissed me again. "You need to sleep," he urged. Reluctantly, he placed distance between us and attempted to open the door.

"Stay with me."

He nodded, allowing me to lead him to the bed. He toed off his shoes, slipped off his shirt and pants with me shooting furtive looks, and I got undressed. With him climbing into the bed with me, skin against skin, sleep was the last thing on my mind.

"Erin," he purred against my jaw when I nestled my face into his neck, my hand running along the hard, corded muscle of his abs. He kissed my brow, securing my roaming hands in his.

"Sleep," he whispered. I calmed my libido, which I tried to convince myself was unspent adrenaline from my fight or flight response coursing through me. It was a lie on a grand scale. I liked sex and I liked it with Mephisto. But I did need sleep. He rolled me on top of him, the warmth of his body snaking around me. I relaxed into the comfort of his arms. Sleep came quickly.

CHAPTER 8

I awoke to Mephisto gone and an enticing smell of food that made my stomach rumble. Throwing off the sheets, I went to the bathroom and washed my face and brushed my teeth. With a poor attempt at taming my bed head, I brushed it. I still looked as if I'd fought with sleep and lost. The bed was similarly a mess, but there wasn't any denying it, I was rested.

Slipping on underwear and a shirt, I made my way to the kitchen, picking up my phone from the sofa where I'd left it the night before.

I'd slept just shy of twelve hours.

Mephisto, dressed in just his slacks from the day before, turned from the stove, his dark eyes giving me a cursory sweep before he greeted me with a light kiss on my cheek. His hand brushed against mine then lingered.

I'm still here, I thought and gave him a reassuring smile before taking a seat at the counter. Checking my phone for missed calls or messages, I only had one from Madison, telling me that she had spoken to our parents last night about my return from *my job* and they were looking forward to seeing us. Madison was trying to deal with the subject in a way that would keep them from worrying. I wasn't convinced they should be kept in the dark.

Ways of broaching the subject of my imprisonment in the demon realm with my parents occupied my thoughts until Mephisto placed a plate of pancakes, bacon, apples, and hash browns in front of me. Because I was sure Madison and Cory had included the fridge in their stress cleaning, I was surprised by the selection.

"Grocery delivery," he explained at my inquiring look. "No berries or eggs," he added with a smirk. I might have gotten off track a few times, ranting about never wanting to eat berries or eggs for the rest of my life.

"Nothing for you?"

"I ate earlier. The second time preparing food was the charm—you slept through the first one. I thought the first attempt would wake you with me moving through your kitchen trying to find things. But I guess it was hard to hear over the *sound effects* you provided."

"Did I snore?" I asked.

His fingers stroked over my hand resting on the counter. "No, you were just sleeping soundly," he politely corrected.

"Is it possible that it was sexy snoring? That has to be a thing, right?"

His laughter erupted in the room, and I noticed he hadn't moved his hand, as if the contact would tether me to the space. It was bizarre for me and very apparent that this wasn't easy for him, either. He moved to the coffee maker once I started eating. Placing a cup of coffee next to me, he sipped on a cup he had set next to the maker.

He glanced down at my phone. "You should call Nolan again," he suggested once I finished eating. I made another attempt, but once again, the call went to voicemail. I repeated my message from yesterday along with sending a text. My finger hovered over the send button as I reread the message: *Dad, I need you.* I deleted it and changed it to *Nolan, please call me. I need your help.* Several moments passed before I sent it.

No messages from him felt wrong. Our last interactions led me to believe that despite what Elizabeth wished, he would somehow be in my life. Had Elizabeth ruined that, too? I tried not to let my thoughts spiral into darker places and wonder whether or not something had happened to him.

"Maybe removing the oath should be my priority," I suggested.

"I'm not sure my magic, or anyone else's, can do that." Mephisto grew silent with contemplation. "There seems to be an undeniable link between demon and elven magic, Erin. I've been trying to figure it out most of this morning. Benton is doing more research on it. Elves can make demons corporeal. If anyone else could've have done it, I'm sure the demons would have bartered a way into doing it. And your ability to be banished to the demon realm. Is that something they've always been able to do? Seems highly unlikely that they've never done it before when they had a body."

"Most bodies aren't able to contain their magic."

"Exactly. Elizabeth did the spell, sending you to the demon realm."

"Maybe there's a connection between fae and demon magic," I speculated. "Perhaps Madison can banish people to the demon realm." Another clench of his jaw at the mention of Madison. There was no mistake, something was going on between them.

"Ian was a fae." I reminded him of the fae who escaped the Veil and killed a demon after he'd given him immunity to iron. With his animancer abilities, Ian tormented the shifters, leading me to finding a way to connect the shifters to the ones in the Veil, giving them magical immunity.

"Speaking of Ian–Mephisto's tone was acrid and

54

contemptuous—"you should contact Asher before he contacts me again. He's challenging my patience."

"I spoke with him briefly, yesterday."

"Ah." His response was simple and with no animosity in it. Reluctant curiosity eased into his look where he seemed to let it settle. Undeniable and unquestionable jealousy. It reared its head and made him uncomfortable. Stretching his neck, like he was trying to remove a kink in it. *That's not how you get out jealousy, Mr. Huntsman.*

"After I called you." I didn't know if that was the issue or if he just disliked Asher. Probably a combination. However, that was one of the least-pressing issues I had to deal with, so I put it on the increasingly crowded backburner. I made a mental note to call Asher, to let him know what was going on. I didn't want to leave him out; I knew telling him everything would lead to him getting involved. This situation required a scalpel not a blade.

Mephisto cleared away my plate and glass when I hopped from the chair to answer the door. Cory responded to my expression of disappointment with a frown.

"I thought you were Nolan," I explained, stepping aside to let him and Alex in. Cory's visit wasn't unexpected. My return ensured that he'd be around more than before, taking on the role as Madison's eyes. It would ease his worries, too.

"How often should I expect these check-ins?" I asked. He made a face and nudged Alex forward under the pretense of him being the reason for the visit.

"Welcome back." Alex handed me a gift bag in response to my inquiring look.

I peered into the bag. There was a beige decorative spa box, the fragrance of lilac, eucalyptus, orange, and a few scents not easily identified wafting from the box. I was sure a loofah, candle, and exfoliation gloves were packed in it as well. Along with the spa box was a small plush howling wolf and a metal keychain of a fire station.

"Should I thank you or Asher?" Alex's visit was clearly Asher trying to unobtrusively check on me. I leaned in and gave him a knowing grin, despite the stoic look he maintained.

Alex flashed me a wayward smile. "The box is from me. I don't get the firehouse reference." He met my eyes with a little twinkle. "The wolf is cute, right?"

"Wolves are apex predators. Thinking they're cute little fluffies can be dangerous," I countered. "I think you know that better than anyone." Whatever disarming smile they offered or the breezy mien they donned, behind each one of them was a predator lurking close to the surface. It was a mistake to forget that. Even when one was dressed in a tailored suit and giving me a genteel smile.

I handed Cory the bag, extended my hands, and did a slow spin. "You can tell him I'm fine. No injuries, broken bones, or scars." The shirt hid my demon oath, and I had no plans to share that with Alex.

His head barely moved into a nod before he stepped farther into the apartment and sat in the chair across from Mephisto, who was on the sofa.

"Madison will be here soon," I told Cory over my shoulder as I went to my room to take a quick shower and dress.

"I know, she invited me."

Madison had already established an exit plan from our parents, considering the circumstances. Cory would come up with an excuse of having to leave, and since we were his ride, ultimately, we'd have to leave with him. He'd suggest taking a share ride and our parents would be appalled by the very idea. We used the tactic so frequently, it was surprising they hadn't caught on. But maybe they had and were just entertaining us.

I didn't feel great about needing a plan, but they tended to be adamant about us staying—an effort to protect us from whatever they deemed we weren't handling. Telling them I'd been trapped in the demon realm was going to spark their protective instinct. Who could blame them? While I showered, I debated sticking with Madison's story, but by the time I had showered and dressed, I decided they needed to know everything—although perhaps not all the details, a palatable version.

My coloring was still wan, so I added a little blush, mascara, and peach-colored gloss to give me some color. I'd changed twice, trying to find clothing that would hide the weight loss. A patterned flounce shirt and jeans were the only things I had to camouflage it.

Mephisto was waiting by my bedroom door when I emerged. "I need to leave. I'll see you later and let you know if Benton finds anything," he said. Madison had arrived while I was in the shower and was waiting for me near the front door. With an audience, Mephisto's kiss was feather light as his lips brushed mine before leaving. Giving Cory and Alex a nod goodbye, his face was carefully neutral as he approached Madison. She moved away from the door, giving him a wide berth. Despite the mere seconds of interaction, the friction hung between them.

"What the hell is going on between you two?" I asked her once he was gone.

"Nothing." She waved a dismissive hand. A glow highlighted the bridge of her nose and ran up her cheeks, a response that usually occurred when she was embarrassed. But she didn't look embarrassed; she looked defiant. "We're fine," she tacked on.

Cory craned his neck to look over his shoulder at her. "Really?" he asked with a cocked brow.

Alex stiffened at his question.

I have to know.

"You two aren't fine. What happened?" I pressed.

Madison's lips drew into a tight line. "Nothing."

"What!" Cory squawked, wide-eyed as he approached her. His lips parted in awed incredulity.

"Everything I did was legal," she snapped through clenched teeth.

"And you hold on to that sentiment. It will serve you well if he ever decides to lodge a complaint of abuse of power against you."

Her skin illuminated more, but defiance remained in the jut of her chin. "We should leave. We don't want to keep them waiting. We're going to get panic calls," she said in a poor attempt to change the subject.

"Madison?" I urged.

She took in a long breath and released it in an exasperated huff. "My only goal was to find you, Erin. Nothing else mattered and it was important that everyone who was there to help, actually did so. There was no time for games or half-assed efforts. I made that known. Distractions hurt the search and would not be tolerated."

Okay, that answered none of my questions.

"She arrested him," Cory blurted. "Don't be coy. She arrested both of your boyfriends, Asher and Mephisto."

Too shocked by the arrest revelation, I didn't correct him about my relationship with Asher because it wouldn't have changed anything. Cory liked Mephisto and Asher but was unabashedly in the Team Throuple camp.

"What?"

Madison sighed. "It had to be done. He was hindering the investigation and…" She let things trail off as if I had any idea how to complete her sentence. Embarrassment faded to stalwart insolence.

"Okay, since you're being sketchy with the details, let me take over." Cory hopped from his chair and came to stand next to me. He tossed a look over his shoulder at Alex. "You might want to leave. There will be a lot of brutal commentary about Asher that may offend your sensibilities," Cory warned with a grin.

"I'm not blind to Asher's flaws," Alex shot back.

Cory shrugged. Sometimes he was a little too Cory and he was making a show of his preparation for the telling. Readying me for a fantastic recapping with extensive commentary.

"You know how Asher is a little much. Mister I Run This City, Master of the Wolves. King of Arrogance. The big bad wolf who keeps his toe firmly on that line between being charmingly confident and a total and complete asshole." He side-eyed Alex, who fidgeted in his seat. Alex might be aware of Asher's flaws, but Cory's candor surely shone an unflattering light on them.

"We got a lead, someone who claimed having seen someone who looked like you. At that point, we had nothing to go on, just sightings from randoms. The person made it sound as if you were being held against your will. Unfortunately, when it comes to missing person sightings and rewards, you get a lot of bogus claims."

"Something that I had made known and quite clear. I encouraged people to refrain from offering rewards. Neither Asher nor Mephisto listened. It resulted in too many false sightings and dubious leads," Madison interjected.

"This one appeared to be legitimate. They'd described Harrison. His body hadn't been discovered so we didn't know he was dead and that Dareus had his own body," Cory continued. "Madison and STF had it under control, despite having to fend off River, who had taken a special interest in finding Harrison and you." Of course he had.

"STF was there, along with Mephisto and Clay. It was an efficient search party. Asher got wind of the hunt and arrived in the only way he knows how. Without an ounce of subtlety. Five SUVs filled with shifters. That's not offering assistance, that's a dramatic statement if ever I've seen one. It's a declaration of a war that no one was aware was taking place."

Alex stood and eased over to Cory, giving him a reassuring pat on the shoulder before giving the excuse that we needed privacy. Then he left.

"Can we get to the arrest part?" I pressed.

He gave me a quelling look. "I'm getting there. Patience is a virtue."

"Being less dramatic is one, too," I shot back.

Cory gave me a grit-smile before continuing. "I'm assuming Asher was there to offer assistance, but the moment he saw Mephisto, he changed course and headed for him. I have no idea what was exchanged between them." He looked to Madison for input.

She rolled her eyes. "Asher accused him of being the cause of you being missing. And pointed out that you had been injured and placed in more dangerous situations ever since you increased his presence in your life. And then told him that he needed to do a better job of protecting you. Mephisto didn't take it well, and instead of deescalating the situation, which he could have easily done, he taunted him."

She huffed. "He told Asher nothing thrives in captivity and snidely pointed out it was the reason the friendship between you and Asher didn't flourish into something more. Went on to tell him that Asher could be assured that Mephisto was far more suited to providing safety than a glorified dog."

Madison's frown etched deeper. "Of course, Asher offered to introduce him to the 'glorified dog' bite. They were in each other's faces, holding up progress, and their interaction had devolved to a measuring contest that I had no time or patience for. A fight was inevitable. I could see it brewing. I attempted to deescalate the situation…it didn't work."

"You getting between them and telling them to stand

down before you made them was deescalating the situation?" Cory inquired.

Madison glared at him. "They were hindering an investigation and needed time to cool off."

"You arrested them?" I understood Cory's shock. That was extreme for her.

Her voice softened along with her strident expression. "I just wanted to find you," she admitted.

Being trapped in the demon realm wasn't my fault and I knew it. But pushing away the guilt of putting my friends and family through that, despite knowing it wasn't my fault, became impossible. "I know. I hate that you were put in that position."

Heavy, sorrow-laden silence continued, until Cory broke it. Leaning in closer to Madison, he said in a stage whisper, "Are you going tell her about threatening to arrest Clayton, too, or should we leave that part for later?"

"We're done with the story," she hissed, and his dimpled infectious grin did nothing to relax the stern look she lobbed at him.

"Mr. Suave was all smiles and deep sexy voice as he attempted to charm your sister into releasing Mephisto. You should have seen his face when she asked him if he wanted to join Mephisto. Clearly a man who's never failed at getting his way with a smile and sweet talk," Cory blurted out, quickly finishing the story while Madison jabbed a warning finger in his direction. "I'm finished. Nothing to see here. The story is over. Just a retelling of a woman on a mission arresting friends, allies, and lovers, with absolutely no fucks to give."

Madison sneered, turned on her heels, and stormed out of the apartment. Cory and I gave each other a look. Madison, when motivated, was an unstoppable force. It was necessary, but it left her blinded by her purpose.

CHAPTER 9

Standing in the middle of the living room in my parents' house, the dynamics of our family was undeniable. It was weird. *We* were weird. The operation of my and Madison's parental unit was weird as hell. We accepted it, but even when we managed to view it through the eyes of a casual observer, there was no denying that it was objectively odd.

I was surrounded by Sophie and my mother in the circle hug, where she embraced me from the front and my mother from the back like a well-practiced synchronized performance that spoke to their connection, the tightness of their hugs an indicator of their fear. Something was off. After casting a look in Madison's direction, it was clear she had noticed it, too.

The absence of the infamous purple suitcase that stored the games we played when they wanted a family day was another indicator that something was wrong. Regarding my family with suspicion as I ambled back and took a seat next to Madison on the sofa, I prepared to answer whatever questions they might have. Reading the tension and uncertainty in the room, Cory offered to leave.

"I think that would be best. We need to talk to our daughters," my father suggested in a tight voice. Madison handed him the keys to her car, and he took them, instructing her to call him when we were ready for him to pick us up. He forced a rigid half-smile, knowing it probably wasn't going to be anytime soon, and stuck his hand up in a wave before quickly leaving.

"Where were you, Erin?" my mother asked, her sharp tone insisting on the truth.

Out of my periphery, I saw Madison shift and look away from her parents and their inquiring gaze fixed on her. *How much truth do we tell them?*

"No lies. Truth, Madison," Sophie said before flicking her eyes to me and giving me a reprimanding look. "You too, Erin."

"We aren't fools. You've never been away on a job this long. In your absence, Madison just happened to be working twelve-hour days?"

With a slight nod of her head, Madison urged me to disclose the truth. I gave as much as I could, withholding the details that would cause them to unnecessarily worry. They were informed of everything except the deal I'd made with the demon.

The furtive looks our parents exchanged made me suspicious. Madison didn't bother hiding her expression, her assessing eyes narrowed on them.

"What?" Madison blew out.

Sophie sighed and was the first to start for the kitchen, beckoning us to follow. She prepared a pot of coffee while the others sat at the table, pulled into their thoughts. When she returned with the pot, she filled everyone's mug. My mother fiddled with her mug, the creamer, the sugar. Our dads busied themselves pining over the choice between the biscotti or shortbread cookies. Blatant stalling tactics.

No one seemed to be comfortable with broaching whatever topic was causing the tension in the room. Dread snaked around me. They were being cagey and weird even by our family standards.

My mother was the first to speak. "We know that you two have always kept secrets from us. We've ignored it. The bond you two have and the dedication to protecting each other and even us is admirable. But turning a blind eye to the dangers of whatever is going on is reckless and irresponsible. We're aware of a lot more than you two know. We might not have the specifics, but we know things are bad. We are family, we protect each other," she said softly. She opened and closed her mouth several times, but no more words came. Frowning, Sophie touched her hand.

"We think it would be best if we all stepped away from this. Keegan still has the family home in Ireland, and we can stay there for as long as we need to until things are resolved and it's safe for everyone to return," Sophie provided. In anticipation of Madison's refusal, she tacked on, "Relocating won't be an issue. I'm in a position to transition without any problem."

She flicked a look in my direction. "Your mother has been planning to take a break from her work, and for the past two years, Gene has been considering taking early retirement."

Madison and I both turned to Keegan. Unlike Madison's mother, who was a semi-retired nurse practitioner, working two to three days at an urgent care clinic, or my mother, who had an Etsy shop, or my father, who blamed the thinning of his hair on his job as a financial advisor, Keegan owned a construction company. He'd have to be the one to infuse some reality into this plan of packing up and leaving the country.

He placed his hand on Sophie's back and my dad took my mother's hand into his, a sign of solidarity. "I trust my manager and my foreman. At this point, most of what I do is administration and that can be done remotely. If not, I can take time off. Or sell the company. Thanks to Gene, financially we're in a good place to do this."

"Are you kidding!" Madison sputtered, coming to her feet. Her mouth parted in an obvious state of confusion. "What about *my* job? *Our* lives? We're adults, and you've reduced us to children by making a decision for us all to leave without consulting us."

They were expecting her to leave the job she'd worked so hard for, dedicated a significant part of her life excelling in, to do what they expected: protect me. It was unfair. Ridiculous. And it wouldn't solve anything.

My debt with Asial wouldn't go away because I was in Ireland where I wouldn't have resources, Mephisto, the Huntsmen, Cory, and my daily life. Massaging my temple where I felt the beginnings of a headache, I inhaled a cleansing breath. It wasn't just my deal with Asial, I also had a debt with Landon. Hiding wasn't an option and Landon would take offense at the mere suspicion of an attempt to do so. Which would make my return significantly worse.

My rebuttals dissolved into the uncertain silence in the room. The collective concern and sorrow sweeping over our parents' faces forced a defeated sigh from Madison. She dropped back down into her chair. "This is scary," she said, "and I understand you feel the need to protect us, but running isn't an option."

"Staying here so we can bury you two is?" Sophie asked, her tone desolate.

"Madison's right. Being in another country won't solve it. If anything, it leaves us more vulnerable. We don't have the resources there, the connections, or the home court advantage. Here we have a chance," I reasoned, catching each one of their eyes, taking measure of whether I was getting through to them. Raw emotions showed in their expressions and made me desperate to find the right words. I didn't have them.

I'd placed them in a position where they felt they needed to upheave their lives and run for our safety, and that hurt.

"The only way this will end is if you kill your mother and your aunt," my mother pointed out.

"Malific and Elizabeth," I corrected.

"Malific, your birth mother, and your paternal aunt. One is a god and the other has command of magic that neither one of you has. Your resources and connections didn't prevent her from sending you to the demon realm." Her flailing hands showed her despair and feelings of help-lessness.

"She did it with the help of a demon. It's not something she could do alone," I countered.

"That doesn't make it better," Sophie blurted, taking the words out of my mother's mouth, who nodded her head in agreement.

"I'm a god, like Malific, and an elf, the same as Elizabeth," I pointed out.

"Doesn't seem like enough, honey," my mom said. "You're just part god, part elf, and *human*. I don't know if that's suffi-cient. And Mephisto and the other"—she searched for the right word and gave up—"god people or whatever his friends are don't seem to be able to stop her. If they could, wouldn't they have already?"

It was obvious they had deliberated extensively over this.

"We don't want to lose you two. Everything that you've revealed to us is bad. What you are withholding from us is probably worse." Four pairs of accusatory eyes looked at me and Madison.

"Mephisto and the others are gods," I told them, putting the weight of conviction behind my statement in an attempt to ease their apprehension. "The only reason they never had the opportunity to stop her was because Malific was impris-oned. Now, she's not. But she's the reason they're here, living among us." I went on to tell them about the Laes no longer being in her possession and therefore not a bargaining tool for her.

They were quiet for a while, taking in the information. "Who has it, Elizabeth?" Sophie guessed.

Poker face. It was easy with clients, with people I needed and desired to deceive. But I didn't want to deceive my parents, or Madison's. Concession made Madison's shoulders slump. The abridged version was no longer applicable.

"Yes, Elizabeth has it," I provided. "We are looking for her. But Malific no longer having the Laes gives us control. Gives *them* control. I have magic that can be used against her, that she can't counter."

"Oh, then this should make things interesting." Malific's voice was hauntingly cold and tinged with humor as she stood after easing into our kitchen nearly undetected, just inches from Sophie and Keegan, a blade at Keegan's throat. He'd never summon his magic fast enough to defend against the swiftness of her movement. His eyes cast down, looking at the blade held at his jugular.

Perspiration pooled along Malific's hairline. The slight tremor of her hand made me nervous. How much magic and energy had she exerted to break the ward that the Huntsmen had placed around the house? Had we been so comfortable in our sense of security or immersed in the debate that we'd missed the influx of magic that allowed her to dismantle the barriers? It had taken effort; that was noticeable in the diminished fluidity of her movement, the subtlety of her magic. Was her magic weakened enough and her movements diminished enough to improve my chances against her?

Easing to my feet, I quickly assessed the situation. A protective field could be placed around me and Madison, and it might be able to reach my parents, but Sophie and Keegan would be left vulnerable. Malific's cold ruthless glare was a reminder of her killing a shifter in cold blood for failing to assassinate me. Breaths coming at short clips, I met her gaze. "Let go of him," I demanded.

Keegan shrieked when the blade pressed into his skin and blood trailed down his neck. Malific bared her teeth. "Make me. Show me what gives you an advantage over me," she taunted, but her expression held genuine curiosity.

Her cool calculating eyes swept away from me, homing in on Sophie's face first then her hands, which were rising to perform magic. Malific shook her head in warning. I knew it would be the only one. Silently I pleaded for Sophie to listen. My magicless parents' gazes drifted around the room, looking for a solution. No solution would leave them unscathed if it wasn't Malific's will.

Madison shifted in her chair and looked at the butcher block, but she wasn't inconspicuous enough to escape Malific's notice.

"I'd take my cues from Erin. It might save your life. You make a move for it, use your pitiful magic against me, and I'll kill him."

"Do not threaten my family," I hissed through clenched teeth.

Quickly sheathing the knife at her thigh, she threw Keegan's six-seven frame aside with the ease of tossing a rag doll. Her eyes fixed on me, a strike of her finger sent explosive magic fanning out in my parents' direction. My mom hit the wall on the opposite side of the kitchen so hard, plaster rained down on her. My dad slammed into a high shelf in the corner. A plant, ceramic vase, and decorative knotted clay crashed down on him. Sophie landed a few feet away. Keegan recovered enough to return a breeze of the limited defensive magic afforded to fae. Without the earth to borrow magic from, it was even more limited. Like all magic, it had no effect on her.

Narrowed amused eyes landed on him.

With an imperceptible sweep of movement, she was

suddenly inches from me and Madison. I struck her in her chest, the hit seemingly more shocking than painful. She stumbled back. I erected the field impressively quickly. Her lip quirked as her magic shimmered over it without penetrating.

"Family?" She let her eyes move to them briefly. A baleful look slid across her face. "I am your family."

"No, I'm the child you gave birth to in order be sacrificed for your escape. I was never family. I was an instrument."

"Even in your infancy, you were a disappointment." Disdain punctuated her words.

I balled my fists at my sides. "Do you really want to do this?" This. What was *this*? How would *this* end? I wasn't under any illusion that I and my family were alive for a reason. But in the mind of someone like Malific, the drive to keep them alive was tenuous and could easily be revoked.

A soft tsk escaped her, and with the ephemeral movement that I had not yet managed to duplicate, she'd grabbed my mother. Malific placed her in front of her, positioning one hand under her chin, the other secured on the top of her head. I couldn't breathe. Tears blurred my vision. Fuck. I hated the helpless defeated whimper that escaped from me. I hated Malific with my whole heart.

Her attention abandoned me, switching to the figure holding the Obitus sword and advancing toward her. Mephisto.

Her lips pinched into a sharp frown. Vehement anger cast a dark look over her face.

She appeared to be resolved to violence, accepting of the death that would eventually come. Rapidly, I culled through every possible scenario, calculating the risk of everyone getting out of this alive or unharmed. It didn't look good. The hopelessness on my mother's face lit something in me.

"Let my mother go. Now," I demanded.

Malific dismissed me with a razor-sharp look then

returned to watching Mephisto's movement toward her. She met his cold savagery with twisted amusement.

"Will she still care about you, knowing you're the reason her family is dead?" she asked.

"She won't have to because you won't kill them. If you wanted them dead, I'd be stepping over their bodies," he asserted with a level of confidence I didn't feel.

"I came to talk. She forced my hand. Will you do the same?" she retorted, light humor in her voice as she jerked my mother's head, causing her to cry out in pain. Her shrewd eyes swept over the room, taking in everyone's position. She chortled at Madison, whose sharp glare promised a wrath that would have intimidated anyone else.

The violence-laden silence was breached by a large body smashing through the sliding door, hitting the ground with a resounding thud and sending shards of glass flying in all directions. Pieces of it cut my mother and embedded in Malific's face, who didn't flinch or loosen her hold on my mother. She simply closed her eyes for a few seconds, to protect them. Other than that slight movement, she seemed unaffected. It was a sharp reminder that she wasn't subdued or deterred by pain like a normal person. The perverse symbiotic relationship she had with it was another weapon at her disposal.

The positioning of my mother's head prevented damage to her face, but glass cut into her shirt, surrounded her body. She was hurt.

Malific's anger flashed at Clayton standing over the person lying on the kitchen floor. His violence swift and brutal. Effortlessly he twisted, and the crack of bone lingered in the air. When the body slumped to the ground, Clayton was out the broken door again, his sword yanked from the scabbard. I could hear the vicious-ness of the fighting outside but not see it in its entirety. If I couldn't see it, neither could our parents. But we got glimpses of movement and sprays of crimson over the green grass.

Malific's lips thinned into a tight angry line. Hate radiated from her. Her suppressed violence couldn't be ignored. Eyes darkening with deliberation, her eyes flicked to Mephisto then over my family again. She sneered at Madison, who kept glancing at the butcher block. Her magic couldn't work on Malific, but it could on the objects.

"Do you really want to make a sacrifice of your life for a fleeting point, especially when I come in peace?"

"You don't come in peace," I snapped, waving at her holding my mother, the dead body on the floor, the blood splattered on the grass, and the minacious soundtrack of fighting in the background.

She shrugged as if she'd suddenly become bored. "I needed someone to keep the Huntsmen preoccupied." Apparently they'd arrived sooner than she anticipated.

"Last time you claimed to come in peace, you'd made a deal with Dareus to capture me."

Unmoved, she tugged her hand again. A warning. My mother responded by clawing at her hands. For the first time, Malific displayed something other than self-assurance and bristling brutality. It wasn't defeat—maybe caution. Acceptance of a mangled plan.

Her eyes went to Mephisto, where they remained locked. He was waiting for her to drop her guard for a microsecond. The scheming and calculations showed on their faces. I was becoming increasing annoyed with reminders that I was out of my depth when dealing with them. Mephisto had replaced the refined mask he donned daily with an intense savagery that he wore like a second skin. I recalled Madison inquiring if the Huntsmen were really the good guys. I couldn't give her a definitive yes then and couldn't now.

"Another time, daughter." Malific heaved my mother away from her, just inches from the body Clayton had left.

Malific was gone. My mother scuttled back from the dead body in her kitchen, panicked eyes darting around the room.

"Breathe, Mom," I instructed. Something so simple and automatic seemed to be out of her grasp. Approaching her in the same manner I would an injured animal, I kept offering myself soothing affirmations. *She's all right, uninjured. Breathe. It's okay.* When I reached her, tears rolled down her cheeks. It was worse than anything I'd seen on her before and my heart sank.

My father joined me. "We have to leave," Mom said in a weak, tiny voice.

But more than ever, I couldn't.

Mephisto was at my side in that swift unsettling manner that had my and Madison's parents taking sharp breaths. They were getting the full version of him, unrestrained and undiluted. Of gods and their abilities. And more unsettling insights to the world.

"You two need to go home and pack your things. We should be able to get everything in order to leave in two days," Keegan ordered. His Irish brogue was thick and unyielding and delivered in a tone that reverted us to children and limited decision making. There was more to his tone than insistence; there was ignominy and defeat.

Magic wielders knew their limits, but they were never powerless. That was the reason, when their magic was limited by the respective metals, they railed against that more than the possibility of imprisonment. Magic was their identity, an essence of their being, another limb. If you possessed magic, you were never rendered completely powerless. Keegan and Sophie had never been completely powerless until faced with a god who didn't respond to their magic, moved faster than vampires, and had a lust for violence they'd never experienced.

I could sense it, and so had Madison. Looking at each other briefly, no words needed to be spoken. We were the anchors and had to reel the situation back. We made a concerted effort not to let our eyes wander to Simeon and Kai, who had joined Clayton in cleaning up the mess outside to keep our parents from focusing on it.

Shaking my head, I said, "Madison and I aren't leaving, but you all are."

"Nothing can be done if we have to worry about your safety," Madison tacked on before they could argue. She looked at me for cues. How long did they need to be gone? I was on the clock, and I had to figure out how to break my oath with Asial or satisfy it, which might mean I needed Elizabeth or at least Nolan. I had to do something with Malific. "Something" was quite a flippant way to say murder.

I turned to Mephisto. "Can you make this an easy transition for them?"

CHAPTER 10

*I*t was shock that made them so amenable. We'd broken the chain, done the unspeakable by defying Keegan and taking control. Telling our parents they were leaving and getting them to do it was an entirely different thing. Giving the kitchen another once-over, their eyes filled with frustration, unable to vocalize what they felt. Or rather unwilling to vocalize it.

I was out of my league. Despite trying with all the bravado I could muster to convince them the situation would be handled, they thought otherwise. They didn't want to be the bearer of bad news. Eventually they migrated to another room, away from Mephisto, Clayton, Simeon, and Kai, who seemed to be unwanted reminders of Malific and her capabilities. The bodies, six to be exact, were gone, and sans the neighbors seeing the discolored grass or a camera that would show the activity, there shouldn't be any issues. If so, Madison felt confident she could handle it.

Still in the kitchen, we periodically looked over at our parents, who were huddled discussing things, calm enough to keep their voices lowered. A feat they were incapable of ten minutes ago.

"This is the package you get," I whispered to Mephisto, who had glanced in their direction. I wondered if he'd over-looked my weird family dynamics when he thought about taking things with me to the next level. He responded with a faint smile.

"Are you sure sending them away is what you want?" Clayton asked, moving closer to Madison and trying to get her to look at him, although he directed the question to us both.

Madison dragged her gaze from his blood-speckled shirt up to meet his eyes. His earthy brown eyes softened. If he harbored any ill feelings about her arrest threat, he was doing a good job hiding it. The tension between her and Mephisto wasn't on display, but there was a noticeable disconnect that I didn't recall existing between them. A casual despondency.

Madison's face filled with uncertainty. She was displaying a vulnerability that she wasn't entirely comfortable revealing. This was our parents' safety and lives we were dealing with, and the weight of making the wrong decision was debilitating. "I don't know," she admitted. She couldn't stay still, pacing the few inches of space not taken up by the Hunts-men. "There's too much activity from the Veil," Madison acknowledged. "How can we stop this? We're not just dealing with other supernaturals, but those who can't be managed with our magic." She blew out a frustrated breath.

"What do you propose to be done with that?" Kai asked. Madison's unease seemed to bother him.

I knew what she wanted: to keep the Veil from being accessible, but that wasn't an option. Keeping her wishes to herself, she sighed. "I just want to protect our parents." Whatever image came to her mind, it caused her face to blanch.

"I don't think them being farther away will help. It will limit the help you can give and make you worry about them more. That would be counterproductive to your goals," Clayton stated in an even tone. A voice of reason and strategy. It wasn't coming from the place where we and our parents were—pure emotions.

"It will be harder for Malific or anyone to get to them," Madison countered.

"And harder for you to as well," Simeon reiterated. "If Malific wanted your family dead, they would be. It is to your advantage to understand that. She's never exhibited any self-restraint from violence unless it benefited her."

I knew that. Had been told the many stories of the pitiless acts. A woman who'd kill her own brother for daring to rein in her tyranny.

"I just want them safe," I admitted.

"She broke the ward, and we were able to respond swiftly. She wasn't able to enter from the Veil here. None of them were. The larger the ward, the weaker it is. It's best to keep it around the homes. We'll know if it's been compromised," said Clayton.

Mephisto remained silent, deep in his thoughts, energy humming from an expected fight that never occurred. "She's using them as leverage. It's all she has. Malific will not allow her impulses to derail her goals. If she hurts your parents, she loses that advantage." He added, "If you want your parents to leave, I'll do my part, but I agree with Clay. It won't ease your mind."

"I wonder what she wants?" Kai inquired, his eyes on me, sharp with intrigue.

Shrugging a response, I was curious as well. What did she need that only I could give her?

Madison was expressionless, and I had no idea what was going through her mind. Clayton watched her, looking for some feedback. Eventually he touched her hand, a light sweep of his finger across her skin. Before she could respond, our parents approached in their familiar formation, Sophie and my mother in front.

They'd do the emotional appeal: mom guilt and then sorrowful exasperation. Leading to Keegan intervening, his accent purposefully thickening to the point understanding him was difficult. As if we'd agree to whatever he said for not wanting to admit to our lack of understanding. If he failed, my father would come up with more rebuttals in the low paternal voice that belonged on a child's TV show. We had our tactics and they had theirs.

"We're not leaving. If you are staying, then we need to be here, too."

Madison and I looked at each other and nodded in agreement. Shocked, they silently looked around at us all. So many things were left unspoken because me having to deal with Malific to end this was a topic no one wanted to broach, a dark, corrosive cloud that lingered as the wards were re-erected.

"You can do a protective field that can't be broken by Malific. Have you tried to do a ward?" Madison asked me as the Huntsmen continued to work.

"I have to actively hold up my protective field, and my wards aren't any stronger than theirs. If I knew how to isolate the elven magic, maybe?"

That was the main issue, the very thing that could solve many of my problems. I needed to harness my elven magic more efficiently. Taking my phone from my pocket, I was disappointed to see no messages from Nolan. Madison was equally disheartened.

Nolan, I need you.

Several hours passed before my family felt comfortable with us leaving—or at least they made a better performance of it. They were left with a schedule of the guard rotation of their homes. I considered asking for Asher's help with surveillance.

His pack's immunity to magic would help in this instance, but I could be putting them in danger unnecessarily. Clayton was right. Malific wanted something and my family's connection was a double-edged sword. She'd use them as leverage, but she understood that killing them wouldn't make me amenable.

Not having a car was a problem I needed to rectify soon. It seemed like a frivolous thought as I entered Mephisto's home, driven by Benton who'd picked us up because Mephisto had Wynded to my parents' home. Clayton had arrived on his motorcycle and, against my objection, had taken Madison home. Gods were hard to injure and if by chance they suffered injuries, they healed fast. Essentially, Clayton drove his motorcycle as if that was at the forefront of his mind at all times. Before he left with her, I reminded him that Madison didn't possess that ability. I may have mentioned it more than once, because it took Madison glaring at me to stop with the reminders.

Benton went straight to the room he'd made into his office. I headed for Mephisto's backyard, appreciating the setting sun, the thicket of trees so lush and verdant they looked like an illusion. The woodland creatures that didn't seemed bothered by my presence and occasionally feeding and interacting with nature's hodgepodge oopsie, the okapi, made a great distraction between me checking my phone and texting Nolan.

I'd made two more calls and one text, making alternative plans. Elves existed, more than just Nolan and Elizabeth. I just had to find them. They weren't in the Veil but living here among us. They were thought to be extinct. Finding one was the problem: We didn't look different, and the hypothesis that we'd have the distinctive pointed ears was wrong. Or maybe it was right. I hadn't met a pure-blood elf, just magical hybrids.

Two hours and I hadn't come up with anything that would help me find another elf. I considered summoning Asial, to ask if he had something similar to the Black Crest grimoire. He'd probably consider it a sign of arrogance—or naivete—to summon him for a favor and not to satisfy my debt. My mind had become a whirl of thoughts, ill-conceived ideas, and terrible plans by even the most ambitious standards.

Assuming that Mephisto hadn't joined me outside in order to give me time to process things, I searched the house. Benton stuck his head out the office long enough to direct me to Mephisto's office and tell me he was there with Clayton, Kai, and Simeon. I eased toward the slightly ajar door.

"The raven is here," Kai announced when I was within a few feet. He said it purely for my benefit, because if he knew of my presence, so did they. Padding in, I found Mephisto leaning against the desk, his arms crossed over his chest. The hours that had passed hadn't diminished the intensity that radiated from him earlier. A fight denied. I watched them: the careful assessment of their eyes, solemn concentration, and obvious conversation from which I was being excluded.

"How does it work? Are you all always in each other's heads and have to actively enable it, or is it the reverse?" I asked.

Clayton lips twisted into a mischievous smirk.

I shrugged. "Now that I know that it happens, it's easy to recognize when you all are having your exclusive conversations. The chats always bring a notable but indecipherable look to your faces. Especially yours," I said, singling out Kai. His head canted, awaiting an explanation.

"If anything were to ever happen and you were all suspects, you would be the unusual one. They look like they're up to something or at least thinking about it. You don't. You never do."

He found that humorous, probably because of whatever silent exchange had occurred. But I couldn't shake the feeling that of them all, he was probably the most dangerous. His senses were more acute than theirs. And after seeing him spar with Mephisto, he definitely thrived on violence. His cherubic appearance didn't hint at any of that. Underestimating him could be fatal.

They looked at each other while another private conversation took place. If the tight pinch of Mephisto's lips was anything to go by, I was requesting insight to something personal, information that left them vulnerable.

"It's a modified closed loop. When we are close, it opens automatically, but we can close it," Simeon supplied.

"When we are apart, it isn't the best form of communication. I may be able to get things across, but it's fragmented, so efficiency and directness are important," Kai added.

"It's only between us. A spell was done when we accepted our positions," Clayton said, "so, no, you can't get in on the group chat." He smirked, preemptively answering my follow-up question. Clay's lip twitched with amusement. "Nor can we share the spell," he tossed in. I was uncomfortable at the ease with which he anticipated my questions.

"We're trying to figure out a way to track Malific," Mephisto provided. "Most of her time is being spent in the Veil. Now that she can't make an army, she's recruiting, but she doesn't have as much influence with the use of violence since her magic is limited." All eyes moved to me—the cause of those limitations.

"If something happens to her, will I inherit her magic?" I finally asked the question that had been nagging me since the discovery of what my existence did to her magic.

"No. If so, we'd have a lot of parricide. Life is the gift bestowed by the parents."

"If I have a child or children, then I'd be weakened, and their magical ability would be barely discernable," I theorized.

"That would be the case, but it doesn't happen often. The reduction of power only occurs in the mother of Arch-deities. They typically don't mate with lesser. At the mini-mum, they procreate with a god. It ensures a strong progeny and bloodline."

Not only did the woman have the child but she lost some of her magic because of it. I couldn't hide my disdain for the situation.

"Magically, the women are stronger. Oedeus couldn't create life from inanimate objects, but his sister could. Malific treasured her magic over having a child."

"Oh." She only had a change of heart when having a child would benefit her. A subject change was needed. "Do you think there's a way to nullify the contract with Asial? An object, spell, or anything?"

"That's what we were discussing. We're going to try the Cupio." Apparently, they were out of ideas, too. Because that object was the fable of fables. The wish rod that everyone wanted. No one had ever seen it, yet people were convinced it existed based on tales that continued to circulate.

"You believe it exists?" I asked, searching each face. They were having another insular conversation. "Please stop doing that. I'm going to assume you all don't believe it exists and are just trying to give me some semblance of hope. I'm not fragile. I want the truth, straight no chasers. Please. Since I can tell when you're having these private conversations, it seems rather—" I shrugged the ending. Rude. So. Very. Rude.

"Sorry, Raven," Kai offered. The title seemed to serve as a reminder, and based on the rigid severe line of Mephisto's lips, had been directed at him. Kai may have stayed behind for them, but he wasn't above reminding them why they made the choice to stay.

"I've been hired seven times to find it. Nothing ever came of it. It's an elusive hire object that I'm convinced doesn't exist."

"Perhaps." Mephisto sighed. "We're just brainstorming." It was an admission he didn't seem comfortable making. "Like elves, demon magic works differently. It's the reason witches and mages turn to them." His glance at me was a reminder of the conversation we had about there being a link between elves and demons. The grimace on his face deepened.

"I'll talk to Victoria," Simeon said. "She doesn't practice, and without her coven she doesn't possess the same level of magic she once had, but she could be a resource."

And a reason for him to go play with the apex predator, Pearl, that she kept as a house cat. Victoria and Simeon were the only people who saw an adorable little kitty when they looked at the hundred-pound feline.

"And you can visit the ice tiger," I teased.

"Ice tiger?"

"I saw a guy on TikTok refer to snow leopards being genetically closer to tigers than leopards," I pointed out, my voice trailing off at his expression that indicated that my name for Pearl wasn't warranted or appreciated. As if I had subjected her to some indignity.

"She's a snow leopard. Snow tiger, perhaps. But ice tiger." He frowned. Something about that name bothered him. "They're far more passive than a tiger and choose not to harm humans if leaving is an option," he said in a stilted voice. It was obvious the ice part bothered him, attributing it to her personality, which admittedly was quite friendly and needy. Mephisto cleared his throat. Further discussion about Pearl wasn't going to go my way and would only dig me deeper into the hole I'd found myself in.

"I'm glad you'll get to see her. She's a beautiful animal." My insincere flattery softened his look some, but I had clearly offended his sensibilities. I couldn't imagine him taking such offense on the behalf of two-legged animals.

After more discussion that didn't yield any results, it really came down to me needing help from Nolan or finding another elf. Elizabeth was out of the question because it was doubtful that she'd help. Benton was locked away in his library/office and might come up with something. Although even if he found a link between me and demons, I wasn't sure how that would help. Could it somehow void the agreement?

CHAPTER 11

"*M*ay I see your room of objects again?" I requested from Mephisto once everyone had left.

He nodded and grabbed my hand. "After we have had"—his eyes flicked to the clock. It had been hours since I'd eaten and he'd clearly heard my stomach grumble—"dinner."

Watching him prepare our meal, I wondered why he had a cook when he seemed to enjoy doing it himself. "I know how to cook," I declared when he relegated me to sous-chef, which entailed occasionally retrieving a spice, and dicing garlic and mushrooms for the chicken marsala. After I was done, I sat on the counter next to him, glass of wine in hand, idly watching him and occasionally glancing at the entrance, hoping Benton would burst through with an idea or a solution.

Nothing came, and dinner was eaten, our discussion reduced to trivial exchanges. Neither of us wanted to list the limited options.

Seeing the many magical objects he had collected over the years wasn't any less impressive that it had been before. A plume of sadness overshadowed my admiration because even with such a collection, none of it helped him find a way out of my situation with Asial.

"Will you take me to get a rental car?" I asked, entering the bedroom. Mephisto stopped, his brows inching together in confusion.

"Rental car," he said slowly.

"Malific destroyed mine," I reminded him. "I need to search Harrison's home and follow some potential leads and I can't do share ride-hails for those."

"Why do you need a car when I have several?"

"Do you have any that don't cost the salary of middle management or could reasonably buy a home in a small town?"

Smirking, he said, "I wouldn't know. I've never been a middle manager and I only have my house."

"This isn't a house, it's a mini mansion complete with a chef, Druid/butler—who at this point should drop the second title, he's an occasional room direction pointer—and land expansive enough to keep exotic hodgepodge pets."

Chuckling, he made his way toward me, his finger gliding across my cheek in a need for a connection before dropping his hand to his side. The energy from his denied fight still hummed from him. "I do enjoy our little debates, but this doesn't have to be one. You need a car, and I have one, so why is this a discussion?"

"I don't want to be unequal in this relationship," I blurted.

Rearing back as if I struck him, he asked, "What?"

"Unequal," I admitted in a quiet voice. The confession stung. "I don't want you to think that the things you give me is why we're together," I said. "You keep giving me expensive things, buying me wine I can't afford. I put ketchup on a Matsusaka steak, and you looked as if I'd given the queen a kiss and crotch contact hug."

"Did that bother you?" He seemed genuinely bewildered.

Everyone had their insecurities, but food shame wasn't where mine lay.

"Not at all. Give me one now and I'll drench it in ketchup again. I'd definitely try harder to get Clay to try it."

"It won't happen, he doesn't like ketchup." He shrugged. "Says he doesn't get it."

"Who doesn't get ketchup? How can you not *get* ketchup? It's the fry and burger condiment. What strangeness is this?" I had to shake off my ketchup defense although it was definitely something Madison needed to know about. It was deserving of a "proceed with caution" label.

"Today, when I wanted my parents to leave, I turned to you without a moment's thought. I knew you'd be able to take care of it efficiently." Having him and his resources made life significantly easier. "I just want us to be on equal footing. I don't want to be a person you have to take care of."

I had hang-ups rooted in the fact Madison took care of me, sacrificed for me, and her life was made more complicated because of me. But I was in a different place now than I was then. I didn't want that from anyone. Burdening someone about transportation seemed trivial.

"But we aren't equal," he pointed out.

I am of the belief that everyone has a trigger word. Something said that sparks the flames. Shoots you into fight mode. I never thought "unequal" would be one.

Backing away from him, my arms crossed, I snapped, "Excuse me?"

His flash of movement that closed the distance between us was a harsh reminder of my demigod status. Leaning in close, his nose brushed against mine. His warm breath wisped across my lips. The crisp notes of the chardonnay he'd paired with dinner lingered on his breath.

"You create wards that I can't break. I can glamour my appearance, you can cloak yours and be invisible to the eye.

You have the ability to render me magicless with a circle," he cited.

"A circle that you can step out of," I reminded him. It wasn't much of a defense against a person if they could just step out of it. I knew it worked on fae and witches, and assumed it worked on mages as well. The spell was untested on demons and other elves.

"But you can do it." He kissed my bottom lip. "Keeping me confined becomes the task. I am quite hard to contain, but if anyone could find a way to do it, my demigoddess can."

As he stepped away from me, my hand slipped from his waist where it had found itself.

"Equality seems quite simplistic in its definition, but only if you ignore the nuances. Do you approach a deer the same way you would a lion, despite them both being animals?" he asked.

"Who's the lion in this example?" I asked, the flare of my anger dying down.

His tongue moistening his lips was the only answer I got before he continued. "Not equals but complements. You need a car. I need a woman who manages to frustrate and possess me in the most tantalizing way."

I smiled. "Undeniably Erin."

He nodded.

"Okay, just a borrow. As soon as I have time to research and find a car, I will get one, okay?"

When I was met with silence I prompted again. More silence. How in the hell was I the frustrating one?

Desire rolled into his gaze before he responded with a voracious kiss that made my request melt into a groan. Despite no longer craving his magic as I had before, it was impossible to be in its presence without taking notice. It was all-consuming. He pulled me closer, the warmth of his body slinking around me, his hands cupping my butt, lifting me to him, against the hard bulge in his pants. I groaned against his lips, curling my legs around him as he walked me to the bed.

Commanding hands caressed my body as he removed my clothes, smoothing his hands over my exposed skin, kneading it, teasing me with lips, tongue, and touch. He inched up to me, covering my lips with his. I craved his touch even as I moved away long enough to jerk off his shirt and toss it aside. Running my hands along the defined cords of muscle of his abs, the toned grooves of his back, I slowed my touch. Languidly stroking the hardness between his legs elicited a deep throaty rumble from him. Quickly he rolled from me to remove his pants and underwear, and nestled between my legs.

His kisses were ravenous, becoming increasingly fervent, warm, and wanton as he pressed into me. His warm sensual lips running along the curve of my neck, the pulse of it, my shoulder, until he came to my breasts. Laving over the hardened peaks of my nipples, he continued to tease until I was panting, moaning, and clawing at the duvet. Giving me a dubious chuckle, he continued to explore my body, nestling between my thighs, exploring the sensitive area with his kisses and tongue. Licking, teasing, lazily tasting me until I exploded with release, leaving me compliant and relaxed under his touch.

Holding his impressive hardness, he teased me. A devious grin lifted the corners of his lips at my groans and pleading.

"Mephisto," I whined at the persistent teasing. His fingers slid against my wetness, amusement twinkled in his eyes, and he taunted me with a kiss. A gentle teasing at my lips. When I thought I'd shatter with anticipation, he slid his cock in me. My legs wrapped around him, pulling him into me, meeting his thrusts, surrendering to his touch. My fingers kneaded into the muscles of his back. The fire raged again and I needed it to be extinguished. Lowering his face to mine, he kissed me, trailing over the edge of my jaw, biting the lobe of my ear.

He whispered in my ear, his voice deep and rough, matching his movements. "Come for me, my demigoddess," he growled. And I did. Yielding to the command, I found my release, Mephisto soon after.

I melted into the bed. Mephisto nuzzled my neck, his hand palming my breast, his thumb grazing over my nipple. He lay next to me, nudging me onto my side and pulling me into the curve of his body. He lightly nipped at my ears before inching even closer until our bodies seemed to be one.

CHAPTER 12

*C*ory slipped into the passenger side of the car and leaned back against the buttery soft leather. He ran his finger over the upholstery that caressed his body and made it apparent this was a luxury car. The Audi RS 5 was the least ostentatious car in Mephisto's garage. It was debatable whether the velvet black coloring was less obtrusive than the pearl white Maybach he offered. His nod to my suggestion of adding a Toyota to his collection could only be described as amused placation.

"Don't get used to it. I'm giving it back as soon as I can. After I deal with Asial and Malific, getting a new car is my next priority."

"I know but"—Cory sank deeper in the seat—"it's nice to be in a vehicle that rides smooth and doesn't constantly remind you that it needs a tune-up. Don't judge me for enjoying being cradled by supple leather and its appealing smell as opposed to being enclosed in the upholstery scent of fries, coffee, and cinnamon bun."

"Are you implying that's how my car smelled?"

"Implying? I thought I was being brazenly direct."

"Sorry my car can't smell like annoying Type A personality, lemon, and verbena," I snipped back, wrinkling my nose.

"Don't be so touchy, Erin. I'm still on your team. Eat the rich." He growled, bending his fingers as if they were claws.

"You know that's not how I feel. The self-indulgent magically powerful elite believe in the ruthless pursuit of whatever they want. From the outside looking in, it can be enticing. But that world will draw you in, tempt you to drop your defenses, and when you're vulnerable is when you find out you've been outmatched, betrayed, and played for a fool. They enjoy it. There are very few boundaries. Keeping the worlds separate lets me stay focused. It prevents me falling for the allure."

"Having nice things doesn't make you self-indulgent, Erin."

"I know. I have nice things."

"You have nice and clever weapons. A few expensive clothes, but most of them help you do your job better. Leather pants, modified shoes with blades in them… You know that's not normal, right? And the compartments you have in your jackets and clothes are nice but not personal. Items just for you. Nice *personal* things."

Who asked him to call me out?

I shrugged. "I've been involved in the dark entitled underbelly and I can't help but hold a level of disdain for it. Compartmentalizing things is how I survive."

"It seems that being with Mephisto would help."

I gave him a quick glance that spoke volumes. Thinking the Huntsmen were strictly white knights and never dabbled in the gray or sank deeply into the bowels of the underbelly was naive. They were restrained in this world, but when unleashed, they exhibited a raw, chilling demonstration of power and violence. I'd seen their room of magical objects, Mephisto's dedication to possessing them, and the ease with which he navigated that world. It wasn't an act to infiltrate it; he belonged there.

The reason he hadn't joined us today was because of that ease. He was attempting to acquire the Cupio and find Elizabeth, and he was also digging into the existence of more elves. Despite seeing the flaws in the grayish world, we both inhabited it for different reasons. I couldn't deny that it had its benefits. It was the fear of becoming like Malific that made me impose boundaries and prevent my morality from becoming more ambiguous than it already was. However, because I was committed to doing whatever it took to stop Malific and Elizabeth, it might be too late. My only solace was I didn't start it—they did. I had to end it.

"He's not as bad as most. But I don't want my relationship with him to compromise my defenses and forget the type of people I deal with in my job and what I could become if I do. It could have cataclysmic results."

As if summoned by the word "cataclysmic," the car notified me that I had a call coming in from Landon. I ignored it.

"You're going to have to deal with him sooner or later," Cory said.

"I know but it has to be later. For now, we need to search Harrison's and Elizabeth's homes."

Silence thickened between us. "I thought once you were unbound and had your own magic things would get easier for you," he whispered, keeping his attention on the scenery out the window. "I wanted it to be easier for you," he added. His voice was wistfully sorrowful.

Out of my periphery I saw the brief anguished expression when he turned to look at me. "Your struggle was so painful to watch, especially when there wasn't anything that could be done for you. Now you have magic, and things seem worse. I didn't think that was possible." He heaved a sigh.

"It's not worse." *That's debatable.* "It's just more complicated. The issues can be resolved." I just had to murder my mother and my aunt, nullify a deal with a demon *or* figure out how to make him corporeal, figure out what do with Dareus—whose inactivity was surely temporary and him being cautious—and satisfy my debt to Landon. Easy peasy.

Cory knew me well enough to find the insincerity in my words and my effort to ease his worries.

"What's the plan?" Cory asked, ending the uncomfortable silence that ticked by once I parked the car on the gravel area a few feet from Harrison's trailer.

"To see if anything was missed. Find a clue as to how we can locate Elizabeth or Dareus." I was too embarrassed to admit to the sliver of hope that part of the Black Crest grimoire had survived the fire Elizabeth set to it. It was unlikely, but that's where I was in the grand scheme of things. Grasping at the improbable. Searching and hoping to find something that STF and River had missed.

Desperation left very few options. Nolan still hadn't contacted me. I needed a way to get to him or Elizabeth. From there, I'd have to figure things out.

"If you can't break the contract and find a way to make Asial corporeal, our next course of action needs to be figuring out how to imprison him and Dareus in their corporeal form," Cory said, getting out of the car.

I was thinking more along the lines of restricting their magic or sending them back. "Imprison them for what, being a demon?" I asked, lengthening my stride to keep pace with him.

"Should we wait for them to do something?" he countered.

"It would set a bad precedent to imprison people because they *might* do harm, no matter how high the probability. Dareus has been quiet and not caused any destruction—or any that can be traced to him." It wasn't an endorsement that he wouldn't. There was a reason behind his good behavior, I just wasn't sure what. His realm was the best place for him.

"They removed the tape?" Cory observed, approaching the trailer. The door was locked. He looked over his shoulder, whispered a spell, and stood back. "Checking for wards or detection spells," he explained.

Smoke and turquoise coloring spooled around the door. Caustic energy buzzed in the air. I hadn't seen him perform this spell before and wondered if it was something new or one he'd taken from the Mystic Souls book.

He invoked another spell to open the door once there weren't any indicators of wards or detection spells. Stepping over the threshold, I wasn't prepared for the lurch of anxiety I felt at the appearance of the home. Inhaling a breath, I inched into the trailer, my eyes immediately going to the space where I tried to cling to this realm.

There weren't any nail marks or gouges in the floor from that failed fight. My chest tightened and breathing became more difficult. My nails cut into the palm of my hand, as my hands balled at my side. Two months I was gone and I spiraled into the dark territory of what-ifs. A lucky turn of events was the only reason I was here.

No matter how I tried to claw my way out of the grim thoughts, I was spiraling.

Get it together, Erin, I coaxed myself. Forcing myself to take slow, controlled breaths, with a great deal of effort, I summoned some modicum of calm. Feeling Cory's eyes on me, I turned to give him a reassuring smile.

"I'll search in here and you see if there are any leads outside," he suggested.

"I'm fine," I lied. It was over. I had escaped despite the cost.

After a few minutes of searching, my anxiety had reshaped into determination. I was resolute that this wouldn't end well for Dareus and Elizabeth.

Before we exited the trailer, I looked again in the trash can where Elizabeth had burned the grimoire, as if I'd missed something the other three times I'd checked it. Would a search of Elizabeth's home be equally fruitless? She'd had two months to scrub away any means of locating her. Cory and I noticed the unoccupied car next to mine.

"Put your hands where I can see them," River demanded, from his position at the side of the trailer that had kept his presence hidden. He kept his gun trained on me while dividing his focus between the two of us. "What are you doing here at a crime scene?"

"A crime scene from two months ago," Cory pointed out. "There wasn't any police tape and the door was unlocked."

Unlocked by magical intervention, but nice wordplay.

River's lips puckered, and his baleful eyes sharpened on Cory before snapping back to me.

"They always return to the scene of the crime," River noted in soft condescension, slowly putting his gun away. In turn, I lowered my hands, crossing them over my chest where he could see them, not wanting to give him a reason to feel threatened into reacting.

Cory followed suit, clasping his hands in front of him and returning River's cold stare. It was always a little disconcerting to see the side of Cory that illustrated military training: hard-assed and capable of a strategic strike if provoked. Donning that aspect seemed to bother Cory as well. A destruction mode that he clicked on. He didn't seem to have a gradient to it. River noticed the change.

"What do you want, River?" I asked, redirecting him to me with hopes to deescalate Cory.

"Just pointing out you returned to a scene where you are a suspect."

"If I was a suspect, you would have presented irrefutable evidence and used your influence to pressure STF into arresting me."

His lips furled at the reminder of his attempt to question

me when Harrison was initially reported missing, which turned out embarrassingly bad for him. He bristled.

"You seemed to have been MIA for the past few months."

"A person can't take a vacation?" I shot back.

"Seems suspicious that you decided to vacation during the investigation into the disappearance of someone, an investigation in which you're a potential suspect."

"You're the only one who considers me a suspect."

"So smug," he sneered.

If it came off that way, it wasn't intentional, but any refutation would have been perceived by him as smug.

"Expensive lawyers, friends with the pain-in-the-ass Alpha, and a sister who will use her position at Task Force and connections to protect you at all costs, has made you feel invincible."

"Not too invincible, since I'm standing here being illegally detained."

His hand dropped from his gun where it had been resting. "You're not being detained."

"I'm free to leave?"

"Of course." He stepped aside from the pathway to our car.

"Someone decided to leave Harrison's body at my door," he offered with a pointed expression.

"We've already established I wasn't here."

"Yes, but we also *established* how well connected you are."

"What? You think Madison had something to do with this?"

The mention of her name brought a dark scowl on his face. Madison played the bureaucratic system to her advantage and could end his political career before it started.

"Or is Asher under suspicion? Do you seriously think he'd take time from his duties as Alpha of the largest pack in the county to play a prank on you? Because there's no way you would have been considered a suspect. Why would I have that done to you?" I softened my voice during the questioning. If I could get River off my back, life would be a lot simpler. "I just want you to leave me alone. The hits your reputation is taking are the results of your own actions. I wish you no harm."

To my surprise, River took in my comments with consideration.

His response was cut off when a hand wrapped around his throat.

"Well, he's annoying, isn't he?" Dareus bit out.

The shock of the ambush showed on River's face. Before River could protect himself, Dareus invoked a spell and moved aside, letting River collapse to the ground. His head lolled to the side, giving Dareus perfect access to his neck. He eyed it as his claws extended from his hands and he slowly shifted to his demon form. Rust-colored leathery skin sheathed his body. His face misaligned to accommodate the ram's horn that protruded from it, and the pointed chin. When his transformation was complete, his dark thunderstorm slitted eyes fixed on mine.

"Erin," he drawled in a low, taunting, throaty sound. "I should have known there was more to you than elven touched. What have you done to make such an enemy of someone as powerful as Elizabeth?"

The only thing Elizabeth revealed before I was banished to the demon realm was that she'd kept her promise to Nolan by keeping me alive. Serving my intended purpose. As far as I knew, he wasn't aware of my relationship to Elizabeth or that I was an elf as well.

"Elizabeth will be quite unhappy to know you've returned. What is it about you that she loathes so much? Make no mistake, she loathes you."

"So, you've been reduced to her errand boy. How the mighty have fallen," I retorted, ignoring his inquiry.

A slow smile curved his black lips.

Cory appeared to be having a difficult time adjusting to the new shape.

Stepping forward, Dareus's cloven feet bumped into River's sleeping form, bringing his attention back to him. He descended on River with his claws.

Cory reacted before I could.

The bolt of magic slamming into Dareus made for the perfect opportunity to run. And I did. Charging toward the wards as the aggressive sounds of magic being hurled, thuds of bodies hitting the ground, and Darius's barks of anger and promises to rip Cory to shreds for his interference started to fall away.

That threat made me halt. Should I leave Cory alone to take on a demon? Cory's chortle and his urging Dareus to try eased me enough to continue with my plan.

My decision to delay picking Cory up in order to swing by my apartment to retrieve my scribing chalk was a good choice. Quickly scribing the neutralization spell, I tore up grass and hid the circle. My ears perked up at the sound of approaching footsteps. Dareus sing-songed my name as he navigated in his human form. Perhaps he thought he could hunt me more efficiently through the populated trees in human form.

"Your friend is a coward. He ran away. I don't have time to play with him when you're the one I want."

A calming wave of relief moved through me. Cory knew me. He knew me well. He didn't run; he gave me time. It brought a smile to my face as I stood in plain sight, but cloaked. Patiently I waited for Dareus's approach.

"Come on, Erin. Tell me, what is it about your existence that makes Elizabeth uneasy? What will having you in my possession be worth?" Greedy jackass.

Closer, I silently urged. But he wasn't moving, just slowly circling, on high alert listening for sound. He raised his face to the air. "I know you're around. You have a peculiar essence to your magic. I'd come if you summoned me, sheerly out of intrigue." He took a few more steps, listening for the patter of movement. I didn't give him any feedback.

Dammit, he wasn't close enough. I didn't have access to magic in my cloaked state, so I tossed an electric pellet to Dareus's right, drawing his attention.

His eyes darted around frantically, looking for more signs of movement. "Your mother said you were clever. I don't believe it was cleverness that is responsible for you being out. But I'm quite interested in finding out."

His curiosity was met with silence. Magic twined around his fingers as he waited in anticipation of sight of me. I tossed another pellet. He moved a few more feet toward the circle. At a full run, I slammed into him, knocking him the distance necessary to slam him on his butt in the middle of the *adligatura* circle. Dropping my cloak, I swiftly activated it.

Pulling my shoulders back to stand taller, I refused to reveal how much I'd exerted myself. With his magic gone, he melted into his demon form. Standing, his lips drew into a grim sneer. After a third attempt to use his magic, he plopped to the ground, extending his legs out and lounging back on his elbows in an attempt at indifference. I wasn't buying it.

"You are a slippery little thing, aren't you? How did you escape?"

My long sleeves hid the oath marking, so I left him to speculate.

"Did a demon help you?" He tossed away that idea with a shake of his head. "No, someone like you would have been kept or put on the market."

A shudder of fear ran through me at what could have been my fate if Wendy hadn't summoned a demon. Whatever favor she requested—and I know there would be one—would be honored without hesitation.

"How did you know to track me?" I asked.

"My mark has returned," he blurted, then snapped his

mouth closed.

"Now you can be sent back to the demon realm," I pointed out. The thought brought a satisfied smile to my lips. "You're safe unless someone makes you incorporeal. Without a body to use, well…" I gave him a wiggle-fingered goodbye and watched the smug arrogance seep from his face. After several moments, it returned, but it was hard earned.

"It won't be by you. If you could do it, you would have upon seeing me," he huffed. My lack of a response returned his expression to conjecture. Turning from him, I stepped away to speak with Cory, who had joined me.

Pondering the various metals and their effect on magic, I wondered if the combination of them all could subdue Dareus enough. Iridium worked on witches and mages, iron on fae. Zirconium weakened vampires. Combining them would probably have some effect. Limited interaction with demons left us at a disadvantage when dealing with them. Most of the focus was on containing them, not on what to do with them once they were among us. When they borrowed bodies, their magic was limited enough not to be a dire threat and they did what was necessary not to draw too much attention.

"We need my bag from the car," I told Cory. "I have various cuffs in them."

"Which cuff?" Cory's aversion to the mention of the magic-restricting cuffs creased a frown.

"All of them."

"Ah, the kitchen sink approach," he teased before heading for the car.

"You're a bug that I can't seem to squash."

I whipped around in the direction of Elizabeth's frosty voice. Anger-hardened eyes bored into me before she turned them to the imprisoned demon. She looked at him with the same contempt and disappointment she usually reserved for me.

"Imprisoning her in the demon realm wasn't the solution, was it?" she chided. Drawing himself up to stand, Dareus's eyes followed her as she circled the enclosure, twisting her lips as she studied it. "It's good," she said, opening her hands just inches from it. A burst of illumination wrapped around the enclosure then faded.

"The spells of ours that you have in your possession, you've mastered." Her gaze returned to me and was like ice. "It was a failing of my brother to give you such weapons."

"Where is Nolan?"

Her expression blanked as she moved from the enclosure toward me. My panic was quickly replaced with anger as I relived what she'd done to me. What she'd taken from me. Charging toward her, I called magic, ready to blast her with it and finish her. She wouldn't be my problem any longer.

She pointed a chastising finger at me. "Arrogance is your failing. You can't keep the enclosure around him and attack me. Now you must make the decision, Malific's daughter. Who is the greater threat?" She glowered. "I have an appreciation for what your life means in the grand scheme. He doesn't."

"For that reason, you won't allow him to kill me."

Her eyes glassed over in consideration as we came face to face. Not a sliver of fear of reprisal showed in hers. "I often wonder if we hold a slanted view of history. Perhaps what was done to us was a necessary catalyst to propel us into action. We aren't the same as we were. Pacifism is only effective when dealing with the civilized. Gods aren't civilized." Her expression softened into her thoughts before returning to its cold veneer. "Most who possess magic lose some of their civility."

"Especially you."

Her confirmation that there were more didn't escape me. My insult didn't land or get the response I thought it would.

Insults only work when the person holds you at some value. To Elizabeth, I had none.

"I assure you, I am quite civilized. My intervention is the needed balance and justice among those who deal in magic."

"It seems as if someone wants to be a deity," I said. "You aren't justice and balance. You're a bitter bitch with a highly inflated sense of importance."

Irritation flitted over her expression. Watching her rub three of her fingers slowly together, I prepared for her to retaliate with magic, forcing me into fighting her and Dareus. Instead, she slowly walked around me, driving me to match her step by step to keep her from getting behind me.

"I love my brother." *What does she want, an award?* "I've tried to see what inspires him to protect Malific's daughter, and what hold you have on him." Sadness crept into her voice. She studied me anew, exhibiting a similar scrutiny I saw in Madison when I shared that Landon had saved Dr. Sumner on my behalf. Speculation in her expression as if my father's innate ability to love me and help his daughter was some form of enchantment.

"Perhaps he will forgive me for—"

Not giving her time to finish her sentence, I hit her with a right hook that landed squarely on her jaw. She wouldn't be given more of my time to lob threats, muse over me being unworthy of existence, or Nolan being foolish for seeing me as more than Malific's daughter.

Shock registered on her face. It was clear that she'd never been punched. The left hook I delivered next knocked her to the ground. Her lips gaped into an astonished O before she reacted. A light nudge of magic that did nothing to fend me off. Just placed more distance between us.

Then flames erupted around me from the Mirra she erected. Heat licked at my skin. I prepared myself for the pain of walking through it, as opposed to disabling the Mirra, to keep Dareus in the enclosure. My efforts were in vain. I came out on the other side to find them both gone. The area where the sigils once were had been scorched over by more sigils, and the remnants of energy from the powerful magic lingered around it.

Taking out my phone, I took pictures of it with the hopes of duplicating the magic she used to override mine. Elizabeth had either a mastery of her elven magic or talent of merging her fae and elven magic to complement and enhance her magic. Whatever the case, my magical skills were inferior.

After seeing me emerge from the woods, Cory brought River from under the sleep spell. Confusion settled over River's face as he looked around. An awareness of where he was and that he'd lost time quickly followed.

"What did you do to me?" he barked, his hand going to his now-empty holster. His eyes dropped to Cory, who held his gun in front of him, in plain view.

I stood in front of River. "If I had something to do with it," I said, "and I'd targeted you for retaliation the way you believe, you wouldn't be standing here. You're fighting a unilateral war, River. I just want to be left alone. If you continue with your vendetta, this will be the last time I intervene. You're a nuisance to me, but you're a liability to people who want to harm me. They'll just plow over you to get to me."

Having had my fill of confrontations, I didn't stand around for further debate. Once in the car, I watched as River clenched his jaw and fumed as he accepted his gun from Cory. He scowled at Cory's back as he got into the car.

I searched his face for some resolve or at least acquiescence but saw nothing. He was too deeply rooted into his enmity. There was too much hate for me and the supernatural world. I suspected it extended further than me. I was emblematic of a perceived symptom he believed existed with supernaturals. River was another problem I'd have to deal with on another day.

CHAPTER 13

Several hours were spent dissecting Elizabeth's spell, hoping that it would give me another tool to explore my elven magic and help me spell weave the magic. Grasping at every possible straw of hope, I couldn't stop basking in her confirmation that there were more elves. It wasn't wishful thinking. They existed and that meant they could be found. I just needed to figure out where to start.

The feelings of despair that kept creeping in fell away and were quickly replaced with hope. Enough that I sent out feelers to my contacts in the service industry to let me know if they heard anyone mention the Cupio. They were always the best source of information because, unless they needed something, they were invisible. It worked to my benefit.

Next, I called Maddox, the nicer of the criminal trio who'd I met after they had stolen items from some powerful people during a poker game. Maddox was a shapeshifting dragon who attributed his predilection for theft to him being a dragon, but their collection wasn't a dragon horde; it was the haul from their many burglaries. Plain and simple. Own it. They liked nice and expensive things and they used a five-finger discount. More impressive than the expensive electronics, jewelry, art, and liquor were the magical objects they had accumulated.

When I asked about the Cupio, his roaring peal of laughter caused me to reassert my skepticism about its existence.

"If we had one, it wouldn't be in our possession for long. We'd sell it. For no other reason than to get the target off us. Taking the seven-figure payout would be easier."

"Easy is never fun," I teased.

"The people interested in the Cupio are more trouble than it's worth," Maddox said.

"I'm interested in it."

"You're not exactly a lamb," he scoffed. His comment bolstered my ego more than it should have or I cared to admit. It seemed like I was getting my ass handed to me too often and taking losses more than wins. The people I was dealing with now were at another level, and it felt like I was perpetually failing.

"Let me know if you hear anything or find yourself in possession of one."

"Sure. When I see a unicorn, I'll tell you about it, too," he quipped back. "You still owe me dinner," he reminded me.

"Really? The unreasonable price you charged me for that phylaca urn should buy you more than enough dinners at the fine-dining restaurant of your choice," I shot back, recalling his fee that had one too many zeros behind it. In a desperate situation, I hadn't had a choice.

He responded with what I assumed was a shamed grunt. Although I knew if presented with the situation again, nothing would change.

Intensely focused on scrolling through my phone for any possible missed contacts, I was surprised to open my door and find Elon seated on my sofa, flipping through a paperback. Quickly, I retrieved my dropped phone to check the screen, using that time to tamp down my raging fear at having Landon's cleaner, the main assassin himself, in my home waiting on me.

He was nearly seven feet tall and sinewy, built for stealth and speed, with short matte black hair and cinder-colored skin that showed the radiance of a recent feeding. His bluntly hewn features were attractive, like most vampires, but he'd never be described at pretty. The keenness of his demeanor didn't allow for a good faith belief that any interaction with him would be peaceful.

Keeping his eyes trained on his book, a dubious smirk inched across his lips as he flipped another page and I slowly eased past him, making my way to my room. I closed the door, fully aware it wasn't enough to stop him if he wanted in. But I still had the advantage of surprise. My magical ability was still unknown to the vampires.

Landon picked up as soon as the phone rang. "What the fuck, Landon? Why is Elon here?" I barked.

"Ah, Erin. You're a busy little minx, aren't you? My calls and texts go unanswered. Being ignored by you was quite discomforting. There were moments I thought you were avoiding me to prevent dealing with your debt. That was a foolish thought, because you'd never do such a thing." Despite his cloying tone, his little speech was laden with threats.

"I wouldn't think of it."

"Of course, you wouldn't. I request an audience with you."

"I'm not going anywhere with Elon."

His ominous chuckle sent a chill through me. It was a reminder that Landon was more than just an ostentatious and dramatic vampire who let slights go because he chose to and not because he *had* to. Sometimes I needed the reminder, because their veneer of civility made it easy to forget that the violence depicted in our history books wasn't inflicted by their forebearers or other vampires, but by those who lived among us.

Yet again I was on the ever-present tightrope of maintaining professional respect and maintaining agency by exerting my boundaries while preventing making enemies with someone who could snuff out my life with a simple command.

"Let's clarify, Erin. You might not go with Elon willingly, but if I request that you are delivered to me, you will be going with him."

Clenching my teeth together, I bit back the response that would have challenged him and emptied my voice of any of the anger and contempt I felt for having to perform in this dog and pony show. "I haven't been avoiding you. Things have been a little chaotic. I have time now. Can we meet in an hour?"

"Of course, I'd love to meet with you. See you in an hour."

Before I could end the call, he tacked on. "Erin, no weapons. I'd like to trust you on this. Can I trust you?"

"Yes. As you wish," I said in the same faux cloying tone.

I had no intention of bringing weapons, because I wasn't going to be in hostile territory. Landon had the advantage.

Elon was gone in the few seconds it took me to get from my bedroom to the living room.

Elon opened Landon's door before I had a chance to ring the doorbell. Looking at him eying me with the same dubious smirk, I couldn't help but wonder if he had knowledge of the debt or Landon's plans for repayment. Perhaps he thought I was going to renege and was looking forward to the repercussions. He looked me over, his gaze slowly moving over the fitted long-sleeve t-shirt, leggings, and flats. There wasn't any place to hide a weapon and I made it obvious. He did another cursory measured once-over that landed on my hair, upswept into a hasty bun that I'd ornamented with long decorative pins.

Elon's lips twisted into a frown. "Give me those."

"It's for decoration," I said, flashing him a smile. Technically they weren't weapons but "behave" sticks.

"You need no extra flourish, you're lovely just the way you are," he said. His tone held no warmth or earnestness. I wondered if he was recalling the time I stabbed Landon before threatening him with Amber Crocus. I pulled out the decorative pins and handed them to him. Frowning, he examined them. They were long enough, and the tips were sharp enough, for their intended purpose: ensuring vampires played nice.

I shrugged. "Decorative, aren't they?"

He responded with a sneer and started walking away. Assuming I was to follow, I let him lead me to the den where Landon was seated in his thronelike chair sipping on something from a wine glass that was so viscous and sanguine that despite the open bottle of wine on the table next to him, I remained unconvinced it wasn't blood. At least a very large portion of it was blood.

"Landon," I greeted then turned to the man on the sofa. "Assassin." Dallas's arms were stretched along the back of the sofa, his legs crossed, and a warm affable smile was on his lips. A viper ready to strike, looking as innocent as a lamb.

"It's lovely to see you, Erin," Dallas said. His placid dark eyes welcomed me into his web of deceit.

"May I offer you a drink?" Landon asked, lifting his glass. "It's wine," he added in response to my grimace.

"I'm sure part of it is."

He laughed. His jocund mood made me even more apprehensive. It wasn't Landon's histrionics that unnerved and annoyed me, but his solipsism. He was the world. It revolved around him. His problems were your problems. His annoyance needed to be of great importance to everyone around.

His pleasures were to be shared. For the right audience, that could be enticing. I wasn't the audience.

"I suppose this is more of a champagne moment," he said, standing and walking over to the bar where a bottle was chilling. Taking out two flutes, he opened the bottle and poured two glasses.

Dallas took that as a sign to leave. "Always a pleasure, Erin," he said before sliding past me to exit the room, closing the door behind him. I sneered at his back.

Landon frowned. "I was under the impression that you two got along, but it seems there's some animosity." Understatement of the year. We got along until I found out he was an assassin for Landon.

Dallas looked like he was sculpted from marble. Beautiful flawless skin accompanied a deceptively congenial personality. A vampire who handed out warm smiles like candy on Halloween left me unprepared for his lethality. He had two witches by the throat with such speed and precision that I didn't have time to react. Didn't realize he was the person I needed to watch. I'd been blindsided.

Knowing the major players, and the people I needed to be cautious and highly alert around, was knowledge I had honed over the years. He'd slipped under my radar, and I was sure I wasn't the only one deceived by his bashful sweet persona that belied anything deadly about him. My anger was misdirected. It was Landon who had hired him, but I couldn't help but be annoyed by how well he played his innocuous role.

Landen strolled to me with an exaggerated slowness that was as off-putting as when vampires tried to breathe to seem more human. They made weird, inconsistent shallow breaths, when they remembered to do it. It had been so long since they'd had to breathe, the whole response appeared to come from the neck, only adding to the eerie factor.

He handed me a glass and in a graceful sweeping movement, he was on the other side of the room seated in his chair.

"What are we celebrating?" I asked.

"I'm no longer a liaison."

"What?" I asked, the flute halted midway to my mouth.

"He's dead. Ramos is truly dead." Perhaps the cool apathy of his delivery was his coping mechanism, that, or his indifference was a result of Ramos's new status. He sipped from his glass. "So, I'm no longer the acting Master. This is mine, now."

I needed to know.

"How did he die?"

"I killed him," he said curtly before taking another sip. My sip slipped down quickly, keeping me from choking on it. I was used to the arrogance, the sense of entitlement, the expectation of impunity for wrongdoing, but this admission was so blatant it left me baffled.

"You gave yourself a promotion."

"No, he asked me to. He was ready to go." Sadness seeped into his voice. His eyes moved from mine to the floor. His slow sigh was the most human thing I'd ever seen him do. He grieved.

"This is mine," he whispered. Like Alphas of packs, vampires had territories and there were rules of propriety. With a shudder, he shook off all remnants of grief and sadness, allowing his eyes to lift back to mine.

"Which leads me to you."

Sitting farther back on the sofa, I let one arm rest on the back of it before taking a draw from the glass. This was going to be interesting.

Several moments of silence crept by as he took his time deliberating on his delivery. "I don't have children, but with Ramos's departure, I'm left with the desire to have some."

"Great. Thanks for sharing." I stood. Placed my flute on

the table and prepared to leave. I had an idea where this was going and I didn't want any part of it.

"Erin, sit," he demanded, steel in his voice.

With a sigh, I said, "Look—"

"Erin, sit. Please," he requested through clenched teeth, exposing his deadly fangs.

I sank down onto the sofa and waited for him to continue, my chest tight.

"I need progeny. They can be among my trusted, help me with ruling—be a reflection of me and what I represent. I want a family and I would like you to be their mother."

Landon had been a vampire for at least a century and was too old to be able to make children. New vampires lose their ability to procreate about a month after their transition. When a vampire is sired, they are also considered children of the vampire. Based on vampire canon, Landon had just killed his father. There seemed to be irony in him wanting children. Or perhaps it was poetically symbolic. When he was ready to depart, he'd want his progeny to do the honors.

"Anyone can help you create a vampire. There are plenty of people who'd consider it an honor to help create your family."

He made a face. "Some random person used to create my family? How gauche."

"All it is, is a blood exchange," I pointed out.

"Exactly. I'm particular about who I feed from and need to be even more discerning about who will help create my children. I want it to be you. Of course, it will be stressful for your body, so I will care for you afterward."

It wasn't just stressful, it was dangerous. I'd have to give enough blood for them to survive while making sure I didn't die. The fact that he hadn't done it before made it more dangerous. Would this be his first attempt, or had he never successfully created a vampire? I didn't want any part of it.

"No." I blurted it out without a second thought. "I don't

want to be your baby mama. Find another way for me to repay my debt to you."

His lips stretched into a tight line. "Hmm. I do believe it was an open-ended debt," he reminded me in a crisp tone.

I sighed. "Something else. It needs to be something else." Creating a vampire didn't bother me nearly as much as the significance he was putting on creating a "family" and his children. He was going to fetter me to his vampire family as their mother. I wasn't going to have the freedom to give some blood and walk away from him and his indulgent, entitled children.

He nodded, took another slow sip from the flute, then placed it on the table next to the red wine. "Your friend is alive because of me, correct?"

Considering it a rhetorical question, I didn't answer.

"Erin," he urged.

"Yes," I said.

His eyes turned chillingly cold, a dark gleam to his black onyx eyes. "It was the offering of my blood that gave him life. Should I revoke my gift? Just say the word and it can be done and the debt be cleared." He leaned forward on his chair, exuding all the power, raw lethality, and cruelty that would make him feared among the vampires and allow him to rule without challenge to his authority.

I shook my head. The debt had to be honored.

"I would like to hear your commitment."

"No. I don't want you to revoke it." I gulped down the champagne, went to the bar, and refilled my flute. Staying close to it, I asked, "Why me? All you have to do is make one public request and there would be a line of willing people." He only needed a blood donor.

He mused over the question. "You realize that we weren't always able to Wynd. Then suddenly we were, and that gift was linked to one bloodline. One created by using a witch. I don't know what you are, but it damn sure isn't a death

mage. I'm curious as to what will come from our creation."
He flashed me a wide smile. "I only want the best for my
children."

If it weren't for the fact that I needed to be sober to drive
home, I'd finish the bottle and start on the harder stuff. I
hadn't even considered that angle. What would I create? New
creations weren't always good.

"Are we done?" I asked. He stood, grabbed his glass, and
in a flash of movement was in front of me, tapping his glass
against mine. "To family." He grinned and finished off his
glass.

I didn't repeat it. I finished what was in my glass, set it
down on the bar, and headed for the door.

"Don't worry, they'll be children that will give us the
utmost pride, I guarantee. A boy and a girl, a perfect family.
Just as I wouldn't just choose any woman as their mother, I'll
be just as discerning with who I pick as our children," he
boasted. Nearly at the door, I fought the urge to give him
double middle fingers. It was childish, but my desire for
civility was worn to a nub. Seeing my struggle to leave
without responding induced a roar of laughter from him.
"They'll have my urbane refinement and hopefully your
tenacity."

I breezed past Dallas and Elon on my way out of the front
door. Elon's smirk taunted me. He knew.

"Do you want your pins?" he asked, calling after me.

"Keep them." As angry as I was, I had no confidence in my
ability to keep from introducing him to Mr. and Mrs. Pointy
if he said the wrong thing.

The text I sent Cory earlier had been timed perfectly. He had
just returned from the gym as I drove up to his apartment.
Our search earlier wasn't going to keep him from his

workout schedule. It took a while for him to let me in. His hair was damp and disheveled from being towel dried after his shower. The damp t-shirt clung to his chest, and his basketball shorts kept sticking to his thighs as he walked to the sofa.

"He wants me to be his baby mama!" I blurted, sinking into the sofa and covering my face with my hands. "That's how he wants me to repay the debt."

After moments of silence, I spread my fingers to look through them at him. He was relaxed back on the sofa, his mouth twisted in thought.

"To clarify, he just wants you to help him sire some vampires and not get someone to give you their baby goo to make an actual baby, right?"

"Baby goo? Ew. Just ew. And yes, he wants me to help sire some vampires. And he's very specific about it. He wants two children: a boy and girl. Who thinks like that!"

"He does. He's over a century old. Picket fence, two point five children, and all that other outdated nonsense." He moved from the sofa until he was in front of me, then pulled my hands from my face. "It's not nearly as bad as I thought it might be. If you consider the number of things he could have requested, you got off pretty easy."

"He wants me to be the mother of his children, how is that easy?"

"Oh, calm down. Your Best Actor, Television Drama Series is in the mail. It's not like he's asking you to push a Mini-Cooper out of your lady garage. He's requesting your help in creating two more than likely annoyingly attractive vampires. The only thing you'll have to deal with are more vampires suffering from a case of affluenza and self-entitlement, who undoubtedly will be pretentious knobs you can't stand. It could have been so much worse," he said with a shrug, sitting back and resting his chin on his bent knee.

I sighed. "Lady garage? Really. Make childbirth sound grosser."

"I can't make it sound grosser than it is. My mother seems to have thought I'd like to see me being born. No one needs to see that. Why would you even record that?" He frowned as he regarded me. "Look on the bright side. If he's going to make it weird, like having two grown-ass people calling you Mother and taking you to brunch on Mother's Day and spending holidays together, you just one up him. *Every time.* I'm talking war of attrition. You're good at that. If he's wants you to be a mom—go all out. Pull the mom card all the time. Be weird. Demanding. Outlandish. The baby mamma from hell."

"There's a mom card? Do tell."

"The mom card is powerful. I'm going to Vegas with my mother who actually said 'what happens in Vegas stays in Vegas.' What the hell does that mean? What experience will I have with my mom that needs to stay there?" He grimaced. "Well, she is making me go see Michael Bublé. He's okay, not really my style, but it's not information that needs to 'stay in Vegas.'"

He shrugged it off. "The mom card is why you and Madison spend days at your parents' playing games that you don't like. You'll have two powerful vampires probably being weird as hell—because that's Landon—calling you Mom. Fine. Make them wear matching gawdy activewear and go on long walks around the park. Buy them chunky tacky jewelry and insist they wear it 'for their mother.' Go big and go weird and eventually they'll ignore you. You'll be looking at this situation out the rearview mirror in no time. You would've satisfied your debt and can irritate Landon and his annoying-ass kids at the same time. You have to get your wins where you can."

I laughed. Part of me wanted it to be that simple, but I

knew there was more to it. Landon was hoping to engineer a different breed of vampire.

"It's more nefarious than him wanting a family. He's curious as to what will happen with *me* creating a vampire. He knows I'm not a mage." I stood and started pacing the room under Cory's watchful eyes. "It's all speculation. He's not sure what I am, but he's curious as to how it will influence the vampire bloodline."

Cory leaned his back against the sofa behind him, fingers clasped behind his head. He hadn't considered that.

"Wynding was a special gift for vampires. Landon said it was traced to a single bloodline of vampires. Now it seems that it's not the norm but the exception," I surmised. "Those may be the original vampires and Darwinism has taken over. Witches need a spell to Wynd and not all are powerful enough to do it. The vampires who can do it don't need a spell, they just Wynd."

"But they are immortal, that's steeped in magic. So is their ability to compel. Which is probably why they don't need a spell to Wynd. They are the embodiment of it. Only their blood has the ability to heal. No other supernatural has that ability." Cory's levity had disappeared.

People never explored the reasons behind magic but only ways to counter it because no one wanted to go down that rabbit hole. They'd never crawl out because magic was too nebulous.

"What if I create some other ability, making them more dangerous?"

Cory's frown became more pronounced as I laid out the dilemma.

The more we speculated, the more I understood why some people were puritans when it came to magic. Unlike science, magic didn't follow a lot of concrete rules. $E=MC^2$. Gravity existed. Magic's amorphousness was problematic, and adding interspecies birth could lead to disastrous outcomes.

"Can you imagine a vampire with the elves' cloaking ability? Or one that could neutralize magic? Or perform magic like gods? Or lose their weakness of being able to be killed by a stake? Leaving them indestructible," Cory listed.

He'd stood and was in front of me, pacing. "Stall. You have to do this, but let Landon know that whoever is chosen needs to be mutually agreed upon. We need to figure this out. You're already responsible for making shifters immune to magic. If they ever abuse their new privileges, people will look for the root of it. Asher's protection might not be enough. Vampires with a new gift might cause a situation that will put a target on you. Things could become difficult for you."

"My life is already difficult," I admitted. "Stall for now, send Dareus back, figure out a way to satisfy my oath with Asial and..." The latter didn't need to be said, and it seemed so distasteful. Deal with Elizabeth and Malific. I didn't need to vocalize it. My end goal was clear. For my life to have any glimpse of normality, Malific and Elizabeth couldn't exist.

CHAPTER 14

$\mathcal{T}$ime seemed to be moving at lightning speed. Cory and I walked a circle around the printouts of the spell Elizabeth had used to break mine two days earlier.

Cory moved back several steps, as if looking at it from another angle would reveal something we hadn't discovered in the past three hours we'd spent looking at it.

On the sofa, Madison blew out a frustrated breath. She was looking at the books she'd *borrowed* from work and was using an extended lunch to help. I picked up the Crelic, a flat round stone used to harness witches' magic. After it was stolen from the Supernatural Task Force, Madison hired me for its retrieval. Stolen by a vampire who used it to perform magic, it did nothing to enhance my magic or allow me to perform new magical spells.

Taking in the collection of magical objects and books she'd brought with her, I said, "Madison, don't lose your job for me."

She sighed. "I'm not going to lose it." She gave me a wry look. "Maybe get demoted, but I'm sure I'll keep the job." She was attempting to decrease the intensity that lingered after catching her up with the situation. Her frustration extended further than River and Elizabeth, but there wasn't any legal recourse she could take to prevent Landon from creating new vampires with me. Her intervening on STF's behalf would create chaos and lose the endorsement of other powerful supernaturals.

There was an implicit rule that for the most part, the different denizens policed most of their own behaviors. STF's involvement on most matters was collectively agreed upon, but she'd be overstepping if she attempted to regulate vampire creation. If the parties agreed to be changed, there wasn't anything STF could do. Citing the creation of the potential of super vampires would out me and the Huntsmen. We weren't ready to broach that new set of problems.

Walking over to the circle of the printed spell, Madison looked at it again. "It's not fae magic. I have no idea what it is. Elven?" she asked. It should have looked familiar to at least one of us if it held even a similarity to other spells.

"You need an elven spell book," Cory said before stepping even farther back to look at the string of loops, glyphs, and symbols.

"And someone who can help us understand it." I was sure saying the words was fine, but I'd like to know what spells I was evoking and the meaning of the symbols.

"She did this in a matter of seconds and it broke my neutralizing spell," I said with a sigh. The feeling that I was one book or spell away from unlocking so much stayed with me. So close, yet so far away. Cory had permitted me to do a neutralizing spell around him, the entire time with him in a noticeable state of discomfort as I attempted to use a replication of Elizabeth's spell to break it. Nothing.

Madison and Cory looked at my phone on the table. Picking it up, I checked for a response from Nolan and shook my head. Elizabeth didn't give me the impression that Nolan was missing or worse. But the heaviness in my gut wouldn't go away as that being an explanation for him not returning my calls.

Mephisto's call interrupted our unsuccessful brainstorming. "I need the specifics of your contract with Asial," he rushed out without so much as a greeting when I answered. A car door closed soon after.

I had to give him the specifics from memory because Asial had made the copy vanish. As if recalling the contract evoked a spell, there was a needlelike prickling along my oath mark. Grimacing at the pain caused Cory to give me a look of concern. I relayed the specifics of the contract to Mephisto.

"No transfers of the contract isn't the same as giving him another body if you can't make him corporeal." A keen urgency rasped in his voice. "So another person can be used." It wasn't a question but speculation.

"I'm sure that's possible, but he'd have to agree to it. And he would still be in this world. Another demon with a body. It's doubtful he'd agree. He's forcing my hand to make him corporeal with unrestricted magic."

He heaved a sigh. "That's what I figured." There was a long silence. "How are you, Erin?" he asked softly. In solution mode, he'd abandoned basic phone etiquette. He knew of my run-in with Elizabeth and River.

"Fine." It wasn't a total lie. Frustrated didn't mean I wasn't fine. I updated him on Nolan and trying to mimic Elizabeth's magic.

"If it breaks your magic, it could potentially break the demon oath."

"How did you make that connection?"

"I still believe there's a link between demon and elven magic," he said.

Perhaps, but unless I found it and a way to break the oath, it wasn't going to help me. I winced again at the pain that shot through my oath mark.

"What's wrong?"

"Nothing," I lied. "Why did you ask about the contract?"

"I'm trying to find someone to take your place for the trade." What type of persuasive skill did he have to convince someone to allow a demon to host their body indefinitely?

"What would they get out of the deal?"

"I'm still looking for someone appealing enough for Asial, then I find their price."

"You're buying someone?" Disgust tinged my question. Cory's and Madison's heads perked up.

"No, I'll be negotiating terms for them to be a host on your behalf," he countered.

Tomato. To-mahto. It was the same damn fruit no matter how you say it.

Mephisto still had a tone of urgency, so I started to get off the phone. "Okay, but don't force anyone, okay?"

"Like I said, Erin. Just negotiations. I need to go."

I checked my phone again for a response from Nolan before placing it on the table. No matter how skilled Mephisto was in the art of negotiation, he wasn't going to convince someone to be a demon host indefinitely—or until I was able to make him corporeal.

Madison was tight-lipped as she gathered up everything to leave. "We don't want more demons here," she reminded me.

"I know. You don't have to say it. I'm not cool with using someone else as a host, either. These are just contingencies."

No one said it, but we all knew it. They were bad contingency plans. Fatigued from the research, my mind started to wander.

"What?" I asked in response to Cory's look.

"When are you going to tell M about Landon?" he asked. His eyes widened at my furrowed brow. "You are going to tell him, right?"

"I guess," I offered, trying to understand the shock and reproach in his expression.

"When is Geppetto going to make you a real girl?"

I rolled my eyes. "With everything going on in my life and his, do you think me being Landon's baby momma is going to even rank in the top five of the things he cares about?"

"Yes, it very much will." He closed the distance between us, canting his head to study me. "When we first met, I thought you were peculiar because you were dealing with a lot. Being a death mage along with your oddball and quirky family dynamics, how could you not be...*unique*? But you're just weird. Not in the 'oh she's cute and whimsical' way but more like 'she should be studied' sort of way. Although she hides it better, Madison is a little odd, too."

I glared at him. "How am I weird?"

"Relationships. You're distant in all your relationships." After giving me a considering look, he added, "Probably because you've never really had one."

"I've had relationships." The prickles of discomfort made me shift.

He shook his head. "No, what you've had are hook-ups, shallow, depthless relationships that were nothing more than one-night stands that lasted for weeks or months. You once had one of your hook-ups introduce himself because you couldn't tell me his name with any level of certainty. You were with him for three weeks."

I flushed. Casual relationships were a distraction from the magical cravings. They helped. When things were over, they went on with their lives, I went on with mine.

He pecked the tip of my nose. Something he did infrequently. With anyone else, it was off-putting. It always seemed like something someone would do before they tried to eat your face or something. But with Cory, it didn't seem like a psycho cannibal getting a taste before devouring you with a side of vegetables.

"I'm not trying to shame you, Erin. I say live and let live. There's no judgment about those relationships, just an observation. I know you're capable of deeper because of what we have."

"I trust you." He'd earned that trust.

"Do you trust Mephisto?"

Dropping down onto the sofa, I took a seat, examining my feelings.

I nodded.

"You two seem to be in some type of relationship. What happens to you indirectly affects him. M—"

"Stop calling him that."

Annoyance fluttered in Cory's eyes. It was doubtful that he wanted to call him that; he just wanted to flout the implicit rule. Clay seemed to be the only one allowed to call Mephisto M, and it pricked at Cory's defiance. "Mephisto needs to be let in. Especially if this is going to be something more."

He draped his arm over my shoulder and pulled me to him, pressing a kiss to my head. "Tell him. It probably won't be a big deal, but he should know. Let him in. Really in." He gave me a squeeze. "You're still freaking weird." He leaned in closer. "Maddie can't know I said she was odd, 'kay? I've seen rogue Maddie and she gets a look in her eyes that makes me think I'm about to see a scene from *John Wick*."

"Really. Now I'm starting to question the strength of our military," I teased.

He shot me a dramatic look of horror. "You haven't seen rogue Madison." His look was replaced by concern as my jaw clenched, absorbing the prick of pain that came from my oath mark.

"You okay?"

I nodded my lie. "I guess you won't be calling her a Disney Princess anymore."

He shook his head. "No, and if I ever go missing, please put her on the case."

"Of course. But you think she'd be more relentless in finding you than I would."

"It's just you, whereas she has a whole department of supernaturals behind her and she knows the rules and laws and how to circumvent them and use them to her advantage. You're tenacious, she's pragmatic."

I grinned up at him. "Your secret's safe with me."

We both looked at the door when someone started knocking—no, pounding—on the door. Looking through the peephole was another reminder to put in a camera. The front door was the only exit, but I'd have more time to prepare.

"What?" I demanded through the door. With a defiant jut of her chin, Malific looked into the lens.

"Daughter, let Mommy in." Her voice was softer than usual with a mocking trill of amusement, finding the use of the term as absurd as me hearing it.

I opened the door. When she attempted to enter, she smashed into the protective wall I'd erected between me and the threshold. Her smug expression became vapid anger at the reminder of the abilities I had that she didn't or couldn't use her magic against. She glared at me.

"We need to talk," she insisted, making another effort to breach the barrier.

"So talk."

She glared, her rage clinging to the air. Being divested of control was definitely something she wasn't emotionally equipped to handle. Malific needed to be feared and in control.

"Drop the field," she ordered. "You are in no danger from me."

"You said that before, then you made a deal with a demon to link me to the Laes. I don't trust you."

"You'll need to. We share common enemies. My desire to

punish those who have betrayed me is the most important thing to me."

"You're shameless," I sneered.

"Shame is for the weak," she said. "I will align with whomever is necessary to exact my revenge. I want the elven oath I made broken and I want to make Elizabeth pay for her hand in my betrayal." Her expression creased into a wrathful scowl. "I will have Dareus's head."

It wasn't figurative—she would probably put it on a platter and traipse around with it for show. A reminder of the cost of betrayal. "You have an army of shifters, the Huntsmen"—she looked over at Cory, who glowered—"and even some lesser beings that may be of use. I have knowledge and—"

"And what? No morals? Questionable ethics? An insatiable thirst for violence? Lack of scruples?" I huffed in insult. Unfortunately, Malific didn't take it that way, a smile flourishing as if she'd been complimented.

"Yes. Based on who we are dealing with, I do believe it is what will be needed. You have the Huntsmen, yet you have not used them to their full potential." She shook her head. "So much untapped power at your fingertips and you choose to be mediocre."

"You need to work on your flattery. The platitude of flies, honey, and vinegar still applies in a civilized society."

"I have no desire to catch flies. Even that creature has more ferocity than you." Her lips furled in disgust before she shook her head. "I find it more preferable than what you are. At least it's effective in its annoyance," she snapped.

True disappointment shone in her eyes. Even if the sole purpose of my birth wasn't for me to be killed to release her from her prison, it might have been preferable to becoming what she would have made me. I swallowed, dropping my gaze from hers. It was a bad idea, but looking into the cold hatred and disappointment was becoming increasingly difficult.

"Drop the damn field and let me in," she demanded.

"No."

Emotionless. She was a maven of violence and strife and I denied her the response she desperately wanted. The type of response she thrived on.

Her sharp gaze sent a chill through me. She flicked a look over her shoulder, and the door and wall of Ms. Harp's apartment was blasted. Plaster, debris, splinters of wood violently sprayed into the room. Malific was unaware that Ms. Harp had been at Asher's since her last attack. If she'd been in her apartment within ten feet of the blast, she would have been badly injured or even killed.

Not getting the violence and bloodshed she intended, Malific looked at the other side, quickly taking inventory of what was there. What else she could destroy? Would she level the building to make a point?

Believing she would, I dropped the field. The petty bitch bumped my shoulder while entering the room. Giving Cory a dismissive glance, she quickly turned her attention back to me. "Daughter, don't challenge me, you'll never win."

"But haven't I already? You've sought me out for assistance, not the other way around, Mother." Her title hissed through clenched teeth. The same disdain and contempt in her pronouncement were mirrored in mine. "Whether it's my knowledge or my allies, I have something you need. It might be time to show some humility and consideration."

My hubris cost me. Moving faster than I could react, she grabbed me and held me tightly against the wall by my throat. I gasped for breath that wouldn't come, feeling the color drain from my face. "Erin, you have those things, but I have the one thing that trumps it all. Power. I have it and the thirst for more of it at any cost. I'll sacrifice anything and anyone for it. Because, ultimately, I can acquire anything you have because of the power I possess. Do not let overconfidence be the reason you die."

Out of the corner of my eyes, I saw Cory inching closer, looking for an advantage.

"Or your friends." Her eyes slid to Cory. "You move—*any move*, I will rip out your heart and drop it at my daughter's feet," she said with the virulence of a promise. The threat wouldn't deter him, determination fixed on his face. I shook my head as much as Malific's grip would allow. When he stopped, she released me.

"Let's not make this any more complicated than it needs to be. I want Elizabeth and Dareus dead. My oath will not allow me to hurt her. You need to find a way to break it. That is your task," she cited with cool indifference.

I shook my head. The tension in the room thickened. Narrowed flint-cold eyes gave me an evaluating look.

"You were missing for two months. Where were you?"

I didn't answer. My defiance didn't bother her. It was doubtful she cared. It was mere curiosity to determine how invested I was in getting revenge against Elizabeth and Dareus.

"Do you need the demon's body or him alive for any reason?" she asked. Disturbed by the clinical detachment with which she discussed murder, I gawked at her.

I scoffed. "I don't need your help for any of this."

"Yes, you do. We need each other. And you will do this."

"If I don't?" I challenged.

"The oath is for the elves, not for you, your friends, or family. Do you think they are no longer in the confines of my reach, daughter? They are alive because it is my will. *But*, if you don't comply with the alliance, I will kill them. It won't be quick. Long and torturous and you'll have yourself to blame. Because you will not hold any value to me, I'll kill you, too. I will give you the courtesy of saving you for last.

127

Then I will create my army and exact my revenge. Eventually, I will find a way to break the oath. I have the gift of time, something your human blood has stolen from you."

Removing her eyes from me, she spared Cory a small look and made an elaborate curl of her finger. A blue illuminated light snaked around his neck. He gasped and clawed at the hold on him. Another swift move of her hand and he was hoisted into the air. Color drained from his face. Veins crawled along his face as he struggled for breath.

"Put him down!" I demanded, hitting her with a blast of magic that sent her back against the wall. Laser focused on delivering her point, the noose around Cory held. He emitted strangled gasps, his eyes losing the light of life, his hands moving feebly to conjure a small burst of magic in her direction. It swept over her and disappeared without any effect.

I continued pelting her with more magic, but it seemed to have a diminishing return. Keenly focused on Cory, she accepted the pain with small shudders. Desperation flooded Cory's face as he started to lose to asphyxiation. My oath mark twinged with a burning sensation that made my stomach clench.

"Release him, please." Showing the humility that just moments ago I'd demanded from her. With a slow, satisfied smile, she slashed her hand through the air, severing the magical snare and dropping him to the floor.

She meandered to the sofa and took a seat. "You will do this for me."

Malific was pure fire and vengeance. I had to accept that she would get her revenge and plow over anyone who got in her way.

I agreed with a barely discernible nod.

How the hell was I supposed to defeat a person who didn't possess a shred of humanity? I planned to figure it out because this was going to end. It had to.

Cory glared at her as he stood next to me, but it only fueled her gratification at my capitulation. Malific shook her head. "Your challenge was admirable, Erin. You have the makings of being powerful enough to offer me a challenge. To be more than what you are."

She waved her hand over me, a tense Cory, and my modest apartment. "You have squandered it to be mediocre. Denying the thirst for power that has to dwell in you. How can it not? How does it serve you, for others to think you are incapable of horrible things? That you will make them an example and think nothing of it. Erin, that is a better weapon you have at your disposal. These alliances, friendships, and resources are being wasted. Why would you do such a foolish thing?"

Her disgust was acrid as she nestled back in the sofa. "Where is Nolan?"

So, I wasn't the only one looking for him. "I don't know."

"He does have the uncanny ability to remain undiscovered," she sneered. "Damn elves." She stood, giving me another dismissive look. "Find him. You two share a commonality—weakness for those around you. He more so for you." Her words sharpened at the admission. It was the reason she was prevented from using my death to release herself from imprisonment. He'd never be forgiven for the betrayal. "If he can't remove the oath, I'm sure he has the means to lead you in the right direction. Let him know that your life depends on it, because it does."

"You want me dead anyway, so does it matter?"

She chuckled. "But this is a stay of execution. It breeds hope, and you've lived around humans enough to actually believe in such frivolity." She opened the door and looked over her shoulder, a dark humor in her expression. "Our alliance is not without benefits to you. I'm giving you the gift of knowledge."

"Knowledge?" I scoffed. "That I'm the offspring of a

129

heartless, psychotic bitch? I was given that education quite early."

Depthless despotic chestnut eyes gave me a withering look. "The knowledge of knowing whether Nolan will choose your life over that of his sister. Because that is the choice he is making."

She presented me with the same diamond-shape piece of metal.

"Say *venio*, and it will call me wherever I am," she instructed before vanishing. Leaving me speechless at the cruelty of her secondary purpose: making Nolan choose between his daughter and his sister.

CHAPTER 15

*S*earing pain that felt like someone was sliding a razor across the oath mark had me up examining it under the muted glow of the moon, before turning on the bedside lamp. Eventually the pain stopped and I dragged myself to the bathroom to brush my teeth. The bottle of tequila Cory and I finished after Malific's departure… After not being able to reach Ms. Harp or Asher, I was reduced to leaving a message about the destruction of Ms. Harp's apartment. The more we attempted to problem solve the evolving issues, the more we had to face the fact that fixing most of my problems hinged on finding Nolan. Which made me spiral even more because if I found him and he couldn't help, I was beyond screwed. If there was ever a tequila moment, it was last night.

I brushed my teeth, staring at my image. The undeniable familial resemblance. It was so stark I closed my eyes to get away from it. Then I hissed at the jolt of pain that shot through my wrist.

"What?" Cory asked, rushing into my room, disheveled and clearly woken by what was obviously more than a hiss. The pain was getting worse.

I flashed to the oath mark, grabbed my scribing chalk, and marched into the living room. Drawing the demon circle with such deft precision, I understood Cory's concerned look. Having seen it from both sides, the image of it was burned into my mind. A muscle memory that was unlikely to go away.

"This mark links me to Asial and the oath. He's doing something to the oath. That's the only explanation I can come up with. Maybe he's trying to change it. I have no idea," I explained.

Cory worked at removing his strained frown of exhaustion. Another problem. Problems were piling up, and not buckling under their weight was increasingly difficult.

"He can't change an agreement once it's been established and signed. Does anyone follow the damn rules or give one iota of a fuck about the propriety of magic?" he growled. He shoved his fingers through his hair aggressively. He stepped back, took a few breaths. He held up a finger requesting I wait. After several drinks of water and a few cleansing breaths, his anger abated.

"Erin, he can't do that," he said, his voice heavy with annoyance.

"I know," I gritted out before summoning Asial. He answered in his true form, claws exposed like knives.

"What the hell are you doing to the contract!" I hissed, returning the angry glare he was giving me.

"The contract can't be changed," he barked. "It's a blood agreement. I needed to get your attention. It took you long enough."

"You have it. What do you want?"

He moved closer to the barrier between us. "Dareus has returned," he pushed out through clenched teeth. His accusatory glare bored into me before he directed it to Cory, examining him with suspicion as if he was the reason for it.

"What?" I blurted.

"He's returned. Did you have anything to do with it?"

I shook my head, but that didn't seem to be enough. "No." My voice didn't betray the relief I felt. He was gone. A demon at full power wasn't among us. One less problem. "I had nothing to do with his return. It was Elizabeth." It was probably the penalty for her dissatisfaction. The lines between Elizabeth and Malific were blurring daily. Elizabeth was mirroring the very person she despised.

Asial moved closer, his demeanor still fierce and challenging. "Our agreement is ironclad. If you betray me or try to circumvent it, there will be consequences."

"I am aware of the terms." My even keel made it difficult for him to read me. He seemed to be searching for a way to rile me up to the level he was. "He's vowed revenge."

That's not going to anger me, either. Have at it. I can just check that off the list, too. I wasn't petty enough to care if someone else got to Elizabeth before I did. It wouldn't be as easy as Dareus seemed to believe. He'd put a price on my head and amateurs came after me—if they pursued her, it was doubtful Elizabeth would be as lenient as I was.

"Since I'm still here, I'm assuming she hasn't told you how to make me corporeal?"

"No. But I'm working on it."

"*Working on it?* What has your work yielded so far?" he asked, the sharpness of his voice easing.

"I've contacted another elf who has the same knowledge as Elizabeth. I expect to hear from him soon." Not quite a lie.

"Time is ticking," he reminded me. As if I needed one.

"It's best that Elizabeth is left out of this," Asial suggested. "She'll be too preoccupied trying to stay alive."

Stop threatening me with a good time.

"She sent me to the demon realm, so she's the last person I'd get to help. The oath will be honored. Are we done here?"

With another assessing look, he nodded. "If I need you again, I know how to reach you." My jaw clenched. He could hurt me from the other side of the realm by attempting to modify the oath. "What happens to the oath once it is satisfied?"

His smile widened. I'd given him too much. He savored my distress like the masochist I was convinced he was. There was no way I was letting him out of the demon realm.

"It is complete and void. Nothing can be done with it. Until then…"

"Until nothing." I eased closer to the barrier and held his gaze. "The thing about using pain to make a point is that it's not sustainable. Deal with it long enough, you become inured to it. You learn to deal with it and move on. Do you think I won't get used to it? Don't threaten me. If I don't find a way to make you corporeal, then you get to host my body. Your magic would be limited, and it wouldn't be the life you so desperately want. If you need to contact me again, find another way. Don't do it through pain."

His lips pressed into a tight line as he scrutinized me. Whatever showed on my face made him stand taller and quickly agree to my terms. I was at the end of my patience. Stretched to a shadow of existence and it snapped on him.

"Good day, Erin." He exited and Cory and I breathed a sigh of relief.

"She's pissed off a demon. That can't be good."

I crossed my fingers. "Let's hope so."

CHAPTER 16

In the coffee house, the barista's voice had the impatient edge and exasperation of someone who had called several times. Taking the coffee, I returned to people watching and wondering if there were elves among them, existing in plain sight. Shaking off the absurdity, I took a long sip.

White peppermint mocha did nothing to clear the fog of last night's tequila and the new information. The potential plans that I was sifting through my mind all hinged on elven magic. I decided to go through Mephisto's copy of Mystic Souls; perhaps there was something in it I'd overlooked.

I sighed into my coffee cup at the second idea that came to me. Dareus. He was the right answer in its absurdity and simplicity. Elizabeth had made him corporeal, and maybe he knew how to do it. In my rush to return home and summon him, I barely missed crashing into someone in front of me.

"How unexpected," the woman gasped. Robyn, Landon's niece. The principal dancer for her ballet company, she wore that title with erect posture and lithe, graceful movements. She was tall, slender, and toned, with sharp features and an aristocratic nose that lifted ever so slightly and gave her a presence that commanded attention with the most minute movement, even drinking from her coffee cup.

Despite being clearly human, she made an effort to pay homage to the TV's canon of creatures of the night, millennial circuit. Black and white ombre-dyed hair, and heavily lined eyes accompanied by a thick coating of mascara on her lashes. Black off-the-shoulder shirt and black leggings, with a pair of patterned ballet flats.

Our meeting wasn't by accident at all. She might excel at the art of the dance, but her acting skills left much to be desired.

"Did you get any of my calls?" she asked. Early this morning when a missed call from an unknown number showed, I listened to a message from a woman with an air of self-importance declaring that we needed to have a meeting. That should have signaled the familial relationship. But I had pushed all things Landon far from my thoughts. A meeting with his niece wasn't on my list of things that needed to be addressed.

"Yeah, I got it. I had a busy morning and haven't had a chance to get back to you."

Ignoring the scathing look she gave my cup, I took another sip from it. She pulled me aside to an empty booth in the corner away from the crowd. After giving the room another sweeping look to make sure our conversation couldn't be overheard, she spoke.

"Uncle Landon's starting a family."

Yep, fully aware of that. I'm the one he chose for their mother.

Teeth scraped over her bottom lip before she continued. "I've learned that you will be helping him with this," she whispered again, her eyes darting over the room.

I nodded, unable to find any words. It was better as a loathsome thought in my head.

"I want the position of his daughter." The words spilled out so fast they lost some of their airiness. "Uncle Landon thinks very highly of you, which is why he's chosen you to be the—" she searched for the right word because it seemed like me she found the word "mother" distasteful—"co-creator."

Not fond of that either, but it was better than mother.

"Okaaay?" I eased out between sips of coffee.

Her brows slowly inched together. She pushed her coffee aside. "Have I offended you in any way?"

"No."

"Uncle Landon hinted that you weren't agreeable to me as a candidate."

Did he?

Picking up her cup, she took a sip. Her thoughtful eyes looked at me over it.

"You're okay with me as a potential?"

I wasn't okay with *anyone* as a potential. And wanted nothing to do with it, but I definitely wasn't going to be Landon's scapegoat. "Yes. Let your uncle know I don't have a problem with you being his..." *Daughter? Niece/daughter? If she doesn't have a problem with the weird situation, have at it.* "Potential."

Her face brightened. She quickly took out her phone and called Landon before I could react. Moving closer to me, she smiled into the phone's lens. "Guess who I bumped into, Uncle Landon?"

His amiable smile vanished when she shifted the phone and I came into view. Lips pressed into a tight line. His dark onyx eyes held mine with piercing attentiveness. A nonverbal warning. Even through the phone, the changes in his demeanor were profound. Untethered and under no requirement to answer to anyone. It was a chilling reminder that Landon had a place in the history books. He featured prolifically in the violence and macabre doings of vampires. Their civility and restraint were by choice. I swallowed, forcing down any fear that may have been displayed.

"She doesn't have a problem with it," she gushed. "Right?"

137

She looked to me. Holding his gaze became harder with the same difficulty I faced with holding an Alpha's or shifter's when in their animal form. I shook my head.

"No," I answered simply, using taking a drink from my cup as an excuse to tear my eyes from his.

"Then it's all settled. I know you want to do things at the same time, so I'll have to wait." She looked around to make sure no one was in our space as she continued to speak cryptically to her uncle.

"She's okay with it, I'm not."

Robyn flushed, her mouth dropped open. "What?"

"No, Robyn."

She blinked several times as she attempted to reconcile her emotions. Obviously favored by him, I didn't think she'd ever be denied. Based on the designer bag, the expensive-looking jewelry, including a solitaire benitoite ring, he lavished her with gifts. What a principal dancer earned was limited, and I was willing to bet that what she wore today was worth more than what she made in a month.

She inhaled sharply through her nose. Her lips remained tightly clenched.

"Is there anything else, Robyn?" he asked in a professionally cool voice.

"No," she managed.

With a slight nod, he turned his focus from her to me. "Erin," he addressed me. Malice caressed each word. "Until we speak again." We'd be speaking sooner than I intended. Once he'd ended the call, Robyn was on her feet and rushing out of the door. Watching her get into a Z4 only confirmed that she was probably living a lot better than most principal dancers in a small company as a result of being her uncle's favorite. And now she was in shock at being denied.

I wasn't the least bit surprised that I received a call from Landon half an hour later. I sent it to voicemail. He didn't call again, which I chose to take as a good sign that he got the message. Coddling a vampire was low on my list of priorities. I had an aggrieved demon to summon.

Still not keen on letting the entire demon realm know of my existence or that of elves, I asked Cory over to do the summons. After eight summons didn't get Dareus, I wondered if me summoning would get better results. Demons could tell the magical signatures. Everyone had one, which was how they knew if someone had summoned before and whether to ignore it.

"We need to summon him specifically," Cory suggested. "Which means we need his name."

"Harrison was the only one who had his name, as far as I know," I said, plopping down on the sofa next to him. "It's not like other witches or mages advertise having close enough relationships with demons that they have their name."

"No, but you already know there are witches dealing with demons quite frequently."

With a nod, we both came up with the same person. Wendy. Her denial would come too easily over the phone, so we decided to go by her home. Showing up without a call was rude, but Wendy was shrewd, and I hoped she wasn't so prolific at lying that we couldn't see through it. If she agreed, I would accumulate a greater debt.

As we made for the door, there was a knock.

Looking through the peephole, I cracked the door open to see Dr. Sumner's reserved face. Hair longer than I remembered, slightly disheveled. Wide, square-rimmed midnight-blue glasses, despite their intended efforts, served to highlight his crisp, emotive eyes. I wasn't sure if he was being ironic with the hipster look—slim fit striped shirt, vest, jeans, and messenger bag—or leaning into it so thoroughly he'd become their idol. Greeting me with a bashful half smirk, he fiddled with the messenger bag in front of him.

"Hi," he said with uncertainty. "I know I shouldn't have dropped by, but I left several messages and you never responded. And then your response of 'I'm good' gave me the impression you weren't," he rushed out.

"It's fine. I'm happy to see you." It wasn't a lie. Moving aside, I let him in. Cory introduced himself with a handshake. Dr. Sumner's discomfort with someone witnessing him breaking patient/therapist rules of propriety by showing up at my home caused a flush to creep over the bridge of his nose.

They exchanged pleasantries. Recognizing Dr. Sumner's unease, Cory made a quick exit, confirming his plans to speak with Wendy. Keeping his intentions cryptic, he let me know that if she agreed, he'd wait for me.

Dr. Sumner appeared to be turning Cory's name over in his mind, trying to piece who he was in the complex labyrinth of my life.

I offered him a seat and sat across from him.

His warm eyes and smile made it hard not to flood him with all the new occurrences in my life. Giving me a weak smile, he steepled his hands over his crossed leg.

"How are you?" he asked. I had every intention of the last time seeing him being the *last* visit. Him across from me now, giving me permission to be completely open, honest, without any expectations, was liberating in a wholly different way. Dr. Sumner offered a space of vulnerability that I desperately needed.

His question was the nudge I needed. I disclosed everything, without filter or pretense that I had anything in my life under control. He didn't waver under the deluge, just took several deep breaths and nodded for me to continue.

"I have less than a month to figure out how to make a demon corporeal. Malific wants me to break the oath protecting the elves or she'll hurt my family. I need Nolan but can't find him. And Elizabeth—"

"Your aunt," he clarified.

"Nolan's sister," I corrected. "She has the means to send Mephisto back and no one knows where she is. And to make my family safe and have some semblance of a normal life, I'm going to let my mom kill my aunt. And in turn I'm going to kill my mom."

Stony-faced in the admission of premeditated manslaughter, he sighed and rested his head back in thought. He didn't say anything for a long time, then lifted his head and looked at me.

"How does this make you feel?"

The warmth in his words and the entreaty in his expression caused the snarky retort I usually made about that question fizzle. It was a sincere question, and I sat in silence searching for the best way to answer.

"Like I'm drowning and survival isn't guaranteed, or the safety of my family and friends, either. There's a weight that if I don't figure out how to succeed, it won't just affect me but so many people I care about."

"You're putting the entire burden of this situation on yourself?"

"Because no one else can do anything about it. Gods don't have access to, nor can they affect elven magic, and that's the magic I need to break the oath Malific has with the elves and to satisfy my debt to Asial." I exhaled an anxiety-ridden breath. "I want to kill Malific."

The admission felt oddly cathartic. Said with the determination of a promise. Dr. Sumner shifting in his seat was the only thing that kept me from saying it again and making it a daily affirmation.

"Everything would be better. I'm not subjected to the curse of killing someone from the Veil—and I hate her."

I felt freer, unburdened by the usual sense that killing my

mother would change me. Of course, it would change me, but I didn't think it would be in a bad way. The scar of it would heal over and it would prove I survived something—survived her.

After I'd finished espousing the virtues of offing my mother, there was tension between us. Dr. Sumner busied himself with writing notes, which I knew was a distraction to gather himself.

"Do you feel better?" he asked.

"I do." I waited for him to chastise me. Maybe dampen the excitement with which I was contemplating killing Mommy Dearest.

Seeing his difficulty in forcing a mirthless smile, a pang of guilt hit me. I'd pulled him deep into this world.

"I'm sorry," I said.

"Erin, there's no apologies with us. Okay? With me, you have the freedom to be unapologetically you."

When he slipped his pad into his messenger bag, I knew it was the ending of the session but the beginning of another discussion.

"What's up with you, Sumner?" I had unloaded on him and was curious what he was feeling. I remained unconvinced by his casually neutral expression that he wasn't holding on to something. "The incident with Landon had to be life altering for you."

"I'd never been that close to death," he admitted quietly. "But it's what happened after the attack that was so profound. The situation with the vampire blood." His eyes held mine, brightened with vibrancy. "Never in my life have I felt so—empowered. Alive. It was like seeing the world in ultra-HD. You said it would only last for a few hours, but it was longer than that. For nearly two days that was my experience."

The ebullience or the obvious desire to feel that way again was apparent. "Sumner, even if you can get a vampire to do that for you again, it's not something you should want. It'd be too easy to succumb to the feeling of being that powerful. You'd end up giving more and more of yourself and becoming so indebted to them that you'd be their property."

He'd been exposed to the unvarnished violence, power, and cruelty of the supernatural world; how could I not expect him to seek a way to protect himself from it? I wanted to protect him. He wasn't acting out of curiosity or desire, but fear.

Taking in a ragged breath, it took a long time to gather my thoughts and even longer agonizing over the words I needed to say.

"I want this to be our last visit."

His eyes widened, his expression a glaze of frustrated bewilderment. "What?" he sputtered out.

"Before you started seeing me as a patient, you only had a casual understanding of this world. Your life had never been put in jeopardy. You nearly died. Indirectly, I'm responsible for that. You wanting to feed from a vampire in order to feel safe, or to have the ability to protect yourself, is because of me. I don't want that for you." I raised my hand, stopping his response. "If you try to see me again, I won't see you. Don't be persistent." I let all emotion and warmth drain from my voice. "Do you understand?"

He didn't answer, just stared at me. "I'm competent at kickboxing and Tae kwon do. Capable of taking care of myself. After the 'incident' with Landon I felt better prepared. I would have been able to deal with your mother —" Seeing my expression he corrected himself. "Malific."

I shook my head. "No, you wouldn't. I survived my fight with her because she hesitated, and that microsecond of hesitation cost me. She destroyed my car. *My car*. That *incident* you've brushed over was you *nearly dying*. You want to really protect yourself? Keep your distance from me."

Before he could respond, I stood, averting my eyes from his, and moved to the door, opening it a crack. "It's safer for you this way."

He hesitated briefly with a confusion-warped frown. "Erin—"

"I've made the decision. I have that right, correct? You released me from the court-ordered visits. Neither one of us is obligated to this. So, we won't."

His warm, caring eyes were hard to hold, and I was already missing the ability to be totally Erin with him, not having to show bravado and confidence when there wasn't any. I felt cold and cruel as I continued to silence him with a raised hand. "I need things to be less complicated. Okay?"

"Erin," he pleaded. "You don't believe that."

"I do. I'm serious, and I need you to respect my wishes." I choked on the words and blinked back tears, feeling utterly ridiculous for already mourning his absence in my life. His eyes rested on my face as he kept searching for something. Me wavering or reconsidering my stance. It wouldn't change. It couldn't change.

"I need you to go." I dragged the door open wider.

He hesitated before barely moving his head into a nod. Closing the door behind him, I swiped away the tear that had escaped.

CHAPTER 17

$\mathcal{T}$he hits kept coming. Cory wasn't able to meet with Wendy. He was convinced that she was home but refusing to see him. Perhaps Cory had earned persona non grata status. I was probably on that list, too. Maybe Wendy had concluded that accrual of debt from me wasn't worth having to deal with us.

Making a mental note to attempt contact with her, I scanned the restaurant until I found Kath. Her eyes directed me to the couple seated at the table. When I'd put out my request for information about the Cupio, I hadn't expected to get a response so soon. Kath was my most useful informant. There was always a fee, and if it yielded results, I paid. Often handsomely. Being a reliable source of information was financially more beneficial to her than the two jobs she had as server and bartender. At this point, they were just tools of the trade, a front that allowed her to make money from her side hustle.

Despite it being after the lunch rush, the contemporary casual venue appealed to supernaturals and humans alike who enjoyed the fusion food in a restaurant that would look good on social media. Surprisingly, despite its popularity, the restaurant had an intimate appeal. Small round tables allowed distance between seating, keeping conversations private. The décor of pale wood chairs, beige leather seating, and linen-colored walls was unassuming and relaxing. The restaurant's popularity meant that seating was limited, and a person ate their food, conducted their business, and left.

"I'll send your fee in a few minutes," I said as I passed Kath on the way to the bar.

Her lips pressed into a tight line. "No compensation required," she said, her tone replete with remorse.

"Kath, you didn't betray me. Your dog's life was in jeopardy, and you did what was necessary."

Ian, the fae with the ability to control shifters and who had escaped from his imprisonment in the Veil, had threatened harm to Kath's dog as a way to get to me. Ian killing me was the reason Malific had been released from the Omni Ward.

Giving me an appreciative nod, Kath said, "They've only been here about forty-five minutes." She glanced over her shoulder at the table. "The woman isn't particularly discreet."

I nodded, knowing she wouldn't be and not letting my disappointment show. I was familiar with both people at the table. Although most could only control one element, the mage Kieran had the ability to control both fire and ice. The woman, Brier, preferred the misnomer of acquisitions manager. It was better than peddler-and-acquirer-of-counterfeit-and-poor-quality-goods. She remained relevant because she occasionally stumbled upon authentic goods. A golden sheath of hair framed a round face that had enough distinctive lines along her jaw and cheeks to give it character. Clouded gray eyes that held narrowed-eye suspicion followed Kieran's gaze as he trailed my migration across the restaurant to the bar. I

'd made no effort to be inconspicuous, fully aware that

he'd come find me once he knew I was there. I ordered an iced coffee and appetizer while I waited.

He'd lost interest in his conversation with Brier, his gaze repeatedly slipping in my direction. I tried to determine the purpose of their meeting. Was she a purchaser or an intermediary? Nothing in my prior dealings led me to believe that if the Cupio existed, Brier would have access to it. Kieran, on the other hand, with his money and connections... If it existed, he'd have access.

I'd become a distraction for Kieran. Brier's puckered-lip look of disdain made me wonder if she'd been aiming for more from this meeting. Kieran's charming smile and alluring green eyes had been pulled from her and were resting on me.

It didn't take long for him to pay the check and saunter toward me, still holding his drink. The incarnation of trouble. There was a reason I kept my distance from him. The very reasons people feared my ability to siphon magic and place them in a death-like state, drew him to me.

Kieran spent a great deal of money and time chasing that euphoria of cheating death. Thriving for the thrill of it. He used my struggles to his advantage. He studied his glass, then placed it on the bar, his fingers slowly moving around the rim of the glass, freezing the lemonade in it. A devilish glint sparked in his eyes as fire twined around his fingers. The bartender shot him a disapproving look.

His eyes remained locked on me, evaluating my response to his demonstration of magic. When he invaded my space, I nudged him away.

"Erin, how unexpected," he said as a vulpine look slid across his face.

"Is it?" I challenged.

Amusement skated along his expression, a rekindling of our last interaction when he proposed a deal. *Fun*, he'd called

147

it. I couldn't escape the morbid and aberrant curiosity he held for me.

He shrugged. "There might have been whispers that Mephisto was looking for the Cupio. I figured he'd hire you to acquire."

"Do you have it?" I asked, trying to tamp down my growing excitement, although it could be heard in the high pitch of my voice.

Rose color flushed over his face. "Do you remember the time you borrowed magic from me?" he asked, his scrutiny of me intensifying.

I remembered, and his response to it. The feeling of his magic being taken from me again and the desire I had to reclaim it. His presence became a reminder of how things used to be for me. Now, despite the problems that came with it, I appreciated having my own magic.

His smile faltered when he didn't get the intended response. Inching closer to me, the frenetic energy of his magic filled the space. "I remember it," he whispered. "Quite fondly. I haven't been able to replicate that feeling," he admitted.

"Do you have the Cupio?" I repeated, changing the subject before he could question why being close to him and the promise of his magic no longer appealed to me.

"No." He ran a hand over his flushed face. "You've ignored all my efforts to communicate with you."

I tucked my hand between my legs as a reminder not to choose violence or throw a drink in his face, because I wanted to do both. "You wanted a dupe. For what, to get a meeting with me? What is wrong with you? Do you seriously think it's not easy to authenticate it? That I wouldn't know it was a fake? What did you think would happen?"

"No, there were rumors that Brier had one," he blurted his lie. Even if there were rumors, I was a thousand percent sure she started them and even more positive no one in good faith believed that she did have it. If I'd known it was Brier claiming to have it, I would have met with her but with zero expectations.

"I'm not the only person who believed she might have it. She told me she had a meeting with another potential buyer."

"The meeting is over," Mephisto said from behind him, slipping past Kieran like an ominous wave. Whetted dark eyes slowly glided over him then turned to me. Easing into me, his hand cupped my face, his lips soft as they covered me in a long intense kiss that I relaxed into, inhaling him and his magic. He moved slightly to my ear, laying one hand over my hands. "You look like you are about to choose violence," he teased, his warm breath bristling against my skin.

"Very much so," I whispered.

"Go," he commanded, keeping his attention on me.

His command promised a less pleasant follow-up for Kieran, who took in a shuddering breath. The mage enjoyed danger and was possibly a masochist, but he needed it on his terms and under his full control. Something Mephisto wasn't offering. He'd snatched away both: control and power of it to be on his terms.

Mephisto was waiting for me when I got to my apartment. His fingers clasped mine as we walked to the door. The look he gave me, as if he was expecting me to be swept away.

"Neither one of them has the Cupio," he informed me once the door was closed.

"You know this because…"

He shrugged off his jacket and laid it across the back of the sofa, then rolled up the sleeves of his black shirt. "I searched their homes."

"I figured they didn't but wanted confirmation. And if they'd had it?" I asked although I knew the answer.

"I would have made a tactical purchase," he said.

"*Tactical purchase*. You mean taking it and leaving its estimated value in its place, fancy pants." I wouldn't have expected anything else from him. And he was the one who called *me* a retrieval specialist.

"Getting a Cupio might not be an option." Resignation was heavy in his voice as he sank onto the sofa.

"Using a host won't be an option, either." I told him about my exchange with Asial. Despite giving him the unabridged version, Mephisto seemed unconvinced that an alternative wasn't an option.

"It just has to be someone compelling. He'll be limited with any"—his lips formed "lesser" but he thought better of it —"supernatural. But the stronger the host, the more enticing they would be." A wicked glint flashed in his eyes. "Perhaps a mage with powerful elemental abilities would be appealing enough."

"It seemed like you were prepared to rip Kieran in half, so I don't think you'll be getting a meeting with him."

"I'd never do that in the middle of a crowded restaurant."

At least there are boundaries.

"I don't think he'll agree."

Mephisto seemed unbothered, as if there was a line of people willing to host a demon. "It's worth the discussion. He's welcome to say no, but we'll never know until we ask."

Dropping my eyes to hide the fear I was sure was visible in them, I said, "Time's running out."

"We'll figure something out. Between the two of us, there's no way we won't." Where was he getting this optimism from? What about this situation gave him hope? I simply nodded. He looked down at his watch.

"I have a meeting in an hour. Will you stay with me tonight?" he asked.

"How about here? Nolan hasn't called, but there's still a chance he could show up."

He nodded, grabbing his jacket from the sofa and heading for the door.

"Who are you meeting?"

Several beats of time passed before he answered. "Someone who *claims* to know the location of several elves." Responding to my piqued interest, he added, "I don't want you there in case it's their attempt at gaining information."

The list of people who knew there was more to me than a death mage was growing, and it was becoming a problem.

"Landon wants me to help him make more vampires." The words spilled out like water from a broken dam.

Mephisto eased away from the door. Instead of the usual eerily fast way he moved, this was slow, measured—a hesitation. He blinked once and I repeated it, slower. His hand rested at my waist, his thumb stroking it lightly. Easing into him, I relaxed in a manner that surprised me and rattled out everything that had occurred between me and Landon, even tacking on how I didn't think it was a big deal, but Cory thought I should tell him, so I was telling him. It was such a long string of words that I sighed heavily at the end, because I hadn't taken a full breath since I started.

Silence loomed for so long it became uncomfortable.

"Why didn't you call me?" he eventually asked.

"I didn't have the luxury of time or being wrong. Dr. Sumner's life was in jeopardy. Vampire blood could save him."

He nodded but remained silent, his frown easing with his continued reflection. "I'm glad you're sharing this with me. Cory was right, this is something I would like to know." Regarding me with an unreadable expression, he said, "Would you like me to handle this for you? I'm sure Landon and I can come to an arrangement."

"Should I be concerned that the 'arrangement' will be something along the lines of telling him to do what you ask or else?"

A wolfish smirk curled one side of his mouth. "Not at all. As I said before, I'm very good at negotiations." Didn't take shifter senses to know that was a big lie. I considered it for a moment and shook my head.

"When I start to pull the remnants of my shredded life together, I don't want to have to contend with a powerful vampire."

He leaned forward, his breath a light breeze along my jawline. Moving to the curve of my neck, his tongue laved over the pulse. "Do you know about the intimacy involved in creating a vampire?"

I'd fed vampires before, during sex, but never with the intention to create more.

"Well, he's not going to do it that way. He can use my arm."

Mephisto reared back and looked at me. He shook his head. "It takes too long and risks an incomplete transition. He'll drain them until they are clinging to life, then his blood will initiate the process. The completion into vampirism will be once they feed from another source. But Landon will initiate it; that's typical during the creation. The vampire will be ravenous, and it will be a challenge to keep you alive. It will require a great deal of caution and care to prevent you having any long-term injuries."

"You don't think Landon is capable of doing that?" When he saved Dr. Sumner, he was careful, gentle even. But would he become so absorbed in the moment that he'd become careless?

Mephisto considered my question, his hands sliding down to take hold of mine. He relaxed into the full intensity of his magic, a reminder of how he—they all—muted it to exist in this world, to go unnoticed.

"It is my experience that it is best to leave little room for vampires to rely on their willpower or sense of integrity. I've found that they are weak in both."

"I can take care of myself, M," I said, trying out the nickname. Based on the cock of his brow, not something he appreciated.

His expression relaxed, not revealing anything, but his hands tightened on mine. His lips became a taut line.

"It's not about you being able to take care of yourself, but your unwillingness to accept my help." He pulled away from me, leaving a chill between us and notable distance. I became very self-aware under the scrutiny of his gaze. "The most challenging thing I find about caring for you, Erin," he whispered, "is waiting for you to relax the barriers you have erected. Accepting help doesn't make you weak or incapable. It acknowledges that you are wise enough to know when aid is needed."

"I do relax my barriers."

"Not with me."

There was a tinge of something. I was reluctant to see it for what it was. Hurt.

I sat down. "It's not that I don't trust you or realize that I need help. I can't let my walls down completely with you or make you a large part of my world because once you leave, I will feel that loss. It's going to be hard."

He nodded, urging me to continue.

"I know you want to get back to your life." I sighed. "It's foolish to think you can exist in both worlds. You can't...*we* can't. You won't be able to treat being a Huntsman like a nine to five job any more than I can treat what I do as one." I spoke with a confidence that I didn't really have. As if next month my life would be back to normal, easy peasy.

A tick in his jaw was the only response he offered for a long time. The silence became heavy with unspoken words and doubts.

"Okay," he finally breathed out, pushing his fingers through his hair and relaxing his back against the wall.

I'd put words to something I was sure he was thinking. "I

will do what I can to help you get back to the Veil. Because that's what you want. Even if not just for you, definitely for Kai. His struggle bothers you all, and I hate seeing how it's strained your relationship."

"He's dealing," he said quietly.

"But he shouldn't have to deal. Just dealing isn't much of a life, is it?"

The quiet stretched. Although his face betrayed nothing and offered me nothing in the form of answer, I had a feeling he felt the same.

"There's more between us than just magic." He repeated the adage he'd made several times before. "And it is not just sex, Erin. From the first time I met you, I was intrigued not just with your magic, tenacity, and your"—he flashed me a rakish smile—"let's go with 'directness.' You are often unencumbered by social restraint. I needed to discover how you fit in my world. Would you just be an instrument, a means to an end? It would have been easier if you were." He sighed. It was costing him something to admit this vulnerability. "It really would have been. Me and easy have never been a fit. Perhaps that is part of the draw. I can assure you, my experience with women is not limited by any means."

"No one needs your humblebrag," I shot back. His chuckling consumed the air and the laughter remained in his voice.

"I was surprised by how much I was drawn to you. I despised and was intrigued by it. And then you died." We both shuddered at that reminder. "For that moment, while we tried to figure out how to save you, I felt empty. It was a surprise to me. The thought of never interacting with you again. Finding another person like you. The thought that I was losing my prospect of going back into the Veil never crossed my mind. I was losing *you*. Clayton was the first to point it out, while I remained in denial. I wanted it to be superficial, a physical attraction only. Life would have been simpler."

His lips downturned into a wry frown. "We don't do simple, do we, Erin?"

"I think simplicity was never an option for me," I admitted.

"Us. I'll make this work because it's what I want. You're what I want," he said with the pledge of an oath.

My barriers had been erected because I was preparing for him to decide that the Veil was where he wanted to be, leaving me and our relationship behind. It wasn't. The relief I felt was so palpable, I slumped back onto the sofa. I nodded in response because words had escaped me.

Eventually he left, but his words remained.

CHAPTER 18

When I answered the door, I was expecting Mephisto. He had left for his meeting over three hours ago. I spent a significant amount of that time persuading Wendy, who had definitely placed me on her persona non grata list, to meet to summon a demon in hopes that Dareus would answer. It was a hard sell because of all the time she dedicated to her poorly performed reluctance to summoning a demon. Behaving as if it wasn't something she did often. Which made her a better summoner. Her magic signature was known.

Wendy practiced dark magic. There wasn't anything gray about it. She summoned demons too often for it to be considered anything else. But to save her reputation and her standing with her coven, she kept denying it. Eventually she'd agreed and I had a meeting with her the next day.

I had the nagging feeling she might not be successful. Could Dareus be too consumed with plotting his revenge against Elizabeth to answer summons? I wasn't going to lose any sleep over it, if it was an all-consuming goal.

To my surprise, Ms. Harp was outside my door. Hip-checking me aside, she entered my apartment towing a small suitcase and her cane firmly secured under her arm. "I request sanctuary," she announced.

Before I could respond, she was opening the room that had previously been my meditation room but was now in a transitional phase. I still meditated but needed it far less than I used to now that I had my own magic and wasn't trying to suppress my magical urges. Finding no extra bed in there, she moved toward my bedroom.

"Where do you keep your clean sheets?" she yelled from the room, stirring me from the shock of her intrusion. I had dealt with my share of people and their unyielding gall, but Evelyn was another level. I truly had no idea how to deal with her.

"In the closet to the left," I found myself saying as I walked toward the bedroom.

As she stripped the sheets from my bed, her easy takeover of my room was off-putting enough to stall a reaction.

"Why are you here?" I finally asked.

"I told you, sanctuary." Her gaze flicked up to meet mine. "I can't go to my apartment. It was destroyed." I wasn't sure if she knew that the person who destroyed it was my mother. She went back to making the bed. "Even if it hadn't been, it's not my apartment anymore," she huffed. "The building owner didn't renew my lease. They decided to make it a model apartment," she tutted, frustrated.

"Without notice?"

"Well, you know how Asher is. That bossy thing just does what he wants," she barked out, finishing with the bottom sheet. This woman was oblivious to hypocrisy. The two of them should decide who would be the pot so the other would know their position as kettle.

"What?" I sputtered, grabbing my phone off the dresser and scrolling through my documents for the lease and notification of new management. There it was, six months ago, when I renewed my lease. New management: Greystar

Management, which must be a subsidiary of the Northwest Wolf Pack. I was about to call Mr. Alpha to tell him about my uninvited guest and to get more information regarding what led to his purchase of this apartment building, when there was another knock on the door. Scarlett, giving me a tight smile. I widened the door to let her in.

"Get out here, old lady," she bellowed from the door's entrance. Agitation and amusement twined in her words and placed conflicting expressions on her face. Humor settled in her eyes through the rigid scowl.

Cane in hand, Evelyn touched it to the ground occasionally as she walked into the living room. Her fist pressed into the side of her hip. "That's no way to speak to me," she challenged.

Scarlett's mouth dropped open, demonstrating the same reaction Evelyn Harp provoked in everyone. Shocked incredulity.

"That's exactly how I should talk to someone who tried to burn down our damn lab. You arsonist!"

Ms. Harp shrugged and gave a dismissive wave. "It was just a little fire. A distraction. You can hardly call it arson. I had to escape. I'm not a guinea pig."

"Great escape. You used the pack's account to call the Uber!" Scarlett's arms were flailing wildly. Her emotions had run right through incredulity straight into full-on dismay.

"Well, I wasn't going to pay for the ride."

Scarlett paced the floor, mumbling about the many ways she was going to strangle Ms. Harp, while the recipient of the threats remained silent in her indignation.

"Get your things and let's go," Scarlett finally ordered.

"No, I've requested sanctuary," she said.

"That's not how any of this works."

Ms. Harp had lived outside the supernatural community, but the premise of sanctuary was quite simple. Denizens dealt with their issues from within. If STF got involved, it was seen as a failure on the denizens' part. That things had escalated beyond their abilities. But at times, it had to be accepted that STF was needed. They had resources others didn't. Entreating sanctuary was a big deal. The request gave one denizen permission to invade the other sect's privacy and the authority to make decisions on matters that should be handled internally.

"Erin can't give you sanctuary because she's not part of a coven, court, pack, family, or consortium. Try again, woman."

Offering sanctuary had tacit agreements and implicit extension of courtesies. The most pressing one was the involved party knowing beforehand that sanctuary had been requested. Ms. Harp's jaw was set in defiance. I couldn't determine if she truly hadn't grasped the nuances of such a request or was intentionally being obtuse. I was leaning toward the latter.

"Asher has referred to her and her friends as a pack," she provided in defense.

"This is the time you decided to listen to Asher. Him telling you stay put, you ignore. Instructing you to take someone with you whenever you left the apartment, you viewed as a suggestion that you never took. He told you to stay in the lab, and you waved that away. But he casually refers to her"—she jerked her head in my direction—"small group of friends as a pack and that's the information you cling to?"

Scarlett shoved her hand through her hair and mumbled more impotent threats, provoking Ms. Harp to glower in challenge. Apparently, Scarlett's initial good rapport with Ms. Harp had earned her the task of being her handler. Asher had complained that they were dual pains in his ass. Now Evelyn was a thorn in Scarlett's.

Scarlett's head snapped up. "Door," she told me.

The shifter weirdness struck again. I opened the door to

find a Hispanic woman about to knock. Her loosely curled dark hair was pulled into a top knot, with a few escaped strands framing her face. Large keen hazel eyes regarded me and softened slightly. Her round face and pleasant features didn't abate the predatory alertness that characterized all shifters. A cinched-waist lab coat covered a silky blush-colored button-down and the top half of dark blue slacks.

"Looking for Evelyn Harp?" I asked, widening the door. She nodded, strolled in, and at the sight of her, Ms. Harp sneered.

"I'm in sanctuary," Ms. Harp announced with a dramatic flourish. She seemed to have forgotten about using her cane for her performance of geriatric shuffle because it was firmly secured in the pit of her arm as she marched into my bedroom and slammed the door.

The recent arrival started for the bedroom door but stopped when Scarlett shook her head.

"It'll just cause her to dig her heels in more."

We waited for Asher. I wasn't sure what Evelyn was doing in my room. It definitely wasn't listening to Scarlett as she attempted to reason with her through the door. The tea I'd offered them had cooled and occasionally when they thought of it, they took a sip.

As the quiet ticked on, they both seemed to want something stronger than tea. I offered them wine, a selection that Mephisto had sent me. Scarlett gave it an appreciative look and took a glass. The new arrival, who hadn't provided a name and seemed in no rush to do so, took a glass as well. But as with the tea, it remained mostly untouched.

Asher's expression was shades of self-satisfaction and smugness as he entered my apartment wearing jogging pants and a threadbare t-shirt. Sporting disheveled hair and a light shadow of a beard, he clearly had not been expecting to leave the house. Asher's attention immediately rested on his cousin, Scarlett.

"So, she rebels against me because... Let me make sure I quote you correctly: 'I'm an arrogant, domineering twat.' Did I get that right, Scarlett? Or did I miss something."

Based on Scarlett's sour scowl, humble crow wasn't very tasty.

"If that's the case, why is she rebelling against you?" He cocked his brow. She responded with a glare. Swallowing the space between them, he leaned in. "Evelyn rebels for the hell of rebelling. She likes control, hates rules, and more times than not, she's the ass in the situation." He kissed her forehead. "That's why you two get along," he added, as he continued to ride high on his Schadenfreude horse. The corner of his lip kinked. "And you really need to stop watching British shows. I don't enjoy being called a twat."

Scarlett definitely had more terms waiting in the wings. And based on her tightly clenched jaw, she was fighting to silence them.

He turned his attention to the other woman. "What happened, Marisol?"

"Dr. Reyes," she corrected. There was a flutter in her tone I couldn't quite place. They were grappling with something. Perhaps she was working to maintain a professional distance from him and the pack. I hadn't seen her before and wondered if she was new to the pack, a visitor from another pack, or one of the rarest of rare—a lone shifter.

"Of course. Dr. Reyes. Would you please tell me what led to this situation?"

She glared and rightfully so. It wasn't what he said, it was *how* he said it. He had slathered his Asher-ness all over his words. Having been on the receiving end of it, I knew the feeling very well. It's the moment when you'd officially won the battle, the argument was in the bag, you were the true victor, and somehow Asher made it feel like anything but a win. The insidious way he claimed something from it.

Whether it was a skill of all Alphas, Asher had definitely perfected it.

I offered a smile of solidarity. *Give up on trying to make sense of it.*

Her glance in my direction seemed to work as a reminder to him that an outsider was present.

"It's fine," he assured her.

"I explained to Evelyn that I needed to observe her before the full moon—tomorrow—the day of the full moon, and the day after. Three days. I just need more data. Then I could return to my territory and send you my findings when compiled."

Following shifters' conversations was a nuisance because their exceptional hearing made them speak in tones several registers lower than most humans would consider a whisper. I strained to hear them. It was apparent they were attempting to keep Ms. Harp from hearing.

"Something triggered this response. She did it for two months, so why did she feel the need to leave now?"

"Who knows." Scarlett scowled. "Words. She had to watch *People's Court* instead of *Judy*. She ran out of *coffee*." She air quoted the word. "Have you seen the amount of coffee she has with a Kahlua? She's a walking Kahlua bottle."

Despite being a shifter who couldn't change, Ms. Harp possessed many shifter abilities. Her father was a cat shifter —probably a lone shifter, which was why she hadn't been discovered until recently. Because of Asher's easy connection with Evelyn, he took responsibility for her instead of leaving it to Sherrie, the Alpha of the Northwest Lion's Pack. After witnessing the fragility of Mr. Harp's state during the full moon, when they're forced into their animal form, Asher questioned whether her inability was devolution rather than advancement in their species. He wanted to study the anomaly that prevented her from shifting.

"You've been observing her for over a month. That's a long time," he said softly.

"We needed the information."

"You didn't mention anything about her shifting, did you?"

"Not as a confirmation that we would. I explained that our goal was to make the full moons better for her. That's why we're doing this, right? If not, why even study her? She's the only shifter with this condition."

"That we know of. If it's a genetic condition or magic, we have to discover the root of it. We need her to do this." He exhaled a slow breath and went to my bedroom door.

"Evelyn," he said, turning the doorknob to find it was locked. "Open the door."

"I'm in sanctuary."

Scarlett rolled her eyes.

Another long slow exhalation gave Asher the patience he was searching for. When you're used to making a command and having it followed without question or resistance, all other interactions had to seem unnecessarily tedious. "Evelyn," he said again in a tight voice.

After there wasn't a response, he commanded, "Evelyn, open the door now." The Alpha command resonated in his voice. It felt bone deep, chilling in the way it grabbed you, broke your will, demanded unyielding compliance. Dr. Reyes and Scarlett winced and curled into themselves. If they were anywhere near a door, I was sure they would have opened it. For me, it was a feeling of uneasiness. And a source of curiosity. I knew it was intertwined with the magic of being an Alpha. They were the only ones who could do it, but I wondered how closely linked it was to a vampire's compulsion?

The door opened.

"Let's talk," he said. He glanced at Scarlett and Dr. Reyes.

"No worries, I got this." That was their cue to leave. Once they headed for the door, he went into my bedroom.

I knew they would speak too low for me to hear, so I busied myself going through the books that I'd been going through with no results. The Ms. Harp situation had given me some respite. Sitting on the sofa, waiting for Asher and Ms. Harp to emerge, my thoughts drifted to Landon and the baby mama drama. No matter how much I wanted to ignore it, I couldn't. I was tired of being linked and bound to people, and he was a tie I wanted to sever completely. Him having me as the "mother" of his new vampires was the opposite of that. Finding him an alternative presented the same issue: the potential of a super vampire.

Cane in hand, Ms. Harp marched out of my room, Asher behind her and carrying her luggage. I didn't get the cane thing; she wasn't fooling anyone. At this point it was like a person carrying a nine-iron or a bat ready to retaliate against anyone who wronged them. Handing her the keys, Asher said, "I need a moment with Erin."

Satisfaction brightened her eyes. Despite the hell she gave him, she was team Asher. If she thought I'd make him happy, she was Team Asher/Erin. But part of me suspected she was just Anti-Mephisto.

"How are those fires?" he asked once she was gone.

"An inferno," I admitted.

"What can I do to help?"

I took some time to answer the question, reviewing everything I had done over the past few days. All the possible avenues. I considered suggesting finding Elizabeth, but how would that help because she damn sure wasn't going to do anything to assist me. Go after Malific? With the spell that protected them from being harmed bay anyone outside the Veil, I was putting him in jeopardy. Even if by chance they were immune to that spell, "hey, why don't you kill my mom" seemed like a big favor. Even if I were bold enough to do this, could he? My thoughts always went back to her destroying my car out of rage.

"Nothing." It didn't ease the crinkle that formed along his brow. "I'm not trying to keep you out of this, I know you want to help, but right now there's not much you can do. Besides, you seem to have your hands full." I waved in the direction of the door where I wondered if Ms. Harp was lingering to eavesdrop.

He frowned at the door. I think it had a lot to do with whatever was going on with Ms. Harp. "I'm always here to help, Erin. Don't hesitate if you need it."

"I know." I attempted a smile that didn't quite make it. "Even with the little things like rent." I teased. "You own the building. You could have put a moratorium on it."

"The Northwest Pack owns the building. There would be a problem if *I* put a moratorium on *my* friend's rent," he said. "Didn't matter anyway since Mephisto handled it." His tone was wrought with tension. It was time for a subject change.

"Ms. Harp?" I asked.

The guise of control remained but his eyes seemed sullen.

"I just need to figure out why she doesn't change. If we can isolate the issue, maybe we can use it to our advantage. For now, what happened to her is an anomaly and curse. Based on what Dr. Reyes has seen, it's getting worse." The last words were clipped as his hands scrubbed over the shadow on his face. Worry. Asher was worried about Ms. Harp.

With a heavy sigh, he seemed to let it go for the moment. "Are you ever going to tell me how you ended up in the demon realm, Erin?"

"It's a very long story."

"I have time."

"There's a woman in your car who will say otherwise." I looked at the clock. "I say you have a minute before she *encourages* you to get a move on."

He sighed. "She's more ornery than usual," he agreed. "Everything had been explained to her in detail. Dr. Reyes was very thorough, and they seemed to be getting along and then this happened." He was obviously baffled. "Dr. Reyes is doing us a big favor being here. She brought a mage with her to help with the study. I don't enjoy being indebted. I owe both her pack and the mages. Something needs to come of this."

I nodded. "Evelyn is a mystery," I said, although she wasn't. I nodded toward the door. "Come on. You deal with her and we'll carve out some time for me to tell you everything."

Increasing my speed past him, I got to the car and tapped on the window for Evelyn to let it down. "Turn your ears off," I told Asher. His face creased into a frown of confusion. "Don't listen to this conversation. Please."

He moved to the opposite side of the building. "Can you hear me?" I said softly, looking in his direction. He nodded and moved farther away. I had grossly underestimated the acuity of their hearing.

Taking out his phone, he allowed his attention to be occupied by it. It was doubtful he could completely turn his hearing off or if he would; it was so ingrained in his mere existence.

I crouched down until we were eye level. "Cut it out," I said in a low voice in Evelyn's ear. She turned to me. Her dramatic wide-eyed look of innocence was her worst performance to date.

"I have no idea what you're talking about."

"Don't play matchmaker. If you like Dr. Reyes, let them know your thoughts, but this elaborate scheme is unnecessary," I told her. "Keeping her here against her will by pulling these stunts is cruel."

Her lips pressed into a tight line.

"That's not it. I like her and definitely her for him.

They're a good fit. It won't happen, though. They'd have to stop challenging and annoying each other long enough to see it." Her lips pursed. "I don't want things to change. Not for me. If... *When* they find out what's wrong with me, and they fix it, I may become a shifter. Forced to change until I'm old."

"You are old," I teased.

"Older," she corrected. "I've seen them change. Most of them have perfected it, but that's with years of practice. I don't want to go through that. Be subjected to a strenuous transformation every month. I would rather have the alternative." Her eyes flicked behind me to Asher who was still busying himself on the phone. "He'd never let that be the alternative."

The tears forming in my eyes were the result of the windfall of issues I was dealing with. That was the excuse I was going with. "I wouldn't be okay with that alternative, either," I said, quickly brushing away the spilled tear.

"Stop that!" she hissed and whacked me on the nose.

"What is wrong with you!" I snapped, falling back on my butt.

Being punched by a person in their eighties isn't on anyone's life bingo card. She glanced past me.

"He's coming and you were crying for no reason. I just gave you something to cry about. Stop being so weepy. What's wrong with you lately?"

I recovered and hauled myself to stand, wiping my face. I glared at her through blurry vision.

"He'll find a solution for you." I wasn't sure of that, but I needed her to get the idea of dying out of her head.

I touched my throbbing nose. "Good luck," I said to Asher, who was grinning after witnessing Ms. Harp's assault.

"Said something she didn't like?" he quipped, opening the trunk of his car and placing her suitcase in it.

Tell him, I mouthed to her while he was distracted loading her luggage. The hardness in her face softened. My nose had to take a hit, but she seemed amenable to my suggestion. The hollowness remained, knowing that Asher may respect her wishes.

He gave me a quick wave and got in the car as I debated whether to reveal the information and make him promise not to honor her wish for the *alternative*. Press the issue that another course of action other than shifting needed to be found. Asher's self-assurance did wonders to ease my concern. In the battle of wills, I was placing my bets on him. He'd proven to be resourceful and would find a way to help her without resorting to the alternative she had in mind.

The unrelenting blanket of worry was starting to get to me. I stood in the cool night air, listening to the rustle of the wind through the surrounding trees. Enjoying the solace of the night and the subtle peace that it brought.

Earthy aura and evergreen wafted through the air.

"Erin."

Nolan's voice had me whipping around and launching toward him and hugging him, tossing aside the incongruency, strangeness, and history. He exhaled a surprised humph at me careening into him, burying my face in his chest. He gently stroked my back.

"I'm so glad to see you," I admitted.

"I'm glad to be here," he whispered into my hair.

CHAPTER 19

$\mathcal{O}$nce we were in my apartment, I called Mephisto to let him know Nolan was there and that I needed alone time with him. His protective urges didn't relent enough until I pointed out that Nolan wouldn't be as free with his information if others were around. Mephisto agreed with my argument; he was just having a difficult time conceding.

"It has been days and he's just now coming around?"

"I know." I had no answer and Mephisto didn't push. After a short, tension-riddled silence, he said goodbye. The question lingered in the back of my mind and caused me to put up a protective shield that had been demolished by my relief at finally seeing Nolan.

The time between making our way to the apartment and calling Mephisto, the hollow feeling of betrayal had settled in. It must have shown on my face. Nolan's warm ebullient smile faded. We were faced with the complexity of our relationship. I grappled with the idea of something good coming from such a faulty foundation.

"Where have you been? I've been trying to get in contact with you," I blurted from the other side of the room. My arms were crossed over my chest, embarrassment from my initial response warming my cheeks.

"I don't have that phone anymore." He dropped his head and when he lifted it, he had the sad, vacant look of someone who had taken too many hits and not had time to recover. "I didn't have the ability to move freely around Elizabeth. Her anger and hate have made her a vestige of herself. She believes you are undeserving of my protection and that I give it too freely to you. Sometimes it leads her to treat me like an enemy. The wards and defense spells weren't used to protect us but to keep me in. I was a prisoner, not a guest." I felt like a voyeur to his pain. "It took time to break the wards and leave. I looked for you for weeks. I thought you were dead." His voice broke, his eyes glistening with unshed tears. "The way she spoke of you, I thought she had broken her promise to me."

She'd promised not to kill me, but she hadn't promised not to make my life a living hell. By those standards, her promise to him was intact. He took a deep shaky breath, and the emotional barrier I'd erected faltered. Slowly, I inched toward him and sat next to him.

"I watched your home, Madison's and your parents, hoping to see you. Waiting for your return. I even considered asking them if they had heard anything." His eyes dropped to my hands as they covered his. "I should have, but why would they trust me enough to offer me any information? I'm Elizabeth's brother."

Using Elizabeth as a frame of reference, it was easy to see how he'd be hesitant to approach them, to experience the same hate and animosity that I endured from his sister.

"They're not like that," I assured him, although I said it with more confidence that I felt as I thought back to Mephisto's questioning. Everyone's desperation, frustration, and anger could have easily been misdirected toward Nolan as an outlet.

"Where were you?" he asked, breaking our silence.

The words spilled from me. "Elizabeth sent me to the demon realm and I made a deal with a demon to escape and I have thirty days to honor it or he gets my body and Malific wants me to find a way to remove the oath so that she can kill Elizabeth and I want to do it."

Color drained from his face and his lips tightened.

I only partially regretted my admission about Elizabeth.

He dropped his head, his long hair forming a curtain around his face. "I knew she was involved in some way, but I had no idea to what extent. She's changed so much. I don't even recognize her anymore." His head lifted to reveal a grim, sorrow-etched expression. "She believes she is doing the right thing. She doesn't understand that her actions are just as misguided as mine were. It's a bad place to be." His assertion wasn't an appeal for understanding or forgiveness. It appeared to be a surrender. He'd given up on her.

After minutes of silence, he shifted to face me. "What do you need?"

"To learn more about my magic. I have to be able to make a demon corporeal and defend myself against other elves."

"And what about Elizabeth?"

I had admitted I planned to let Malific kill her. Did he expect me to recant?

The contention between us was new, uncomfortable, and would be the weakness between us. He may have given up on her ever siding with him, but his love was unconditional. I wasn't sure what his love was for me. Was it a love warped by his hate for Malific?

"She sent me to the demon realm," I reminded him.

"Does her being misguided warrant another elf's death at the hands of Malific?" he asked.

Anger blazed in me. Not even the moment I took for a deep breath to check my emotions and try to see it from his perspective was enough.

"What? How many chances does she get? When she kills me, then will she have gone too far?" I snapped.

His calm in the face of my rage did nothing to ease my frustrations.

"Elizabeth won't kill you," he defended.

"No, but it's not because she doesn't want to. I exist to keep Malific in check. That's the only reason she won't kill me. Not because you want me alive. In the meantime, she'll make my life a living hell. Why can't you see this? You want to help, do something about your damn sister!"

He moistened his lips but remained silent for a long time. I wasn't sure if it was a surrender or lack of defense. "What is the deal you made with the demon?"

"It's more than a deal, it's a blood oath," I clarified before giving him specifics.

"May I see it?"

"After I signed it, he made it disappear. I can try to remember everything in it."

He shook his head. "No need. May I have a piece of paper?"

I retrieved a stack of printer paper and placed it on the table in front of him. Taking a small knife from his pocket, he said, "This spell will reveal oaths linked to your blood. Do you have any other blood oaths that you don't want me to know about?"

I shook my head. After pricking my finger, he whispered a spell, then pressed the digit to the paper. Cool circular threads moved around me as if magic was being unspooled. Markings appeared on the paper, as the marking from my oath glowed in defiance. Once the oath was before him, he read over it.

"It is a very thorough agreement," he observed, frowning.

"Is there a link between elves and demons?" I inquired. "That spell was able to pull out a demon oath. And Elizabeth was able to help Dareus send me to the demon realm."

He pondered the question. "Not that I know of. Calling a blood oath is a simple spell—" He stopped midsentence, considering his statement. "It's a simple spell for me. You weren't aware that it could be done?"

"No, I've never seen it done."

"Let me show you how." Taking another sheet of paper, he wrote down the spell. "There's no agreement required. You just need the blood, not the permission. I find that before making an oath, it is best to find out if any exist that will nullify yours. Magic is funny that way. There is always precedence. Based on this contract, you won't be able to enter an agreement with another demon."

"I'm not in a hurry to make any more deals with demons," I said quietly. "Wouldn't have made this one if there had been an alternative."

He covered my hands with his and gave them a squeeze. "Practice the spell," he urged.

"Will Asial be able to tell that it has been viewed?"

"No. It's a good practice to do this spell if you ever intend to bind anyone to an oath." A frown inched over his lips and reached his eyes, darkening them. "I'm taking you to the Havenage," he announced before his lips pressed into a line as if he'd misspoken.

"Havenage?"

"Elves live among you, but usually hybrids, not pure elves. I wasn't aware so many existed until I was approached by one and he took me to the Havenage." His eyes brightened and pride curled his lips into a pleasant smile. I wondered if being half human made him shunned to the point he never expected to be accepted by full elves. "Their magic makes what we are capable of look amateurish. If you are allowed into the Havenage, you can learn from them. Mastering your magic can only be done when you know its full range. They can teach you in a way that I can't."

"I have twenty-three days to deal with the Asial situation,"

173

I finally noted after grappling with the information about the Havenage. "I'd like you to teach me, not them."

He nodded, sensing my apprehension. Despite wanting to improve my skills, I wasn't enthusiastic about being around pure elves who may not accept me.

Tentatively he touched my hand, giving it a reassuring squeeze. "I will do whatever makes you the most comfortable. You would not be alone. It is where I've been for the past month and a half. If they are accepting of me, I don't see why they wouldn't be of my daughter."

Elizabeth accepts you and hates my guts.

"I won't be able to help you make the demon corporeal, but I can do my best to figure out how. It may not be enough. Knowing the full capabilities of your magic will allow you to make the changes to work spells that complement your dual magic. Mine works slightly differently. Diluted by my human half." His touch became firmer. "You have two very strong magics that you need to learn to master."

"I'm human, too. My magic may not be that strong," I pointed out. In fact, being only a quarter elf might be frustrating rather than helpful, learning my magic's limitations compared to that of full elves.

"God and elf. True, your human part my cause some limitations, but when you know your full range, navigating those limitations will come more easily. Elizabeth has mastered both and you see the extent of her skills."

Yeah, I didn't want to talk about her.

"Why mightn't they let me come to the Havenage?" I asked.

"A number of reasons. As I mentioned, pure elves tend to form stronger alliances with each other. When I first learned of the Havenage, I was denied." Hurt flooded his eyes. "I had encountered a pure elf, and it was through our friendship that I learned of the Havenage. Her request that I be allowed in was rejected. Everything I know about my magic, I learned from my mother and trial and error. At the Havenage, they have more spell books and extensive knowledge of elven magic."

"What changed their minds about you?"

"I don't know." Restless fingers ran through his hair. "Their hesitation to let in outsiders isn't out of malice but fear. They are very cautious." He looked away but not before I saw the concern and doubt. That caution might lead to me being rejected as well, despite his desire for me to be part of their community.

Despite his faux optimism, two issues would hinder my acceptance. I wasn't a full elf and my other half was responsible for a number of deaths in the elven population. If Elizabeth harbored so much hate for me for simply being Malific's daughter, I wasn't optimistic that the elves would be any better.

I remained hesitant. Perhaps it was simply me protecting myself from what was surely going to be a denial. Reject them before they got the chance to reject me.

Giving my hand another careful pat, Nolan made an effort to extend to me the same confidence he was attempting to keep in himself.

"Let's call the oath again," he suggested.

It took several attempts but I called the oath. Within an hour, I was able to do it with ease.

I hopped up from the sofa and returned with my phone and the pages of sigils. "Can you tell me about this spell?"

He studied it with the same look of confusion as I had. When I laid the papers on the floor, he walked around them, intently examining them, rearranging them. For nearly two hours we took turns doing a neutralizing spell and trying to break it in the manner she had, but without any success.

"Elizabeth has always been quite talented with magic," he admitted.

"Has she been invited to the Havenage?"

"No."

His response was so anguished it stopped me from questioning him further. It was difficult seeing the hurt return and the warring emotions he had for his sister.

Nolan prepared to leave at nearly three in the morning. His reluctance to leave me whittled away at the residual negative emotions I harbored about the complexity of our relationship. I found solace knowing it thrived despite its tumultuous beginnings and webs of complexity. It wasn't pretty, normal, or simplistic. It was us and had a place in my life.

CHAPTER 20

$\mathcal{N}$olan's call a few hours after he'd left my apartment lifted a weight I wasn't aware I was carrying. They had granted me entry to the Havenage and expected my arrival in three days. Trying not to dwell on the reason for the delay was difficult. What did they need the time for? To further vet me, to establish a teaching plan, or something more ominous? Pushing the last thought aside, I remained both excited and fearful.

Before I left, I had one pressing matter to attend to: informing Cory and Madison. It would not be easy. Cory remained at my side, casting wary looks at me while we walked to Madison's front door. During the drive to Madison's I'd been able to evade his questions, which led to him searing me with accusatory looks. If something needed to be discussed with them both present, it couldn't be good. It was a hypothesis he was quite vocal about when he'd arrived at my apartment earlier.

"What's up?" Madison asked slightly breathlessly through the small crack in the door, her body obscuring anything behind her. An amber glow streaked along the bridge of her nose and along her cheeks.

"I sent you a message about needing to talk to you," I reminded her.

"I know. I said I'd come to you, to make it easier." Her gaze shifted to Cory, who eyed her suspiciously.

"Were you too distracted to press send?" he asked, drawing attention to her shirt that was being held closed with one hand. She appeared to be more concerned with answering to door and keeping me from letting myself in, than putting on her shirt.

"Do you have company?" I asked in a chipper voice, causing her to become even more flustered.

"One moment." She closed the door. She had an urgent whispered conversation with someone, and when she opened the door to let us in, neither Cory nor I was surprised to see a heavy-lidded Clayton on the sofa, arms outstretched, disheveled hair, and a shirt not completely pulled down. Scrabble on the coffee table was unexpected. Was naked Scrabble a thing?

With her phone in hand, she groaned. "I didn't send the text. It would have been simpler for me to come to you."

"*Yeah*, that's the reason," Cory provided with a hint of churlish amusement.

"What do you need to talk about?"

After taking measure of me and Cory, Clayton decided to leave, which made things considerably easier. My plan was to tell Mephisto later, and there wasn't any way Clayton wouldn't tell him before I had a chance.

"I'll come back later tonight," his gravelly rich, deep voice announced. Lifting her chin, he pressed his lips to hers. A light brush, his arms wrapping around her, his fingers fisting the fabric of her shirt. The kiss intensified, making it obvious we had interrupted them. As the kiss persisted, I cleared my throat, reminding them they had an audience. Something they obviously had forgotten.

"How was your game of *Scrabble*?" I asked once Clayton closed the door behind him.

She rolled her eyes. "It was fine."

With a gaping mouth and wide-eyed incredulity that mirrored Cory's, I said, "Are you kidding me! Scrabble? Really? That's what you're going with? He was over here to play Scrabble? If we weren't here the two would have been on the floor naked going at it. I'm not certain you weren't. And that kiss? What's your issue with us knowing you and Clay are hooking up?"

"Why don't you want us to know you two are ravishing each other and chasing the big O?" Cory asked. He switched his voice to a low falsetto. "Take me to pleasure heaven, you sexy god."

I sidled up next to Madison, mimicking her cringe.

"Really?" Madison chided.

He shrugged. "You're the one being weird about it. I was just joining in the fun. No one has a problem with you screwing a god that hot. So, why are you trying to hide it? May I add, doing a poor job at it, too."

Madison dropped into a chair. "It seems wrong and it's out of character for me. He's so arrogant, and he's more powerful than anyone I've ever encountered."

"And really handsome," Cory added.

"Yeah, he's *very* aware of that," Madison complained. "I never go for men like that."

"He's a god, does that make it better?" Cory was grinning.

"Not even a little bit."

"*And* you threatened to have him arrested. That's clearly a red flag. He's probably a masochist," I teased.

"No, that part checks," Cory said. "It's not the humiliation of her threat of arrest that draws him. It's the loyalty and the dedication to you that she demonstrated when she did it. They all stayed behind because of Mephisto. They value loyalty and solidarity. It's quite apparent that he'd never come across a situation he couldn't charm his way out of. After the initial shock of the threat, you could see his admiration." Cory shrugged. "Clayton being into you makes sense. Your hang-up about it doesn't."

"I don't know," she admitted. "We're such a mismatch but we seem to work." She dismissed it with a wave toward the game on the table. "And he's really good at Scrabble."

"Yeah, I bet he's really good at *Scrabble*," Cory teased, prompting a hiss and another eye roll from Madison. Desperate to discuss anything other than Clayton, she turned her attention to me.

"Why did you need to see me?" Her eyes shifted to Cory for hints, but he shook his head.

I told them everything: Nolan's visit, his inability to make demons corporeal or decipher the spell Elizabeth used to free Dareus from my magic, his rejection and then admittance to Havenage, and them allowing me entrance to learn more about my magic.

"Can we go?" Madison finally asked after several long moments of pacing the room.

"No. They're very cautious about who can enter."

"Yeah, you said that. They rejected him initially and now he can bring guests?" Madison stopped pacing just long enough to question me. "That doesn't seem suspicious to you?"

I shook my head. "I'll be safe. Nolan will be with me." In an effort to keep them from worrying, I put more assurance into my statement than I actually felt.

"What chance would he have against them when he's already admitted to being magically inferior?"

Madison's interrogation came from a protective place. Her opposition dampened my excitement and tugged at the apprehension that I was suppressing poorly. My mind raced with a number of ways this could go badly.

"We haven't yielded any positive results with anything we've been doing," Cory pointed out. His comment was just the acknowledgment of a desperate situation. I gathered from his painfully rigid scowl that he wished there was an alternative.

"Mephisto hasn't come up with anything?" Madison asked.

"Just trying to find another host."

Guilt swelled in me as her eyes misted. "What about nullifying the oath? There has to be a way." She went to her bookshelves. Desperate eyes reviewed the titles. All the books that we'd already gone over and over. Returning to us, she plopped into the chair across from me.

"One of us has to go with you. Cory?"

"Nolan was very clear that I was the only one who could go."

When Madison's hands covered her face, Cory stiffened next to me. Time ticked by as she stayed motionless except for the minute movement of her breathing. Her sob tore through the silence. I'd broken Madison, and it made me feel lower than dirt.

"I can't lose you again, Erin," she whispered, unintentionally pushing the dagger deeper into my heart.

"I'm sorry. I don't want this to be hard on you two. But I'm not sure there could ever be a better option or opportunity. My limited magical ability and limited knowledge of the elves is stopping me being able to efficiently deal with Malific and Elizabeth. How can I turn away from this opportunity? Please don't make me choose between doing what's best for me and hurting you."

When she removed her hands, she attempted a small smile that never reached her worried eyes.

"I trust Nolan," I said. "There are reasons to hold on to anger and distrust him, but he's trying to atone for his mistakes. He wouldn't put me in a harmful situation."

"And they won't let Elizabeth in," Cory pointed out. "If nothing else, you can find comfort in that."

Madison was noticeably relaxing. "You trust Nolan without reservation?"

"I do."

"Nervous?"

I nodded. "Elves have been considered extinct, and I'll get to meet some. To finally tap into all my magic potential. And maybe someone can explain why I keep turning into a fucking cat whenever I try to Wynd."

Madison's laughter lifted the burden that would never have let me leave if she wasn't okay with it. She was trying to reconcile her need to protect me and do what was best. I understood that. It was a burden I wished I could remove for her.

"Mephisto's okay with this?" Madison asked.

I could feel Cory's curious eyes burning into the side of my face. I was fully aware of the lecture I'd get if he had the impression that I wasn't going to tell Mephisto or if it was an afterthought.

"I needed to tell you first. I'm meeting him later to tell him." I turned to give Cory a grin of self-satisfaction. It was better than my puerile inclination to brag and give him the smug "I got this" face. Not because I was better than that—I wasn't. But there were ulterior motives to me inviting Mephisto to dinner to tell him. It was less likely to be an intense discussion in a public setting.

Cory turned to face me. "So, you're going to get the whole *Karate Kid* experience."

"I don't know what that is," I said with casual indifference, watching with amusement as a kaleidoscope of emotions—shock, dismay, and finally disgust—moved over his face.

"You would have if you weren't reading a book when you were supposed to be watching it. It's a classic!"

I shrugged. "I get the gist. Wimpy dude wants to learn karate. Something about a girl. Then there's a bonsai tree and he does something to it. I don't know, dances with it or something. Then he has to wash a car or clean something. So, no, I'm not going to get the karate kid experience because I have no intention of cleaning anything in exchange for magic lessons."

Cory graced me with the same look he had this morning as he gave my apartment a judgmental sweeping look. Taking in the unfolded blanket on the sofa, one shoe by the door and the other by the window where I'd kicked it out of my way, crumbs from the bag of chips I ate earlier, the empty bag crumpled on the table. The kitchen was clean. Or so I thought, until his disapproving eyes went to the dishes in the sink and a half-eaten bagel with peanut butter that I nibbled on during my call with Nolan. There was a small circle of bagel crumbs and the knife I'd licked clean.

"Technically, he didn't clean anything. He washed a car. It helped him with his blocks," Madison offered.

Don't validate this foolishness. I shot a look at her and she grinned, enjoying this exchange far too much. Seeing her ease into acceptance made all the difference to me.

"It's David and Goliath, the ultimate bully story, good conquers evil. It had it all and...*it is a classic.*"

"Big whoop. Guy with no skills washes a car and wins a tournament with a weird front kick. Yeah, classic."

The humor ebbed from his face. "We had a good run. Thanks for all the ups, downs, laughs, and sorrow. I can't do this anymore. We are divorced. This is me divorcing you. I'd like alimony." He kissed me on the cheek and pretended to head out of the door.

I grabbed his arm. "Fine, I'll watch all the Karate Kids, Goodmobsters, and Hello to my little friend.'"

"You know damn well that the first *Karate Kid* is the best

and the only one that should exist. *Goodfellas*. And *Scarface*," he said, his light eyes darkening with irritation.

"Forgive her, she doesn't know that we aren't worthy of such phenomenal cinematic classic works," Madison said to Cory.

The conversation devolved to trite topics. It was needed.

As I was leaving, Madison said, "I hope this turns out to be everything you need." Sorrow remained in her voice; she seemed unable to totally eliminate it. But she was hopeful, as hopeful as I was. It was a step toward having a somewhat normal life—something neither of us had experienced since I came into her life.

CHAPTER 21

*A*t first glance, Chastain would make a person question how a restaurant that never had any customers managed to stay in business. At five in the afternoon, there were just a few people in the restaurant. The deep, muted blue/gray walls were a nice contrast to the cream-colored light-filtering curtains that lent to the cozy feel of the medium-size room. Well-placed sconces provided enough light to see where you were headed but not a full view of everyone in the room. Intimate placement of tables and booths allowed the privacy that patrons desired.

Dark wood tables contrasting with beige leather chairs presented an upscale comfort that appealed to its clientele. I'd had several meetings at the restaurant. The food was passable, good enough to enjoy but nothing to rave about or guarantee a patron would return for any other reason than its intended purpose: private conversation in a public setting. For that privilege, customers paid Michelin star restaurant prices without getting the same quality of meal.

Seated in a small booth in the corner, I had traded my jeans and shirt for a charcoal-colored off-the-shoulder dress, cinched at the waist. A softer, unobtrusive look. It wasn't as if

I was blindsiding him with this setup. Who was I kidding; I was, which explained the heaviness in my chest. Twenty minutes early, I was sipping on a glass of white wine when I pulled out my phone to text Mephisto to change the venue to his home. I felt his presence before I saw him.

Moving with the effortless grace and power that his presence and magic commanded, he crossed the room, dressed in a slim fit indigo-blue suit and white shirt with the first button undone. His attire was a brazen challenge. Seeing my shock at his departure from his typical dark clothing, his lips cocked into a smirk. His statement was made. I wasn't going to get away with "Hey, I'm leaving for the Havenage tomorrow. There's absolutely no threat of danger. What will you have, chicken or steak?"

Despite my overconfident display with Cory and Madison, there was always a threat of danger, no matter how minute. I was aware of it but considered the potential benefit worth it. Nolan would be there. That had to be enough. That *was* enough.

Mephisto moved close to me. Leaning down, he took my chin into his hand with a firm but gentle touch, pressing a kiss on my mouth that matched it. "Erin," he purred in my ear. His teeth nipped at my lobe. It felt like a chastisement. He moved to sit across from me.

Confidence is a very transient trait that wanders into arrogance territory so freely. Mephisto rested back in his chair, fingers clasped over his stomach, his shirt molded around his toned stomach, and his piercing coal eyes fixed on me. The look of cool indifference shimmied over into reserved arrogance. It was the man-spread that did it. He couldn't just acknowledge that he knew my motive for our meeting place; it had to be a production. A less than subtle reproach.

Eh, I have a few minutes to kill. I'll play your game. I took a sip from my glass, then pointed to the menu. "Do you know what you want, or do you need to review the menu?" I knew of this place because of Mephisto. We'd had our share of meetings there. "My treat," I tacked on.

A wolfish glint sparked in his eyes. "I'm sure you're about to treat me to something, so I'll forgo the meal."

The stilted silence twisted into a defiant silence. Mephisto ordered a glass of wine. I ordered two appetizers although I wasn't hungry. Once the server had gone, I addressed the dancing elephant in the room.

"Do you know?" I asked.

Clayton couldn't have known, and I doubted Madison had shared anything with Clayton.

"Not the specifics. But you inviting me to a public place to tell me is beneath you, Erin. You've always been direct. This"—his gaze swept around the room—"is not you."

"I wasn't trying to be indirect," I admitted. "I wanted an environment that wouldn't permit open conflict."

His brow rose. That definitely wasn't me.

"I don't want conflict with you," I clarified.

Mephisto's features softened as he studied me. "Let's get out of here."

He dropped several bills on the table and entwined his fingers with mine as we walked out of the restaurant. He steered me in the opposite direction of the parking lot and toward the small park a few blocks away. Once we found a seat on a bench, I told him about Nolan's visit, what had happened between him and Elizabeth, and his offer to take me to the Havenage. His face remained indecipherable the entire time.

I closed with, "I need to go and I trust Nolan."

"You didn't feel comfortable having this conversation with me?" His tone was tepid but the air between us was stifling and cool.

"That's not it. I'm tired of defending my position. All these battles are wearing on me. I didn't want it to be a big discussion." I had no expectation of him responding the way Madison had, and I didn't want his version of it. A pang of guilt moved through me thinking about how broken she'd looked.

"You can't possibly want people to not care whether you are safe?"

"Of course not. But I don't know how to protect them from getting hurt." It was a foolish objective, but one nonetheless. "Madison wasn't okay with me leaving and it was difficult to deal with. I wasn't ready for another emotionally draining conversation."

Mephisto's deep chuckle caught me off guard. He leaned into me, his fingers tracing along the lines of my jaw. "I don't believe I've ever been so wrong about two people in my existence. Madison and you are quite the unexpected twists," he said, his lips quirked into a half smile. "This side of you, it's different and I like it. The side of Madison that caused her to slap cuffs on me and put me in the back of a squad car while threatening to do the same to Clayton doesn't appeal to me, but I respect it. It cemented Clay's interest." Mephisto's response was tinged with a mélange of irritation, amusement, and disbelief.

"In her defense, I heard you and Asher were in desperate need of a timeout," I teased.

"Asher." He grumbled the name. Mentioning Asher raised more uneasiness than everything that I had just told him. Asher and Mephisto had once had an amicable relationship, but it had devolved into veiled threats, covert displays of dominance, and me wanting to pelt them with ice cubes to cool them off when they were in each other's presence.

"Erin, I don't want you to go because I'm not a hundred percent confident that you will be safe."

"Nothing is a hundred percent, but the benefits are worth the risk."

He sighed. "When do you leave?"

"Wednesday."

He nodded, his fingers rubbing along the crease in his brow. "A community of elves among us. What a peculiar turn of events."

"It is an intriguing turn of events. One that you can't explore. Don't try to follow me there, Mephisto." His intention was very obvious in his expression.

"I have no intention of doing any such thing. They want you and you alone, correct?"

"Nor can Kai," I pressed. "I have to do this alone. If you all follow me, try to track us, or make an effort to find the Havenage, it will ruin things. Nolan was very clear about that."

Mephisto took a deep breath. He was not used to working around the confines of others. He always found a way to navigate on his terms. Being aware of the Havenage but restricted from finding it was probably akin to torture. Mephisto's jaw was so tightly clenched, it could create diamonds out of coal. It took several long moments for him to finally agree.

CHAPTER 22

The next morning Mephisto was called away by Benton at the unacceptable hour of five a.m. I ate breakfast with Isley—or rather I ate with the chef who prepared my breakfast and then made every possible effort to escape. He didn't like small talk and politely made it known. Any questions I asked about the Huntsmen were met with his inquiries about whether I was enjoying the meal.

Through bites of my breakfast, I managed to get some information, but only because he used it as a means to redirect questions about himself and his life. Perhaps that was a tacit rule: Don't get too chummy with Mephisto's guest, which led me to speculate about the number of *randos* Isley had encountered and used this tactic on.

Despite his efforts to give me as little information as possible, I learned that Mephisto's pet okapi had been with Mephisto for five years. That he wasn't happy about the gift and that it had been a point of contention between him and Simeon. Clayton visited more than the others and spent most of his time in the pool and enjoying the luxuries of the house.

Isley politely commented that Clayton enjoyed the

comforts of the home but would never be so ostentatious as to have them in his own. Something Clayton reminded Mephisto of, while eating food prepared by a chef that he would have refused to have in his own home. Little was said or known about Kai, but Isley's fandom of him was evident as he showed off the butcher block, cutting board, and hand carved wine rack Kai had made for him.

Recognizing Isley's intense focus on cleaning the kitchen as his way of politely shooing me away, I returned to Mephisto's bedroom. I showered and traded his shirt for the dress I wore the day before. I was going to take him up on his suggestion to leave some clothing at his house. My reluctance was falling away. Mephisto and I would make this work. Dressed, I checked my phone to see several missed calls and texts from Cory telling me he was coming over later, and from Wendy finally responding to confirm a time to meet.

When I approached Benton's office while searching the house for Mephisto, quiet, tense voices inside came to an abrupt stop. They were fully aware of my presence. I still knocked before entering. In a clear standoff, Mephisto stood across from Simeon, Kai, and Clayton. Tension thickened the air. In response to the Huntsmen's shared combative glares, Benton's fingers were pressed to his nose as if warding off an impending headache.

"Mephisto's raven," Kai greeted. No, not a greeting. A reminder of my place in this world. The sin of being Malific's daughter and the reason they had declined Elizabeth's offer. Their wintry hospitality whirred around me when all eyes turned to me.

Mephisto approached me with slow, measured steps, as if moving toward a wounded animal that he was fearful would scurry away. As he planted a soft kiss on my cheek, I remained painfully aware of the audience. He met their pensive looks with a scowl. I wasn't privy to their private conversation taking place at that moment.

"If it's about me, I'd like to know," I challenged, meeting each of their gazes. Their attention moved from me to Mephisto who remained planted next to me.

"We want to go home," Kai said. Hearing the anguished longing in his voice made it difficult to return the suppressed hostility directed at me.

"I want that for you, too," I whispered. "I'm doing what I can to make that possible." They nodded but the tension remained. An unspoken accusation. "You had the option to leave, and you didn't take it. I can't be blamed for that."

"We wouldn't go without him. And he wasn't leaving without the assurance that you were home safe," Simon said.

"So it wasn't much of a choice, was it? Whether you like it or not, you are the reason we are here," added Clayton.

"That's unfair," Mephisto said, pinning Clay with a hard glare.

Anger flitted across Clay's face, and their eerie shared movement placed them face to face sneering at each other. My heart pounded at the looming threat of violence. There was no denying or ignoring the otherness of their magic engulfing the space, the toxicity of their anger, and what felt like the ties of their friendship severing.

"Let me tell you what's *not* fair. The sacrifices we've made. Before, your actions were grounded and your goals clear. I don't see that now. Before, you used to take our counsel. Listen to our advice. Now, the actions you take are too risky. Dangerous. You don't seem to care what we think or about the consequences of your actions. How could you think of—"

Kai whisked me out of the room. Moving with indomitable grace, he grabbed me at the waist, cuffing me to his side. I was a few feet from the front door before I could register what was happening. Simeon blocked my view, closing the door on the sight of Benton trying to put distance between Mephisto and Clayton.

It didn't work. Thunderous crashes resounded from the room.

Simeon's eyes dropped to my wristlet that held my phone and keys and asked, "Do you have your things?"

Chin lifted in defiance, I squared my shoulders to stand taller. "I'm not leaving," I told him.

"Yes, you are."

I was unable to stop looking at the small space between the muscled body wall he and Kai had formed. Simeon lowered his head to meet my eyes. "They have disagreements all the time. This one will be resolved as well."

There was another boom and the sound of plaster raining on the floor. "Doesn't sound like it's going very well."

Simeon dismissed it with a shrug, giving me the impression that their resolution tended to come with a side of face punching and property destruction.

"If it's about me, I have to the right to be there and speak my piece."

Simeon shook his head. "Of course it's about you. It's always about you." Despite the poorly repressed anger and frustration in his voice, it didn't seem like he was speaking with malice. "You going in there would be another reminder that everything Mephisto has done recently benefits only you. That's the issue, isn't it, raven?" He frowned. "We've been here too long." It was as if he was admitting a weakness, their collective shortcoming.

"I didn't ask for this," I said, glancing at Kai, who hadn't reconciled whatever was going through his mind. His sharp, calculating look made me want to put some distance between us. It appeared he was doing a risk benefit analysis of eliminating the problem—me. And that calculation and answer had crossed his mind more than once. His look was enough for me to ease back a few steps until my back was pressed against the wall.

Kai closed his eyes, took in a slow breath, and when he released it, his expression was calm. "We know," Kai said, looking away from me. "Nor did we."

Simeon sighed again. "We've had our share of fights and disagreements. This, too, will be resolved," he repeated. I was confident that the fraternal bond would survive but not without some bruising to it.

"Please go," Kai pleaded. Then he turned from me and headed back toward Benton's office. The reassuring smile Simeon offered me as I fumbled at the front door didn't quite reach his eyes.

Hauling myself to the car, I reminded myself that their frustration and anger wasn't against me but the situation. Though it was hard not to take it personally when I was part of the situation. I clung to the fact that they'd been through worse and survived.

CHAPTER 23

*H*ours after my unceremonious invitation to leave Mephisto's home, I met with Wendy. Despite my invitation to the Havenage, I still wanted to cover all my bases. Any information Dareus might provide would be helpful, by increasing my knowledge and giving me a better understanding of my magic.

Nothing came of the four demons who responded to Wendy's summons, and they were annoyed when they weren't able to receive any benefits for their trouble. Dareus never showed. Between the summons, I had to endure Wendy's terrible dramatic show of pretending to be emotionally wounded at the insinuation that she practiced dark magic. Her persistent denial of knowing how to summon Dareus made it clear that if he didn't show up with a general summons, I wasn't going to see him. I remained unconvinced that she didn't know his summoning name.

She used our break between demon summoning not only to protest her dark magic status again but to pepper me with questions about being an elf. She seemed less impressed upon learning I was just a quarter elf. Telling her my exile to the demon realm was in response to pissing off the Woman in Black seemed to be an adequate explanation.

Wendy ended our disappointing meeting with a less than subtle reminder that despite nothing coming of her summons, she expected repayment. I was racking up my share of debts.

Now I was sitting across from Cory and Alex, who had shown up unexpectedly. I was grateful for the company and the coffee and cookies they brought, but I could do without the probing looks Cory kept giving me. He knew something was wrong, but I wasn't in the mood to discuss it, especially with Alex present. His gaze tracked my movement as I took a bite of one of the cookies from the assortment Alex offered me.

The assessing looks continued, but they were from Alex, too, whose gaze danced between me and Cory. His head shifted, listening intently to something. Heartbeat? Respiration? Ants crawling outside? A limb falling from a tree? Who knew when it came to shifters?

His look turned sympathetic. "I think you could benefit from a night out, away from this," Alex said, waving his hand at the stack of books on the table, notepads with my scribbling, and runes I had been working on.

"Night out doing what?" I asked suspiciously. Their shared interest of watching classic movies, cult classic TV shows, and critically acclaimed movies was the last thing I wanted to do. Ecstatic for their relationship and how happy it made Cory, I held an equal amount of joy over never having to watch another TV show or movie with him. Alex had taken over that role.

"The Jazz Bar," he quipped, excitement sparking in his eyes.

I frowned. "Only one of those words appeals to me and it isn't jazz."

He chuckled. Cory shook his head. "Despite its insipid

and unimaginative name, the music is phenomenal," Alex said, demonstrating the enthusiasm of a person who adored the genre.

"I've heard jazz before and not one time during the experience did I think phenomenal. Pretentious? Maybe. Boring as hell? *Every time*. Musical noise definitely crossed my mind. But phenomenal? Not once."

I expected Cory to join in, since our dislike of jazz was mutual. "You'll like this place," he assured me.

Betrayer! When I fixed him with a blistering glare, he looked away, rose coloring his cheeks.

"Give it a try," Alex urged. "They host bands and singers with a vast array of musical styles. Everything from John Coltrane to Sade with hints of Ella Fitzgerald. Every third Wednesday, there's a performer whose style is so reminiscent of Thelonious Monk, you'd believe you're hearing him. If you like Frank Sinatra, they feature a singer with a similar sound the last Friday of the month."

My head swiveled in Cory's direction. Alex's enthusiasm seemed to be shocking even him.

"I'm so glad you two found each other, because the chances of finding that special person weren't in either of your favor," I teased.

Matching smirks accompanied by raised brows were a precursor to them shifting their bodies to give me a full view of both of them, along with a challenging look of "really?"

Great, a supernova of arrogance. That's all I needed to complete my day.

"How sober do I have to be?" I asked.

Alex chuckled. "No expectations. This night is all about you."

"Don't give her that power," Cory interjected, quickly ducking to miss being hit by the pillow I lobbed at him.

"Seriously, if you don't enjoy it, say the word and we leave," Alex assured me.

"I've been given that option by this one before." I jabbed an accusatory finger at Cory. "'We can stop watching it if you don't enjoy it,' but he failed to mention the disclaimer that it was predicated on a good stopping point. Apparently crappy movies don't have good stopping points."

"You control the night," Alex insisted. "If you hint at not enjoying yourself, we're out of there. I think you will enjoy it."

After I agreed, they headed out. Cory wrapped me into a hug and whispered, "If you need to talk about it, you know I'm here for you."

I knew he was and so would Madison, but I didn't want to discuss it and reopen the wound of seeing what I was doing to the Huntsmen.

Cory's eyes trailed over the loose waves of my hair, along my bare shoulder of my tiered mini dress, gliding over my exposed cleavage to the fringe at the end of the dress. I shimmied them. "I'm jazzy," I chirped.

"Fringe is more of the twenties," he corrected. Taking my hand, he twirled me around and when we were face to face, he said, "I want you to stay behind me. I'll fend off any hungry babies who try to get at those to seek nourishment." He smirked, pointing at my cleavage.

"You're the only person who thinks you're funny."

Playfully elbowing him in the stomach, Alex pushed him aside. "You look gorgeous," he said, giving me his arm. I took hold of it and allowed him to escort me out the door.

"Just so you know, he's my favorite of this couple," I told Cory over my shoulder.

The Jazz Bar may have chosen a mundane name but that was the only thing dull about it. Uniquely shaped pendant lights cast a warm glow throughout the modern bar that featured curved velvet deep wine-colored chairs and black tables, complemented by a metal music note centerpiece. Seating was close enough to give the illusion of intimacy as the patrons enjoyed the band, but allowed the servers uniformly dressed in a vest and pants to effortlessly navigate around them. Toward the back of the bar, a crescent-shaped table and seating provided optimal viewing of the stage and touted the luminary status of anyone who managed to snag the table. Something that Alex was disappointed wasn't available when he made reservations.

Shifters had their own brand of smugness, and Alex's was on full display after several times catching me leaning forward, watching the band with rapt attention. I was convinced they weren't a band but sirens, because only magic could explain the music. It wasn't like anything I'd heard before, which made me question what I'd heard before.

Alex's knowing smile flashed at a steady clip. It was pleasing enough to ease the cloud of my concern after Mephisto's curt response earlier when I enquired whether his dispute with Clayton had been resolved and the cause of the strife. His only response was, "Everything's fine. Can I see you later?"

I made plans to see him after I ended my night with Cory. Drinks and great music and time with Alex and Cory had me relaxed enough that I wasn't annoyed at spotting Landon seated in the back, at the table so desired by Alex. A location that gave him and his three guests an unobstructed view of the band and everyone present. His dark, bemused eyes fell on me hard before he bared his fangs. I dismissed him and the weapon he'd displayed and returned my attention to the band while trying to ignore the piercing weight of his eyes that I felt on me.

Unsurprisingly, moments later, the server offered me another French martini from the gentleman in the back.

"Are you going to thank him?" Alex asked.

I shook my head. "Maybe later." I made a show of sliding the drink to the middle of the table, where I planned to leave it untouched. When I chanced a quick glance in his direction, he crooked his finger, inviting me to join him. I shook my head and lifted my chin toward the band.

Moments later, my phone vibrated. Without looking, I knew who it was. Debating whether to ignore him, I decided it would be prudent to just deal with the situation.

The message read: "Please join us. One of these men could be your son."

I responded by reminding him that we were listening to a band and it would be rude to have a conversation during their set. Next, I turned my phone off.

I did not believe for one moment that it was a coincidence that within minutes, the band was taking a half hour break. The moment they stepped away from the small stage, Landon approached me with the ease of floating on air. Offering a self-indulgent smile, he picked up my untouched drink and drained it in a few gulps.

Keeping his eyes on me, he addressed both Cory and Alex. "Please excuse Erin. I'd like her to join me and my guests for a few minutes."

Fury had me several shades of crimson. Landon was well known in the city and all eyes in the bar were on me. I was becoming a distraction and the recipient of a lot of unwanted attention. Forcing an amiable smile on my face, I said through clenched teeth, "Of course."

Taking his proffered hand, I squeezed it as hard as I could, aware that it would never inflict the level of pain I wanted.

He leaned into me as we navigated past through the bar toward his table. "You look absolutely lovely, Erin. I wasn't aware that you were capable of such stunning beauty. It's a shame you often choose a more...*carefree* way of dressing, when you could look like this."

"By 'carefree,' do you mean badass?" I countered.

He chuckled but there was no humor in it. "You're such a good judge of character, I do believe your input is necessary for these potentials."

"Of course. I wouldn't have it any other way."

Thrown by my acquiescence, he gave me a sly look out of the corner of his eyes. "I'm not used to you being so amenable." His lips brushed the side of my ear as he spoke. "I really enjoy this side of you."

Don't punch the Master of the City in his man berries. It became my mantra as we made our way to the table. Landon poured a glass of wine from the bottle on the table and handed it to me. Once I took the proffered glass, he extended his hand and introduced the men who were participating in Vampire Bachelor. Who'd get the rose by the end of the night?

I studied the budget version of Dallas, without the expensive suits, modesty—whether faux or authentic—and unassuming lethality. His satin-smooth bronze skin was complemented by the light-gray shirt conforming to a body that boasted of an obscene amount of time in the gym. His smile was dangerous, but so was everything about him, from the calculating eyes to the smirk that hinted at trouble, and his feline movement.

Refined charm was a smokescreen for something far more nefarious. It didn't take a student of body language to know this man would be a very dangerous vampire. Would Dallas be flattered or offended by the similarities? Maybe he could overlook the creepy factor. I couldn't. This was fucking creepy. So. Very. Creepy.

Could Landon not see that he was wining and dining the man who would dethrone him if given a sliver of a chance?

Then there was Mr. Check Out My Profile. He didn't provide a name or care when Landon gave him mine. Diamond-cut striking features turned slightly just in case I'd missed any of his appeal. Whether it was from inherited wealth, an unearned sense of entitlement, or pure arrogance, he was cocooned in the scent of self-entitlement. He gave me a once-over with bored pale-brown eyes. His cool olive skin was definitely a result of tanning or perhaps a recent island visit. The light streaks in his blond hair suggested sun exposure.

He hadn't decided if I was important and it showed in his aloof expression. After the introduction as a special acquaintance, I'd registered as important. So, he smattered on the charm full throttle. Wide smile, affable glint, smooth caress of my hand, all lauding his true sincerity in meeting me.

The third man was the wildcard. Dark curly chin-length hair that fell haphazardly gave him ample opportunity to dismiss the world around him as he fidgeted with it. Flat dark eyes reminded me of rich chocolate, and roughly hewn features gave him a rugged appearance. He didn't seem uncomfortable in the expensive suit he was wearing. His expression hovered between nonchalance and boredom, as if he'd agreed to show up because he had nothing better planned. He didn't strike me as the type to want to be a vampire, so I wasn't sure why he was there. Had his aloofness appealed to Landon so much that he coaxed him into it? An offer of a life that would be anything other than insipid? Landon texted me names days ago, but I hadn't bothered to commit them to memory.

My attention stayed on the third man with the unruly hair, simultaneously intrigued and put off by his indifference. My goal was to stall progress. I gave each a long appraising look while Landon treated me to the same level of scrutiny.

I pointed to Mr. Profile. "This one will be a pain in the ass. He makes your arrogance and sense of entitlement seem diminished enough to perhaps even be charming. Make him yours and he'll be a menace bringing more trouble than it would be worth. If you ever have to 'handle' your own child, you won't get any do-overs with me." If by some chance Mr. Profile had missed my comment, I leaned in and held his gaze. "If you become too much of a problem, they murder you. Period."

Landon's lips tightened. "Handled' was too innocuous a word for such a ruthless act.

I continued. "Depending on how bad the situation is, and the damage control needed, you'll have to pay for the transgression. There's a dungeon. Do I need to get specific?"

As the color drained from Mr. Profile's face, I knew details weren't necessary. Landon's scrutiny turned to a glare.

"This one." I jerked my chin at Opportunistic Dallas. "Don't turn your back on him too many times. You might find a knife in your back and a stake in your heart." I made a face at Landon. "Seriously, Landon, how could you miss this? He's wearing his thirst for power like a fragrance."

A shrewd smirk settled on Faux Dallas's lips. A slight raise of his brow illustrated that I hadn't shamed him by any means. Through his expression was an undertone of mockery as if to display that his intentions were so obvious, I was the inane one for pointing it out.

The third one was easier; he hadn't even roused from the dressing down of the others. "He couldn't care less about being here. And that indifference isn't going to change. If you want a vamp who's going to make you a proud papa, he's not the one." I took a long drink from the glass I'd been holding. "Gentlemen, have a good night." I headed back for my table.

It wasn't unexpected that Landon would catch up. He grabbed my arm and turned me to face him. "The little minx is vicious today, isn't she?"

"Not vicious at all. Just perceptive and trying to make a bad situation work to my advantage. If I help you create this vampire whether I like it or not, I'm forever linked to them and you. I don't want controversy and issues with them causing problems that will likely reflect on me and make my life miserable. You don't want that, either. And"—I moved closer, dropping my voice even lower as I leaned into him —"let's not be coy here. You're hoping the new vamp will start a new bloodline of better vampires. You want excellence, so don't start with a faulty product."

I winced inwardly at calling people products, but Landon reveled in it. Bemused satisfaction brought a wide smile to his face. I moved back just in time to prevent the kiss he attempted.

"You, Erin, enchant me."

It was rooted in the shallowest of reasons, but it worked in my favor. I just hoped all the flaws in the other potentials were as easily sussed out and he agreed with my evaluations.

An hour and a half later, the bar became a hum of chatter with the band's departure. As we stood from the table to leave, I felt Landon's presence before I actually saw him. Glancing in the direction where he was once seated, I saw that the potentials were gone. He took a look draw from a glass filled with a thick, sanguineous liquid. His tongue slid over his lips to remove a small trickle.

"May I have a moment of your time?" He phrased it as a question but there was obvious expectation of compliance.

Alex, although part of the pack, wasn't the Alpha, which meant that in this implicit world of hierarchy, power flexing, and jiggly bits measuring contests, he was inconsequential. Cory wasn't the elder of his coven, so he was negligible. Landon flicked his attention at them but didn't wait for a response, expecting them to leave.

Irritation flared when they didn't immediately comply, the muscles of his neck becoming taut from him clenching his jaw. Powerful, entitled people were exhausting to deal with, but I didn't want a mere conversation with the Master of the City to become an incident between the Northwest

Pack and the vampires over a slight, or Landon proving to the witches that magic didn't supersede vampire speed, strength, and preternatural thirst for violence. I nodded to Cory and Alex. "I'll meet you at the car," I told them.

Landon's narrowed eyes followed them as they left the table and headed for the exit. Committing the implicit insult to his list of things to be dealt with at a later date. Pettiness didn't fade with age or increased responsibility. Acting on his base triviality was now his hobby.

Drawing his attention back to me, his lips eased into a sneering grin. "I can't tell you how much I appreciate your dedication to finding the right progeny for me."

Returning his cynical smile, I was acutely aware that me standing face to face with Landon had attracted the attention of a lot of people who seemed to still find the vampires intriguing. *Be on your best behavior, Erin,* I coaxed myself despite everything about Landon's hauteur making me want to rail against my own advice.

I said, "Of course. I don't want to put you in the predicament of trying to find another person to replace the ones you had to get rid of because they disappointed you in some way." I was sure it was his arrogance, or the relentless weight of my debt to him, or the numerous other things that Landon had done that made me reluctant to put any effort into adding sincerity to my response. His lips tightened and he exhaled an unneeded breath to demonstrate his exasperation with me.

Taking a long drink from his glass, he savored it, then he bent down until our eyes met, his stone hard and wrathful. "I'm so happy we are in accord with this." His voice was rough and steely. "I really hope that such dedication is for my benefit, *not* yours." He backed away. "It would be unfortunate if I felt compelled to invalidate the debt," he cautioned in a low, lethal tone before turning away from me and starting to return to his seat.

The implications of that would mean erasing the entire debt, including what initiated it: saving Dr. Sumner's life.

"I don't like threats," I barked, at the end of my patience with intimidation.

He stopped, his back still to me as he finished the remainder of the contents of his wine glass. "And it wasn't one. Just a reminder of the situation, because you seem to have forgotten the gravity of what was done. I hope you don't require another reminder. While we're at it, don't let what happened with Robyn *ever* happen again." A dangerous energy moved around him, but I wasn't going to be his scapegoat.

"No. You clearly had the problem with turning her. You should have owned it instead of passing it to me. I won't lie for you."

He turned around and studied me, the hardness of his gaze unchanged. Time ticked by, causing my curiosity to heighten.

"Why don't you want her to be changed?"

"She's talented and I enjoy watching her perform. If she's changed, they'll overlook the detail that she possessed those talents before, and her dancing career would be over."

"Maybe that's not important to her."

"It's not." His response was as balmy as his expression. "But it's important to me. As I said, I enjoy her work and find pride in knowing we are related."

"You're taking away that option from *her* for *your* enter-tainment."

"Yes."

"Well, I have to respect that you have no qualms about expressing your selfishness."

"I have no qualms about doing what is necessary to keep myself happy and entertained."

I scoffed.

That amused him. He closed the distance between us. "I

have no problem keeping myself entertained. Listen carefully. This is where our interests must align. I need to be happy. I desire a family, Erin. Make sure you are equally committed to making that happen. I fear that my patience with you will be challenged. I don't want your games and defiance. I require your compliance. Remember that."

Without another word he was gone back to his table. This was Landon unleashed? I didn't like this version of him at all.

Moments later my hands clenched. The Landon situation was no longer on the backburner; it had to be a priority as well. By the time I made it back to the car, I had wrangled my emotions under control. When Cory offered to walk with me to my apartment's door—an excuse to hear about the conversation between me and Landon—I gave him a sanitized version. It wasn't a burden I wanted to place on him, and I didn't want to give him a misguided reason to challenge Landon and his behavior.

Once I was in the apartment, I took out my phone and stared at the contact I had pulled up. Dr. Sumner. But he wasn't the person to call. My predicament with Landon was a result of saving his life, and I couldn't have him hold that guilt.

CHAPTER 24

Still wearing the dress from earlier, I left the overnight bag I planned to take to the Havenage in the car and slung another over my shoulder, filled with extra clothing to leave at Mephisto's.

He answered the door and tossed the overnight bag I handed him aside. After pulling me into a hug, he released me. His depthless eyes and stoic expression left nothing for me to read or gauge. Even his gait as he led me to the living room provided no feedback. Easy and measured, his fingers lightly clasping my hand. His hold tightened as we passed the damaged wall outside Benton's office. The door edges were splintered where the hinges had been torn off. The door rested at an awkward angle against the entrance, offering a partial view of the destroyed room.

As soon as we were in the living room, I let out a gasp of surprise when Mephisto pulled me onto his lap, positioning me until my legs were astride him.

"Tomorrow?" The first words spoken since greeting me at the door.

"Tomorrow," I repeated. His strong fingers kneaded the skin of my exposed thighs. He sighed against my lips before kissing me. Returning the kiss, I couldn't pull my thoughts from the state of Benton's office and wall despite his attempt to distract me. And I saw it for what it was—a distraction.

"How are things between you and Clayton?" I asked. A better question would be how were things between him and the others, but I presumed if he could resolve things with Clayton, it would pave the way to smoothing any animosity that Kai and Simeon harbored.

"We're fine," he answered, his tone cool and the timbre of his voice neutral.

"If I'm expected to share things with you, then it's only fair that you do the same," I pointed out.

Resting back, his hands clasped behind his head, the dim warm lights hit the features of his face, highlighting the sharp angles, creased brow, and downturn of his lips. I stroked my thumb lightly over his brow, smoothing out the unforgiving line.

"It is fine." He blew out a breath. "As fine as it can be right now and what I expect it to be, considering the circumstances."

He reached for the silver torus-shaped object sticking out from the side of the sofa cushion. "It's a Bailer," he offered in explanation as I studied the engravings on the object. "It works like a magical flare. A one-shot deal. My magic is stored in it. Not active magic. But when activated, it will weaken any ward or obfuscation spell enough for me to track its location."

"Your very own Bat signal."

"Except a Bat signal doesn't leave Batman compromised," supplied Benton in a tight voice of disapproval as he entered the room.

Straddling Mephisto with my dress hiked up, I was surely giving Bento a peek at my hind end. Mephisto's arms tightened around me when I attempted to move away, pulling me close, his touch possessive. Mephisto's eyes narrowed to slits in response to Benton's comment. A response that Benton dismissed.

"I did as you requested and found a way to find her if needed. It is not fair that you not inform her of what this help will cost. What it means to you and the others." Unlike with the Huntsmen, they weren't having a secret conversation but were expressing themselves with glares and sharp looks.

I scrutinized the object. It looked fragile. A quarter-size donut-shaped object with powerful abilities. "How does it work?" I asked. Benton moved toward us, showing the same lack of concern about my compromising position as Mephisto had.

"It's not as stable as I would like to have made it, but he wanted you to be able to use it with ease. Bound to him, his magic feeds it."

Responding to my confusion, Mephisto pulled back his sleeve to reveal branded skin with the same markings as on the Bailer.

With a delicate touch, I traced the painful-looking sigils. "Why hasn't it healed over?"

"It won't until the spell is invoked to sever my tie to it," Mephisto explained. When he gave me the words to do so, Benton's expression collapsed into a frown when sigils illuminated. "Then you need to smash it."

Benton studied me for a long moment, allowing his eyes to drift to Mephisto's arm, which had returned to his place around me. With notable effort, Benton held back whatever he wanted to say.

"Take care of it and I hope you won't need it. And its creation is a mere overreaction on Mephisto's part." There was a great deal of judgment and censure in his words that was directed at Mephisto. Once at the door, Benton started to say something else, but Mephisto quelled him with a sharp look. His mouth closed but he didn't leave.

"You put yourself at risk, because you think she'll be in peril." Benton shook his head. Taking several moments of quiet contemplation, he said, "I'm going to stay at the loft. I'll be back in a couple of days,"

I still hadn't established the hierarchy of the Huntsmen or even if there was one. It appeared that Benton, as their advisor, wasn't held to it.

"So," I began slowly, "things aren't really resolved."

"He'll be okay. He understands this had to be done in order for me to let you go."

Let me go? I reared back as far as his hold on me would allow. The countdown from ten did absolutely nothing to squelch my indignation. I blinked, thinking I'd misheard him. Even if I tried to reconcile my emotions and dismiss it as him misspeaking, his look of obstinance and cool self-assurance confirmed it was said the way it was meant.

"Do you want to change the phrasing?" I asked, choosing to handle things diplomatically. He'd made sacrifices and had caused discord between himself, the Huntsmen, and Benton. I wanted to navigate the situation carefully. It didn't need to become a fight, but I couldn't quiet that voice in me that needed autonomy, which he seemed to be taking from me. Recognizing my dilemma, he taunted me with a cocky smirk. The flagrant arrogance wasn't winning him any points, either.

"Which would you prefer, Erin, us to debate semantics to coddle your peculiar need to be an army of one, or for me to be truthful? If the Bailer wasn't an option, I'd be the person stopping you from going. I will not make any apologies for it." He kissed my hands. "You believe this is about control, but it isn't." He held the same look that Clayton had displayed in my barrier in a challenge when he advised me to never lock myself in a cage with a serpent without knowing whether it's a garden snake or a black mamba. The Huntsmen didn't fight for control because they never felt like it was out of their grasp.

"Erin, we all have our weaknesses. A person who believes they don't have any is a fool waiting for destruction. You truly believe that you've seen and can deal with the darkest the world has to offer. You've been exposed to a mere fraction of it. The worst of it hasn't been experienced by you or revealed to you. Therefore, you cannot be prepared for the many forms of betrayal that exist. I want you to find comfort in trusting Nolan and the elves, but it needs to be done safely. These objectives must be mutually inclusive."

"This situation is similar to what's happening between you and Clayton."

He gave me a weak smile. "Similar. They don't think I see their argument, but I do. But I also see the potential of this arrangement. You learning about your elven magic and meeting more elves can help us as well. Elizabeth has the Laes. Hopefully you will be equipped with the tools to find her. To learn the secrets behind magic that keep the elves hidden. They aren't wrong, you are a weakness for me. A weakness that I don't mind." He pulled me to him, kissing me long and hard, his tongue caressing mine.

"We don't have to destroy a room to make nice."

"Not at all. We have other ways," he said, sliding the strings of my dress off my shoulders and running his thumbs over the hardened nipples of my exposed breasts before taking them into his mouth, laving over them as I arched into him. His fingers pressing, caressing my back.

I pulled away enough to remove my dress, leaving me in my panties. Removing his shirt, I pressed ravenous kisses to his warm skin, tasting him as my fingers trailed over him to unfasten his belt and caress his hardness. His hands twined in my hair, pulling my head up, my lips back to him, devouring me in a heated kiss. Stroking and caressing, the heat and need making any distance seem too far.

Slithering down his body, I brought his pants with me, settling between his legs. I took him, tasting him. His deep, throaty growl reverberated in the room, wanton lust filling his steely eyes as they held mine. Panting, his fingers sliding through my hair, he pulled me to him. Kissing me, insatiable hunger in the intensity of it.

He rotated our bodies until I was lying against the sofa, his muscular arm caging me as we continued to kiss. One tug and he ripped my panties off. Settling his broad hips between my legs, deft fingers teased me with their persistent erotic touch. My body pulsed with need, my nipples taut with desire, hungry to feel him, all of him. Lust-hooded eyes trailed over my body before he captured my breast in his mouth. Languid and slow circles coaxed a moan from me.

Entering me with a powerful thrust, his deep kisses swallowed my moan. My hips writhed and rocked under him, meeting his demanding, dominating movements. Desperately, my fingers curled into the grooves of muscles in his back that contracted and relaxed with the sole purpose of delivering pleasure. His breath hot against my ear, whispering my name in reverence. Desire heightened, I craved for a release. With each indomitable stroke, I felt him bringing me closer to it. I shattered into the pleasure, melting into the sofa as Mephisto shuddered over me. He kissed me before resting his face against mine.

"I think we handle quarrels better," he whispered.

"Me too. But I wouldn't consider that a fight. Just a misunderstanding."

He made a deep, throaty grumble. "We're good at misunderstandings."

CHAPTER 25

olan sat in the car with an amused smile while I said my goodbyes. Mephisto was determined to see me off despite me waking up with him that morning. He departed, giving me a quick kiss and hug before driving away. The simple display still drew Nolan's attention.

Madison and Cory made it weird. They were going for gold. It wasn't just the multiple hugs. They took it up to an embarrassing level, Madison handing me a bag of Jelly Belly, then waving in the middle of the parking lot like parents sending their only child off to camp and ending it with their questions. "Did I have enough clothing?" Had they heard of a washing machine? "Make sure you have an emergency bag with food and water in it." I always had an emergency bag. "Take notes." No, I'm just going to stare at them googly-eyed.

The amusement remained on Nolan's face as I managed to untangle from them and get to the driver's seat. The drive itself was somber. I had so many questions, which Nolan answered in an unusually terse manner as he directed me.

"You and Mephisto," he started slowly, keeping a careful eye on the passing scenic view. "It would be best if that's not something you share at the Havenage."

"Why should I keep my relationship with Mephisto a secret?"

"Not a secret. I believe they are aware of it. But it will be best if they aren't reminded of your relationship with the very beings that killed a significant number of our ancestors." He turned to me, a sullen entreaty for understanding.

"You like staying at the Havenage, don't you?"

He nodded, an apparent appreciation for the place alight on his face along with hints of desperation that it could be fleeting. My presence could derail it all.

I nodded, my hand finding his and giving it a squeeze. "Thank you for making this happen."

He returned the squeeze and continued scrutinizing the area. After twenty minutes, he told me to turn into a heavily wooded area that had no appearance of a road and the potential of car damage from the guard rail.

Apprehensive, I turned, driving through the exceptional ward onto a single car dirt road flanked by expansive trees so deeply and verdantly green, they looked photoshopped. The earthy aroma accompanied by an evergreen redolence that denotated Nolan's presence intensified in the car.

"Park here," Nolan instructed. He hopped out of the car, grabbed my bag, and walked closer to the pathway. If I hadn't been looking intently at it, I would have missed the glint of light that periodically pulsed from it. A magical barrier.

An alluring scent of evergreen and meadow rode the air, yet I had no desire to move any closer. The mere thought caused my body to seize in disgust. I wanted to leave. Each step increased the nausea and sharp pangs that shot through me. A portentous feeling increased in me.

My fist balled, trying to ward off the sudden onslaught of unbearable fear, unsettling queasiness, and lightheadedness. I shuffled back and away from the barrier, feeling that if I didn't, everything I'd eaten in the past week would be violently expelled from my body. Nolan placed a comforting hand on my back.

"I'm here," Nolan whispered to the air. Silver fluttered before me, a light shimmer of light flashed, the barrier dropped, and the feeling of repulsion disappeared to reveal a suburban subdivision. Tall mature poplars skirted the vast area. Carefully manicured lawns surrounded modest homes. Vibrant flowers filled the gardens.

We were met by six people. The two people to the side had a small boy, four or five years of age, with them. Bright eyed and lashes so long they brushed his skin when he blinked. His dark, low-shorn hair made his pointed ears more noticeable. He approached me slowly under the scrutiny of everyone's gaze. It didn't make me feel unwelcome but as if my presence was contingent. I had no idea on what.

The boy lifted his hand in a small wave, which I returned a little more enthusiastically. It didn't melt the cold, tension-laden air around me. I knelt down once he was closer.

"I'm Erin."

His attention remained fixed on my ears.

"Pasha," he said absently. He'd leaned in and I knew he was waiting for permission. "May I?" I asked, pointing at his ear. He nodded, and me tracing his ears encouraged him to do the same. Unimpressed, he wrinkled his nose and gave them another cursory feel. His eyes darted to Nolan, who I suspected had been treated to the same. Apparently our curved ears were disappointing.

My interaction with Pasha was a small distraction from the tall, lean man inching closer to me. His hair, terra cotta leaning more toward brown, was styled into loose flat braids. Some curls had escaped. He appraised me with wary acuity. His strident angled features and high hollow cheeks made his appraisal feel severe.

The stranger's vulpine grace made me cautiously watchful as he made a slow, easy glide toward me. Wizened hazel eyes held something behind them and made him seem as if he possessed knowledge beyond the mid-thirty years he presented. The sleeves of his copper-colored tunic shirt were rolled partway, revealing toned arms that I assumed were earned by predominately outdoor physical activity, despite his pale driftwood color. He definitely ran.

"I'd like to speak with you," he said, authority in his breeziness. He walked away from the group with the blatant expectation that I would follow. Rushing to make up the distance between me and the stranger, Nolan kept pace with me. Without looking back, the authoritative elf said, "Just your daughter, Nolan."

I'd dealt with Elizabeth's disgust so much, it felt odd having the stranger call me Nolan's daughter without the twinge of antipathy. Even my mother said it with undertones of condemnation.

"Your daughter will be safe with Fabian. Let's have a cup of tea." The woman who spoke had a flair for dress that reminded me of Elizabeth's. A high-collared white shirt covered her neck with pearl buttons and lace at the sleeves. Instead of a billowy skirt, hers was a pleated circular style, a modern contrast to the shirt. Despite her clothing, she had an understated beauty. Bright, calm, cinder-colored eyes, lightly bowed lips, and short curls of cappuccino brown brushed the top of her pale, wintry ears. She started for one of the homes and the couple with Pasha took one of his hands and trailed behind her.

Nolan hesitated. It didn't register as fear. A protective urge. The complex threads of our relationship seemed to be unraveling and realigning constantly, obscuring our history and making what we had so much more.

"Sanaa is waiting," Fabian urged, his back remaining to Nolan.

Giving Nolan a small smile, I nodded toward the woman waiting for him at the entrance of the house. After several more moments of hesitation, he hiked my bag farther up his shoulder and headed toward the house.

I was unable to make up the distance Fabian had placed between us. He stopped. Turning to face me, he took a bite from an apple he didn't have before, or at least one I hadn't noticed. The fit of his clothing wouldn't have hidden it. I fixated on that as a way to ignore his appraisal as he slowly chewed. His discerning gaze trailed over the length of my body.

"What brings Malific's daughter here?" Despite the implication in his question, there didn't seem to be any judgment.

"I need to understand and improve my elven magic."

He took a smaller bite of the magically materialized apple while subjecting me to more careful appraisal and chewing. "It is my understanding that you are proficient. What more do you want?"

"I need more than that level of proficiency," I admitted. "I need to be more skilled with the use of it and have a better understanding of its abilities and limitations. In the past, I've been lucky by just winging it, which may have given the illusion of proficiency. Coasting on my limited knowledge and skills is no longer enough."

A small smile curled his lips. "Not enough for what?"

"I'm sure you know a great deal about me. I'm sure the reason behind my birth isn't a secret to you. I existed for one reason. Because of a chain of terrible events, I'm alive when I shouldn't be, and Malific has been released. You know of her thirst for power and what she's willing to do to obtain it. I'm the only thing standing between her and unchecked power. She wants to make sure it doesn't stay that way. She wants her army, and I'm the reason she doesn't have one."

"Yes, and you've *befriended* the Huntsmen." He might have kept judgment out of his voice before, but his words were drenched in it now. He chomped on a peach, ignoring the juices running down his hand.

Where the hell is he getting all this fruit? And why wasn't he sharing? Was there some type of enchanted fruit stand somewhere? Briefly, I was distracted by the possibility of hailing fruit.

"If we are able to help you, what are your plans for your magic? What will we be responsible for creating?"

"I don't want to die."

His brows drew together, and he lowered himself to the ground. Sitting cross legged, he looked at a space in front of him. An invitation to sit.

"Go on," he urged once I was seated.

"I don't want to die. The existing situation is something I need to put right, I feel an obligation to do so. Nothing is going to be just until Malific is stopped."

He got the unabridged version. It wasn't done just to purge it from my system, but because I suspected that me being able to stay was dependent on my honesty. I told him about the Huntsmen destroying the remainder of Malific's army, the oath Malific made that prevented her from hurting the elves as a trade for me to be captured and brought to her so she could kill me, and Elizabeth cleverly binding us to prevent it and thereby uphold her promise to Nolan. It was difficult to relate it all since I was doing it while trying to not be distracted by Fabian pulling fruit out of thin air.

He remained impassive throughout my debriefing about Elizabeth allying with a demon to trap me in the demon realm. Not even a flinch or a flicker of disgust showed as I recounted the events and the deal I had to make with the demon in order to escape. His face remained devoid of all readable emotions.

"Ultimately you want the magical tools to stop Malific?"

I nodded. There was no need to be coy or disguise my intentions. Our interests were aligned. He nodded his head slowly, taking in my words without comment. Dark intrigue lay heavily in the pools of his eyes. "Would you be able to do it?" he inquired.

"Do what?"

"Whatever you need to stop Malific, even if it means killing her." He leaned in closer, studying me. I was still consumed by anger and the thirst for revenge. But his question had merit. Malific didn't possess a primitive maternal instinct toward me. She was prepared to commit infanticide, and filicide was definitely in her agenda. Did I have it in me? Could I kill my mother in cold blood if given the opportunity?

"Yes, and Elizabeth, too. I want to stop both of them, by any means." That admission caused a pang in my chest. The knowledge that despite Nolan's anger, frustration, and probably abhorrence, at times, Elizabeth was his sister. My aunt. He loved her and I was willing to take her from him. It needed to be done. I was deserving of revenge against her. Elizabeth's malice was calculated to cause maximum humiliation and trauma. Directing the hate she harbored for Malific to me. Misguided and cruel.

He blinked once before his lips set into a taut line. My intentions needed to be known. I didn't want them to feel betrayed by any omission or dishonesty on my part. They knew what Elizabeth was, her actions, and that she couldn't go unpunished.

It was a gamble and a bold move, but if they had kept her out of the Havenage, part of me suspected that they knew Elizabeth needed to be handled.

He effortlessly came to his feet with a spark of liveliness he didn't appear to have before. Probably hopped up on fructose. I hauled myself up and rushed to his side, staying in step with him.

"You would like to use elven magic to make a demon corporeal," he clarified.

"I'd rather not," I admitted.

"Your plan is to break the oath you made with the demon?" I really wished he'd allow some inflection in his voice, give me an expression, something to work with.

My hand wiped over my face. "My goal is *not* to leave the world worse off by my decisions and actions. I just want to fix the things I can. Demons should not exist in this world."

"On this side of the Veil, shifters shouldn't be immune to magic, but because of you they are. Do you practice that which you extol or just when it comes to demons?"

"I don't know," I admitted with a weary huff of breath. "But I'm trying. The shifters haven't abused their new gifts. I feel confident that they won't."

He nodded slowly. *Good fates, where did the banana come from?*

"You believe the demons will?" He took a large bite from the banana and waited patiently for an answer that didn't come easily.

"I don't know," I admitted.

"You will need to master your elven magic in..." He waited on a timeframe.

"Five days."

His eyes widened with his smirk. "Ah, hubris."

"No, desperation. Malific doesn't have patience and I have less than a month to fulfill my oath with Asial."

"What spells do you know?"

Proud of how efficient I had become at it, I showed him the cloaking spell first. Cloaked, I moved from my original position and watched as he leisurely strolled around the area. His hand clawed at the air, and a strong evergreen scent poured into the surroundings. Fabian turned, moved to within inches of where I stood, and locked eyes with me. "Hello, Erin."

"No one has ever discovered me," I said. Asher had, but it had been by smell.

"I can."

So, want a cookie or an apple?

"Show me more?" Fabian requested.

Losing my previous enthusiasm and confidence, I erected the protective field. He shattered it with the same ease Elizabeth had. Depthless hazel eyes locked with mine and fingers barely brushed the diaphanous wall before it fell away.

"What else do you have?" His lassitude was apparent.

It was ridiculous, but I wanted to impress him, or at least light some spark of interest.

While he's waiting on me to perform another spell, I could sucker punch him. That'll perk him up. Oh, are you waiting for a lame spell? Bam, left hook.

Instead of resorting to puerile violence, I performed a Mirra. The wall of flames divided us. The heat wafted from it, warming my skin. The warmth of the fire wall didn't appear to have any great effect on him. Inching so close to it that the flames licked at his skin, his response didn't betray whether it bothered him or not. Keeping a careful eye on me, he reached his hand toward it but didn't touch the flames. He nodded once.

"Meet me out here tomorrow at eight in the morning," he instructed before turning and starting for the houses.

I could stay.

CHAPTER 26

*A*fter Fabian's departure, I returned to the house where Nolan was having tea with Sanaa. He escorted me to the small house near the back of the property reserved for guests. The quaint rooms were designed with simple comfort in mind. The bedrooms had serene, light-blue walls and small windows that gave a pleasant view of the woods, and hints of lavender from the candle on the dresser scented the room. The waterfall shower in the small bathroom was an unexpected luxury that I planned to take advantage of later.

Covering the twin bed was a fluffy white duvet. A writing table was flanked by narrow bookcases on both sides. Placed on the single nightstand was a lamp and a beginner's magic book. Flipping through the book, I discovered spells that I already knew. Toward the back of the book were more spells written in a different language—Elven, I suspected.

"What do you think of Fabian?" Nolan asked from his seat at the desk after I had finished taking inventory of the room and perusing the books.

"He seems nice." It wasn't the right word. He seemed intense, capable, and peculiar, the arbiter of the Havenage.

Descriptions far more apropos than nice. But it was innocuous enough.

"You made an impression on him," he acknowledged, a smile on his face.

"Really, I wouldn't have guessed. He didn't give me that impression at all."

"Immediately after meeting with you, he told Sanaa that he'd be working with you. Even she was shocked. Usually she's the one who trains elves who are lacking in their skills." A paternal pride flitted over his face. Preening, he could barely get through telling me about the ways of the Havenage without reiterating that Fabian would be teaching me.

Meals were communal, customary but not required. But he urged me to adhere to their customs. There were twelve families who lived in the Havenage. Three part-caste—the preferred name for those who weren't pure elves—were allowed entry to the Havenage but were not residents. Nolan was considered a transient, someone who currently lived in the Havenage but wasn't extended a permanent residence or allowed unlimited entry.

"The three part-caste, why don't they live here?" I asked.

"I don't know. From what I gathered, they are being watched but haven't proven to merit an invitation to live."

"Maybe they were invited and declined," I countered.

Nolan's expression indicated he clearly didn't believe that and was under the assumption that everyone coveted a place among the pure elves. If an invitation to live in the Havenage was what he wanted, I desperately wanted it for him.

"What do they do for money?"

"They have jobs outside the Havenage. Usually where they can telecommute." His voice dropped. "I suspect a great deal of their income comes from using their magic."

Using magic to manipulate stocks, insider trading, or manipulation for sales of property was prohibited and difficult to prove. I suspected humans believed there was some violation of these rules because there weren't many poor or low-income supernaturals, in comparison to humans. But it was done in such moderation that it was overlooked.

"If they work and interact with others, why do people believe elves are extinct?" I touched my ears, the notable distinction between them and us.

"Glamour. We can see it because we have elven blood, but no one else can. The glamour even works on shifters."

It worked on shifters, too. Excitement flared at the prospect of the treasure trove of magic that would soon be revealed to me.

My enthusiasm only heightened during dinner at the ranch home at the center of the property that had been converted to a large cafeteria. An open floor plan with walls that separated the kitchen for the dining areas. The room had long tables for family dining, and smaller ones for more intimate gatherings. Stone fireplaces on each end of the room gave off enough warmth to make the room cozy. Oversized, comfortable-looking chairs were placed near them. A warm beverage station stood just a few feet from the fireplaces. Sandstone walls, burnished orange accents, and landscape art made the space feel welcoming.

The sole purpose of the home was to dine and get to know the people you shared a meal with. Nolan was clearly captivated by it, lapping up every moment, his face the brightest I'd ever seen it. His response to it had me wondering how much isolation he had been subjected to. Or was there an innate need to be with other elves? If his only interaction was with Elizabeth, I could imagine it left a longing for something else. Something different.

The conversation was kept light, but they made an effort to include Nolan and me. Through the chatter I didn't miss the fact that every time I looked in Fabian's direction, I found myself under the scope of his attention. Each time, his response was to raise his glass and give a muted smile.

The more I interacted with the elves, the better my understanding became of why Nolan was so keen on losing the transient label. The familial welcome only heightened when Pascha left his mother's side to sit in my lap. It wasn't until he suggested we share my mango pie that I realized his intent was just a sly pilfering. He then proceeded to eat the lion's share of the dessert and slipped down from my lap as soon as it was gone. When the host noticed the con, he gave me another serving, assuring me that everyone was treated to the same dessert theft. The doe-faced pie thief returned for his share.

CHAPTER 27

$\mathcal{F}$abian wasn't at breakfast. I arrived at the spot where he'd left me the day before with meet time instructions. Fifteen minutes early, I was surprised to find him stretched out on the ground, hands clasped behind his head, the morning sun placing a light glow over his face.

"Erin," he greeted, sitting up and inviting me to sit next to him. He handed me a book. "You read this on your time. Learning Elven will strengthen your magic. Performing our magic in English and Latin works, but for better control and to elevate the results, it needs to be done in our language. Some things are lost in translation."

"Will my protective field, Mirra, and cloaking spells be better if said in Elven?" I thought back to the spell to retrieve my oath with Asial and the one Elizabeth had tricked me into performing to bind me to Malific.

He nodded. "Since that's your foundation, let's start with those." Grabbing the pad next to him, he wrote them down. It took nearly an hour, but I learned the protective spell in Elven. A language far more efficient than English and Latin, there were fewer words to learn. I just had to remember them. Within two hours, Fabian had to put more effort into shattering my protective field. A disappointed frown down-turned his lips at its destruction.

He returned to his position, lying back, propped on his elbows, deep in thought as he nibbled on a pear. No matter how hard I tried to focus, I got sidetracked by the magically appearing fruit.

"Can you Wynd?" he asked. "It's a shared magic from both your abilities."

I shook my head. "I turn into a cat whenever I attempt to Wynd."

"A cat!" he shrieked, laughing as he sat up. His head canted as his eyes brightened. "As in feline?"

I nodded a confirmation. His amusement danced on the edge of mockery, and with effort I pushed down the desire to give him a kitty cat claw hug.

"May I see?"

Agreeing, I stood up. "I need to undress."

"Okay." When he made no effort to move or turn around, I realized he'd taken it as a warning before exposing my lady bits.

After me making no effort to undress, he said, "Oh, of course. Privacy. You'd like some." He turned around. I quickly undressed, attempted to Wynd, which shifted me to a cat, and trotted to him.

He lowered himself down until he was eye level with me. "A domestic cat."

Yeah, a cat. What did he think was going to happen? I tell him I'm a cat and change into a leopard? All amusement drained from his face, replaced with immense curiosity. Returning to my clothes, I changed again, and dressed.

"Thank you for sharing this with me." His statement hinted at an intimacy between us that I was unaware existed. Was turning into a cat when I attempted to Wynd something I should keep hidden?

He invited me to sit with him again.

"I need you to tap into your elven magic. It needs to be the source of your magic. Think of it as the difference between using your diaphragm to breathe and your inter-costal muscles for shallow breathing. You're a quarter elf, so elven magic is the smaller source of magic of the two you possess. Not weak by any means. Just needs to be executed differently. It won't be easy, Erin, and you will require focus."

I closed my eyes and used all the meditation techniques I'd acquired over the years. I tapped into mindfulness strate-gies I hadn't used as frequently since my magic restrictions were lifted.

"Put up your protective field."

Keeping my eyes closed, I erected it. Based on his disap-pointed sigh, it came down with the same level of effort it took yesterday.

"Just keep concentrating. Slow easy breaths," he directed.

The breaths came slower, the control stronger, and I was ensorcelled by the dueling magics. Magic that I had accepted would be frenetic, forever warring inside me, seemingly in a perpetual competition for dominance, didn't feel entwined any longer. Two parallel lines of magic: elven and god.

"Erin, open your eyes."

I did as instructed and found that I was enclosed in a double circle with sigils written between the two enclosures.

"It's like training wheels. Now do your protective field."

It came up with the ease of breathing, magic suffusing through me along with a confidence of being behind an unbreakable barrier.

He pressed his hand against it. The field wavered but never failed. Four more attempts and nothing came of it. My magic held. The same happened with the Mirra; instead of easing toward it as if it was inconsequential, he kept his distance. When he could not detect my cloak, he determined it was time to remove the training wheels.

"You don't need to have the enclosure physically, just evoke them in your mind."

I studied the sigils, committing them to memory as he chomped on a peach.

Come on, Erin, don't focus on the magical fruit stand somewhere in the vicinity and the fact he's not sharing. Concentrate.

"Do you meditate?" he asked.

"That's what I was doing when you asked me before placing the training wheels on."

"Caeni." He provided the name of the double circle. "Try again." He'd inched closer, eliminating the smidgen of space that was between us.

How was I supposed to meditate with him breathing his peach breath in my face?

"You're distracting me," I admitted.

Taking my admission as a compliment on the effect he had on me, he gave me a sly, vulpine smile. I let it go instead of pointing out that it was his creepy invasion of space that was distracting, not him.

It took nearly four hours, but I managed to perform all three spells without the Caeni.

By the end of the first lesson, I had mastered taking down his protective field.

"You are a quick study," he said, ending the lesson abruptly.

"I think it's the teacher."

The attempt at flattery didn't thaw the iciness of his appraisal. It was the first time since I'd met him that it felt like the lens through which he saw me had changed.

Not Nolan's daughter, but Malific's. With a hasty instruction of the time we'd meet the next day, he left.

CHAPTER 28

I'd stretched out on the ground in the same spot. Fifteen minutes past eight and I accepted that Fabian wasn't coming. He hadn't been at dinner the day before or breakfast this morning. Considering the way he looked at me after my last lesson, I didn't consider that a good sign. My curiosity morphed into speculation. Would I be asked to leave the Havenage or my instruction given over to Sanaa?

My apprehension melted when I saw him walking toward me carrying three potted plants.

"My apologies for my tardiness." His brows inched together. "You thought I wasn't going to show," he surmised.

Fabian was perceptive. Afraid that he'd read the truth behind anything I offered, I simply nodded.

He gave me a long considering look before offering a carefully restrained smile. "You're a quick study. That isn't something to fear but to celebrate." Setting the plants down, he moved toward me. Standing so close to me, he didn't have to reach too far to brush away the errant strands of hair from my face. "You have a limited time here, so it is important that we test the extent of your magic and sharpen your skills."

Personal space seemed foreign to him, so I put some between us. Then I scraped away my hair stragglers. Whether intentional or not, there was an intimacy in his touch, a comfort in our closeness, that he claimed whenever he was near.

With a humble smile, he backed away. "Sorry." Fabian clasped his fingers in front of him. Several beats of silence passed.

"Follow me," he requested, breaking the strained silence. I couldn't determine if he felt rejected or embarrassed by my interpretation of his actions. Fabian was an enigma.

"These plants are all Sansevieria, snake plants, but different species. I want you to break a leaf from them all, but only use this plant to do it." He pointed to the plant closest to him, where a spell book was placed. It was in Elven, but a paper was enclosed with the translation. It was a short spell for the magnitude of what it could do. Six words that could do so much. Taking out a small knife, he pricked his finger and then tore at a piece of the plant near the root. Invoking a spell, he pressed his finger to the plant. Magic thickened in the air, and the plant illuminated a bright neon green before fading and the tear weaving together. Focused on the plant, Fabian's breathing increased from the effort of the spell. With a twist of his hand, the stem tore from the root, which forced the others to do the same.

He exhaled a deep breath. "This is the spell Elizabeth performed to give the shifters magical immunity. It's not something many of us have the ability to do. An ability not ever seen in part-caste, but you have proven to be quite exceptional. I would like to see to what extent."

It wasn't to the extent he thought, and we were both equally disappointed that after three hours of practice, I hadn't mastered it. Mastering gave the impression I'd performed it on a rudimentary level. I couldn't even produce a flicker of movement from the other plants. Exhausted, I plopped down on the ground, knees pulled up so I could rest my chin on them. Fabian handed me a pear from the three he had with him.

"Where are you stealing this fruit from? Are you robbing a produce stand or something?"

His laughter was contagious. He shook his head and reached out, his hand disappearing into a prism of color, and when he pulled it out, he had a bunch of grapes. "It's a passageway to my kitchen. They are difficult to create. This one took me seven years to perfect." His shrugged, averting his eyes from mine, a blush of color brushing along the bridge of his nose to his pronounced cheeks. He was embarrassed that he worked on a spell for seven years and that the spell was to get fruit.

I beamed. "If I could, I would, too. But it wouldn't be for fruit," I admitted, taking a bite from the pear.

"Then what?"

Tequila and donuts. When I answered him, I left out the tequila. "Walking down the street or driving in my car, and bam, I get a hankering for a donut, slip my hand in the magical vault, pull out a Krispy Kreme."

"It only works here, and there's a distance restriction as well." He offered me the grapes, and I gratefully took them. The spell had made me hungrier than I expected and I had already devoured the pear.

"Is the reason we're able to make demons corporeal because of a shared link?" I asked.

"No, there's no link between us and the demons. It's just within our magical abilities to do so. I wish they didn't know about it."

Something about his contemplative expression led me to believe he wished little was known of elves. Period. There was power in anonymity and underestimation.

After taking a lunch break, we returned to my lessons,

where he showed me how to break a weak barrier and perform minor elemental spells.

"Erin."

I turned to an apple soaring in my direction aimed at my chest.

"What the fu—"

He wanted me to erect a small shield in front of me to protect me from being pelted by the fruit. And demonstrate enough control of wind to keep the apple airborne.

Amusement skated across his face as he read my intention before I executed it. Instead of blocking the apple, I sent it flying back at him. He plucked it out of the air and took a bite from it.

The lessons continued as he challenged my magic, isolating it and my ability to perform it quickly and with precision. The levity of his mood increased the more we practiced. It was a noticeable shift in his interaction with me. It wasn't until it was gone that I could see the contrast between the aridity and muted intensity that accompanied his teachings yesterday and how it was now.

Feeling emboldened by the change, I excused myself to my bedroom and returned with the pictures of Elizabeth's spell. Fabian studied it with interest. "I have no idea what this is," he admitted. Determination took over his mood as he ended our lessons. I didn't expect to see him at dinner; it was apparent this was where he'd be for probably the remainder of the day.

"Erin," he called after me.

When I turned in response, he flicked his eye to me then promptly returned to studying the papers. "Do you feel comfortable enough to leave the Bailer in the room tomorrow?"

My sharp intake of breath made him look at me. His tone was level without a hint of ire or furor, but the storminess in his eyes was an apt reminder of how powerful he was. They all were. In the strained silence, I searched for an acceptable explanation but came up short.

"Gods are not known for their honor and good deeds. It is admirable that they have extended such to you. It is an impressive feat to receive such attention and protection from them. See you tomorrow."

He'd perfected the skill of the amiable response. It contained a dark hollowness from his effort to hide his true feelings about the Huntsmen. I tried to determine if it was from knowledge of their prior deeds or contempt for Malific, directed at them.

I hesitated, feeling like an explanation was needed.

"Enjoy the rest of your day, Erin."

Message received. I headed for the house.

CHAPTER 29

The next day, I sat in the empty cafeteria where I'd been sent for the break Fabian strongly suggested I take. Fatigue was starting to show in the execution of my magic. Sanaa gave me a small gentle smile before sliding into the chair across from me. She flipped open the large weathered book she was carrying and took a sip from her teacup. My peppermint tea received a nod of approval. I would have preferred coffee, but they didn't have any. This was a tea community for sure.

After nearly a half an hour of companionable silence, she finally said, "You are Nolan."

In the three days I'd been around the elves, I'd noticed that, although welcoming, they were economical with their words. No chatter just to fill the silence. Sanaa was a miser with hers, often not fully voicing her thoughts. And the sotto voce of her voice made me hang on to her every word.

It was a tactic often used by people to make you focus on them to keep from missing anything. A power move. But it didn't seem like a ploy. Her understated features fit the calmness she exuded. Although her eclectic Victorian-style attire was similar to Elizabeth, there wasn't anything similar about them otherwise.

I'm Nolan. From her expression there was great meaning to what she said, but I wasn't sure what. Did she mean I looked like him? Not likely; Malific's features were very distinct in my appearance. Was I blinded by revenge and misdirected? They never voiced it, but at times I could sense it.

"Will you elaborate?" I finally asked, to prevent any assumptions.

She inhaled a deep breath as if readying herself for a feat of labor. "His intentions are good, but I don't think he ever had the savagery and ferocity needed to battle with the likes of Malific."

"She's weakened, and that's because of him. A powerful blow that he landed," I defended. "Although not savage or ferocious, he won that battle."

She nodded once. "I can agree with that. However, Elizabeth yielded better results. The oath she bound Malific to will save our lives."

"She sacrificed me to do so. Nolan wouldn't have done that. It is because of him that I'm no longer bound to Malific. Which was Elizabeth's doing. Malific agreed to the oath because she wanted to kill me."

"That is my understanding. Her binding you to Malific protected you. Your pain became her pain."

"If we were dealing with a normal person, it would have been admirable. But pain doesn't deter Malific. She's a connoisseur of it. If the final result is her having more power, she would walk over broken glass and thank you for the privilege. So, no, Elizabeth didn't do it to protect me. She is fully aware of Malific's inclinations."

Sanaa's lips pursed into a moue. She nodded before taking a long drink from her cup. "It was an unfortunate but necessary sequence of events to get the end results. Like I said, dealing with Malific requires a certain set of traits that many don't possess. Where should your umbrage lie? With Elizabeth or with the woman who was so cruel and hateful, she made us abandon our ways and forced us to become the type of people who can contend with her cruelty?"

After taking another sip, she cupped her hand around the cup, seeking its warmth. "Dealing with Malific...any of the gods, inures a person. Kindness is a weakness that will be exploited. Pacifism makes you a target." Placing the cup on the table, she examined her hands. A finger lingered over the remainder of the tea, creating small circular movements. The tea sloshed around as a waterspout formed over it. Her face screwed in concentration, then she released a slow breath. The columnar vortex disappeared and the tea settled. Lifting her eyes to meet mine, I didn't see malicious intent or hubris as she demonstrated her magic. Just grim frustration and sadness.

"Erin, I must agree with your assessment. Nolan won that battle, but I believe you could win this war for him. How befitting would it be for his daughter to deal the final blow, the final nail in Malific's coffin?" Her expression burned with information she wanted to share.

"How would I do that?"

"I guess our discussion about this was in vain? Were we engaging in it just to sharpen your skills in debate?" Fabian asked from the entrance to the cafeteria, his voice laden with carefully restrained anger.

"Not at all. Just because I don't agree with you doesn't mean I didn't take it into consideration. Fabian, I am right about this. Nolan's actions were misguided, and though some good came from it, Malific is free because of it. He didn't save us. He postponed the inevitable. And you know I'm right, Fabian."

Fabian relaxed into his nod, but I didn't get the impression he was in full agreement with whatever they were discussing. But it wasn't acquiescence. It was reluctant acceptance.

"Erin, will you join me?"

I gathered my things and followed him out.

"Tell her. Let her make the final decision," Sanaa urged as we exited.

Fabian and I walked in silence, he pulling grapes from the bunch in his hand and popping them in his mouth, contemplative throughout the entire process. It wasn't until they were gone that he spoke.

"Nolan's actions weren't as misguided as the others believe. He isn't given enough credit for how much his actions have benefited us. And that's unfortunate. The oath that protects us from Malific could not have been invoked if Malific hadn't been in her weakened state. I believe she only agreed to it because she thought the oath wouldn't take or that she could break it."

"You're underestimating what she's willing to sacrifice to have her full power," I replied. "Letting you all live in exchange for being able to make an army would be worth the sacrifice to her. To return to the way she was."

"Perhaps. Erin, Malific is dangerous to us—to you." He stopped walking. "But you are aware of that, aren't you?"

I'd taken it as a rhetorical question until the space between us closed, and his gentle expressive eyes searched for an answer.

"Yes."

"Were you being hyperbolic when you said you wanted her dead?"

I thought about her threats to my family, her disdain and death lust whenever she laid eyes on me. "No, not at all. Malific has practiced restraint with me because she still needs me. She is blindly driven by her thirst for revenge against Dareus and Elizabeth. If that thirst is sated, or she loses interest, her focus will return to me. She'll kill me and anyone who gets in the way."

I gave him a weak smile. "We fought once and she hesitated. For a naive moment, I thought something maternal had kicked in. That maybe she experienced an existential moment where she realized that her despotic drive was foolish and toxic. But then she betrayed me and was ready to have me killed. I won't survive her. Whether she does it or she recruits someone else to do it, she won't let me live as long as I'm the reason for her weakness."

He regarded me with a pensive frown. "How far are you willing to go to stop her?"

"As far as I need to," I admitted. "But I don't know where to begin."

"What Sanaa was trying to urge you to, in her misguided way, is Blose Chasm. It's like the Veil." He considered his words. "Not quite like the Veil. It's more like a magical purgatory. I can show you how to open it."

"So, the inhabitants are dead?"

"No, just magicless. If you can get Malific to enter with you, she'll be without magic. *But,* so will you."

"Okay?" This sounded too easy; there had to be more. I waited.

He sighed. "There's a cost to enter," he said. "Magic. When you leave, your magic won't be the same. You'll be weaker—I have no idea to what extent. If you decide this is an option, I want you to do so with your eyes wide open and fully informed. It has only been done once, with an elf who allowed their magic to corrupt them. You may lose all your magic. As long as Malific's in the Chasm, magic is the debt paid for her occupancy. Once she's dead, your magic will return."

"Would I go back to the way I was, craving magic, pulling it from others?"

"No. Before, your magic was restricted. If you do this, it will be sacrificed." Moving closer, his fingers outlined the curve of my ear. Based on his look of satisfaction, it was something he'd wanted to do for some time.

"I'll do it," I blurted.

He blinked once, then shook his head. "Sanaa and the others discussed this at length, and I believe it is the best option. I wanted to wait to present this to you, but Sanaa has removed that choice. I want you to think about this, Erin. Give it a day or two."

"I don't need a day. Not even ten more minutes."

He nodded, making an attempt at a sympathetic smile but quickly giving it up. Since he seemed to be content with us violating even the most lenient rules of social distance, and because his gaze had dropped to my lips too many times to go unnoticed, I stepped back.

"I've lived without magic and fought without magic. Malific hasn't. When it's taken away from her, I don't think she'll be able to adapt."

"Once you enter the Chasm, you'll be magicless as well," he reminded me. "You'll have to rely on me to open it. Do you trust me to do that?"

"You haven't given me a reason not to."

A slow smile eased over his lips. "I'm glad Nolan brought you to us." His eyes illuminated with fascination that never dropped from mine. "Erin, I will show you this, but I have one request of you." His hand slid through his hair, getting tangled in the braid. "There are so few of us, Erin. Elizabeth is powerful and quite skilled. We will feel her loss."

"Are you bargaining for her safety?"

He took several moments of thoughtful silence before moistening his lips to speak. "Not just her safety, but any retaliation. A truce. You have every right to want revenge.

But you are one of us, in a manner my elven sister." Unless it was my imagination, nothing he exhibited moments ago was remotely sibling-like. Not the way he touched my ear nor the way he'd looked at my lips.

"I'm negotiating the maintenance of a weakened bloodline. She is strong, not just in elven magic but also in wisdom. Erin, my help must come with the contingency that Elizabeth is free from your reprisal."

Getting rid of Malific only solved one of my problems. Elizabeth wouldn't stop trying to get me out of Nolan's life and making me pay for the slaughter the elves had suffered at Malific's hand. As long as Elizabeth was alive or went unpunished for her actions against me, I wasn't safe. Maybe she didn't have to die, but she needed to know that screwing with me had devastating consequences.

I'd made so many bargains, would this be the worst of them all?

I revealed the marking on my wrist. "Because of Elizabeth, I made an oath with a demon. Can you help me with that?"

Without a reaction to the mark, he nodded.

It didn't seem like a good enough trade. My hesitancy to agree demonstrated how much my anger had ravaged my empathy and ability to forgive.

"Going after Elizabeth proves what, Erin? That you are capable of great brutality like Malific? Or incapable of the forgiveness that you want for yourself?"

Before I could rebut his simplification, he held up a hand, asking me to allow him to finish. "I'm not saying you are anything like Malific, or that you should be held to account for her transgressions. However, you are part god, and gods are not known for their civility or altruism. Viruses, when allowed to mutate, do not get weaker."

"I'm a virus?" I volleyed back with a snarl.

His expression entreated an understanding that wasn't

readily available. It took all my self-control to tamp down the anger and frustration that had settled in my chest and would eventually culminate in a raging display that would surely get me kicked out without any prospect of receiving help. I didn't want that.

But did he realize what he was asking? Giving Elizabeth a pass on all the vile things she'd done to me felt like a surrender, when the prospect of taking revenge on her had driven me for months. It wouldn't even be a stalemate but yet another victory for her. Taking in a fortifying breath seemed to calm some of the emotions Fabian's request had evoked.

Eliminating all the space I'd placed between us, Fabian drew my gaze, which had wandered past him.

"No, Erin. You are a victim of terrible circumstances. Is it unreasonable that I ask you to play a vital role in forging a bond between our shared bloodline, strengthening our magic?"

It *was* wholly unreasonable, but I kept my comment to myself and hoped it didn't show in my face. It was something I needed to think about.

"I need time," I admitted.

"I understand. But will more time really give you more clarity? Despite the improvement in your magic, do you think it's enough to stop Malific? To render her powerless, unable to hurt you and the people you love? Placing Malific in the Blose Chasm is the best way to be rid of her. I can show you how to do it. My only request is the preservation of Elizabeth's life."

Despite agreeing with his stated points, it remained a herculean challenge to consent to allowing Elizabeth to go without suffering any consequences. The time it took me to reconcile those feelings intrigued Fabian and made him noticeably uncomfortable. He was seeing a side of me that he hadn't been sure existed. He needed to understand why it existed.

I shared in great detail everything Elizabeth had subjected me to. Listening intently, horror and empathy washed over his face. It was apparent it was the first time he was hearing the details. Or maybe hearing the victim's version rather than the aggressor's.

"You were brave to come here," he said. "I don't think I possess the level of trust you had to summon to do it." Taking both my hands in his, he bowed his head. "You have my word that I will not betray you. All my actions will be in the interest of you and the elves. You will be protected and treated with all aegis afforded to those of pure elven blood." He made the promise with the devout bonding sincerity of a binding spell.

Despite all the emotions that abandoning revenge against Elizabeth stirred up, I had to be pragmatic. Refusing to put aside my thirst for retribution would only lead me to a pyrrhic victory if it meant that my refusal would result in them rescinding their help.

"I won't seek revenge against Elizabeth, but I require something else, as well," I said in a flat voice, unable to put any energy into the words. The agreement had cost me so much emotionally.

His finger linking with mine gave no hints at the sibling relationship he touted earlier. The simple gesture held an unspoken intimacy, one that he seemed content to continue.

"What?"

"Elizabeth has the Laes. That is what is keeping the Huntsmen here. It needs to be given to them."

He released his hold on my finger. "Is this for all of them, or just the one who goes by Mephisto?"

"All. They want to go home, and I want this for them."

He agreed to it faster than I anticipated. "I will be happy to do this for you."

"Then we have a deal." I extended my hand and he took it, giving it a brusque shake.

"I hope this will work," I admitted. Doubt had found its way into my thoughts.

"I'm confident that it will. You have an advantage that none of us do. Malific will trust you because you have a shared enemy." He smoothed out the frown. "You two share quite a few things. Malific is not only known for her great magic, but also for her cunning and tactical skills. I've heard similar of you."

It was apparent that there were things he'd heard that he didn't want to reveal. I was sure from Elizabeth's POV. I doubted any of it was flattering.

"Even if I could convince her to follow me in, will I be able to exit while leaving her behind?"

"Erin, I trust that you have the ability to do it successfully."

My life depended on him being right.

CHAPTER 30

*T*he open book was in front of the cross-legged Fabian, who had a slight flush on his face and a sheen over his brow. His careful review of the spell made it clear how difficult and rarely used the spell was. The level of concentration held in the tightness of his jaw made me question whether I would be able to open the Blose Chasm, if even he was having so much trouble with it.

"Go ahead," Fabian urged through clenched teeth when the oblong opening of the Chasm appeared before me.

But I couldn't move. My feet were rooted to the ground, grasping at the familiar, unable and unwilling to explore the unknown. Panic rushed through me and I hated every moment of it.

Despite Fabian's clear hazel eyes not showing any hints of malicious intent, I couldn't bring myself to walk through the opening, making me vulnerable to his will. I stood on the edge, recounting every deception and cruelty I'd endured at the hands of Malific and Elizabeth. It had me paralyzed by fear, unable to move over the threshold into a place where I'd be magically vulnerable. Going in meant I had to rely on him keeping it open for me to return.

"Go," his strained voice urged.

Leaning forward, I felt breezy, innocuous air through the opening. Warm hues of light from a clear sky and stone walkway was all I could see from my limited vantage point.

"You'll want to experience it for yourself, Erin, prior to going in there with Malific. Planning is essential, and it can't be done without you knowing what to expect," Fabian pressed, a slight tremble in his voice from the exertion.

He was showing this much strain, and it had only been how long? Would he be able to hold it open for me to get Malific in there and escape? The questions became a distraction and effort to stall going into the Chasm. The opening snapped closed. Fabian's legs were drawn to his chest and his forehead rested on his knees. His body rose and relaxed into the deep breaths he took.

It took a few moments before he lifted his head. His face was devoid of any emotion, eyes empty, his lips relaxed. In silence, he stood and looked away. When his attention returned to me, there was deep-seated ignominy in his grimace.

"There are more spells in the book. Perhaps you can review them," he directed before leaving. His long swift strides had him out of view before I could even inquire whether he was coming back, the time frame in which he wanted me to study the books, or if I'd ruined my chances of staying any longer and getting any help from him or the other elves. There wasn't any ambiguity in this. I had insulted him.

Me ruining Nolan's chances of staying became such a distraction, I was unable to focus on the spells in the book. Some of the Elven language was becoming familiar to me. Someone had translated a significant number of spells into English. A few appeared to be in Nolan's handwriting, and other small quick strokes were similar to Fabian's. Toward the end were elaborate curls and a flourish of loops that looked like calligraphy. I was willing to place a nice bet that it was Sanaa's writing.

They didn't have to do these translations for me; they knew the language. I was the only one who didn't. They were doing their best to help me, and I had insulted Fabian and his efforts with my mistrust.

Before I could look for him to apologize, he returned with Nolan. His gait was easier and more relaxed, keeping stride with Nolan. Fabian's warm smile made me hold my apology.

"Nolan, I think your daughter will feel better if you are here during this portion of our practice." Based on Nolan's confused look, I assumed he had been retrieved without an explanation. It seemed to be a habit of Fabian's.

Fabian explained what we were doing but didn't disclose the reason. It didn't need to be voiced; the understanding showed on Nolan's face along with the disapproval and sadness of me descending into the desperation, unease, and yearning for revenge. He didn't think death was a fitting punishment for Malific. I did.

Ignoring the nonverbal exchange between me and Nolan, Fabian sat cross-legged on the ground, his finger running over the grass.

"Erin, are you ready?" Fabian directed his question to me but kept a careful eye on Nolan. Nolan gave me an inquiring look and I nodded.

Fabian opened the Chasm, reminding me not to leave anything behind because there was a cost for doing that. It wasn't a problem since I had nothing with me, but I took his grave warning to heart. I would have to take the minimal number of things with me, and make sure I left with all of them.

The entrance was inviting. Warm shades of light and a stone walkway.

"May I go in farther?"

"Yes. You need to go past the second entrance. You'll know when you get there."

I did, without a doubt. There weren't any signs of what awaited. Taking a step over an indefinable line, I found myself enveloped in darkness. A caliginous, bleak subspace that reminded me of the demon realm's peculiar dank, dystopian appearance. The light snuffed out, although the glow from the entrance and first space provided enough illumination to see the rough gravel, dried foliage, and rocks that made up the uneven terrain. A few feet of space that seemed to exist as a warning not to proceed. A nebulous threshold that spilled into a new world.

The core of the Blose Chasm. A melon brightness, clear sky, vegetation forming a perimeter and mature flourishing trees. The grass looked thick and healthy. A deceptive paradise where magic didn't exist. Malific's final resting place. Turning my head, I listened for sound. The existence of more life. I didn't hear any. The elf Fabian said had been left here wasn't present. Or at least their presence wasn't apparent.

There was a cool breeze of air, a citrus smell lingering in it. My body settled. Nothing. I was very aware of not having access to magic. When my magic was restricted, I had a craving for it. An ever-present need. I shuddered at the emptiness I felt here. It was worse. This wasn't a craving or need but a void. A riotous hollowness.

It was bad for me. It would be torture for someone with Malific's power, and I was fine with that. I'd even go so far as to admit elated. And I was too far gone to feel shame for that admission. Recalling her threat to my mother, to Madison, her violence to anyone I cared about who was in her path, revoked her right to any kindness or basic humanity. To show it to her was weakness she had no problems exploiting.

I quickly backed away and exited.

When I returned, Nolan's face showed a grim awareness

and concern that he seemed reluctant to voice. I could see the debate in his eyes, the struggle in his posture, and the discomfort as he searched for the words to yank me from a decision that would ensure complication. But desperation had taken me too far. I wasn't sure anything he said would change my mind.

"The session is over," Fabian said to Nolan. "Your assistance was greatly appreciated."

Nolan took the obvious dismissal as a suggestion. Standing taller, he still struggled with what he'd witnessed and the new information he had, his frown deepening with each passing moment.

"Nolan, thank you."

Looks were exchanged. It was the most hostile I'd ever seen Nolan. It seemed to teeter on him taking me by the arm and marching out of there after subjecting Fabian to a few choice words. I desperately needed him to abandon any thoughts of it and tried to relay that in my easy smile.

It's fine. Everything is okay, Nolan.

"She will not be sacrificed for the benefit of the elves," Nolan stated.

Fabian nodded. "This is a belief that we both share," he replied with the gravity of making a promise. His response wasn't enough to ease Nolan's rigid scowl or relax his posture.

"I'll do it. Let me put Malific in the Chasm," Nolan suggested.

Fabian shook his head. "I don't believe your daughter is in the danger you believe she is. But I respect your wish to keep her from harm. Your daughter is deserving of that. I pride myself on being quite skilled in determining the odds of any given situation. With you and Malific entering the Chasm, the odds are not in your favor. With your daughter and Malific entering the Chasm, the success of survival is in your daughter's favor."

What Fabian saw when he looked at me wasn't revealed on his face. But he seemed to have greater confidence in my abilities than even I did. His tone held an unyielding certainty. I had no idea what his reasoning was for choosing me over Nolan. I did know why I would choose me. The pent-up anger, thirst for revenge, and desire to keep my family and friends safe fueled me. Whether considered toxic or admirable, they would drive my actions.

Fabian's eyes moved between me and Nolan, his expression indecipherable. "I'll leave you two to discuss it. I'm here to be of service. I'll respect your decision, but I've made my opinion known. I hope that it is given consideration." With that, he approached me to give my arm a reassuring squeeze before leaving. I got the impression he was trying to let me know the magnitude of what had just transpired.

"You owe them nothing," Nolan said. Fabian was still in earshot. His shoulders stiffened at the statement, but he continued to walk away.

"I know. I'm not doing it for the elves. It's for me, my family's safety, and to have some semblance of a normal life."

"You won't have your elven magic as long as the payment for the debt is required."

"As long as Malific is alive. I have no intention of leaving her in a manner that she's likely to survive."

Creases deepened his frown. His emotions were thick in the air. Pity comprised most of them, as if my empathy had been hobbled and I was a shell of a person.

"It's not out of cruelty but realism. She needed to be weakened and made to atone for her cruelty. I don't fault you for my existence or the reason behind it, but it wasn't enough. I don't want the safety and survival of me and mine to be predicated on Malific not behaving like the monster she's proven to be. Nor do I want to become the person I'd need to be to continue to endure this. I want this over."

"Then let me do it," he suggested. "I'll lure her into the

Blose Chasm and you can open it for me to exit." Desperation was heavy in his voice.

"Nolan. Can you open it? Fabian struggled to keep it open. Are you sure I'd be able to hold it open long enough for you to get out? Malific is a lot of things, but naive isn't one of them. Why would she follow you into the Chasm?" I left out whether he'd be able to get to the exit once I opened it.

He nodded, understanding in his grim smile. "I'm sorry," he whispered.

"There's nothing to be sorry for. Despite the mess that it is currently, I do like my life, and it's because of you that I'm here." My eyes cast down. "I...I just don't want you to judge me the way you were."

It was a hard admission. Our relationship was complex, and navigating the intricacies of it was difficult, but I liked Nolan.

I looked up to find him directly in front of me. He hugged me so tight, breath whooshed out of me. "Never judgment... not against you. I'm so happy that you were born. I am the one who will live with the judgment. Against me, for what I've done." He pulled away. "I understand why you are doing this. I left you defenseless without magic—I don't want you to be defenseless again."

"I'll still have my god magic," I reminded him.

Nolan gave me the same look Fabian gave me when discussing my other magic, a look that contained clear disdain and hints of superiority. But Malific could make life, create armies to do her bidding.

God magic wasn't anything to sneer at.

It was the second day of working on it and required us to put all other lessons on hold. Fabian sat next to me, watching me during the arduous task of opening the Blose Chasm. I knew from the strain placed on Fabian when he initially opened it that it would be difficult. I wasn't prepared to what extent. The exhaustion from opening it was a problem, since I also had to get out of there. Which led to relying on Fabian opening it and keeping it open until I exited.

Fifteen minutes seemed to be the longest he was able to keep it open. Based on the amount of rest and food refuel he needed afterward, it would require the same labor needed to work on the Alaskan pipeline.

We had extended my stay at the Havenage to ensure that I mastered opening the Blose Chasm. It was a good thing the other lessons had been placed on hold. I didn't have the energy to practice anything else.

In the end, I had perfected it. It was time to put Malific in it.

CHAPTER 31

"*T*omorrow," Nolan repeated roughly, blinking twice at my answer of when I planned to enter the Chasm. "So soon."

"It's better this way," I explained. "The information is fresh in my mind and I feel confident doing it."

He moistened his lips and looked to Fabian, whose expression was stolid as he attempted to present a united front. Nolan wanted me to wait, but I feared if I waited too long, I would lose my courage. I didn't believe that was Nolan's biggest concern. It was that I had chosen not to tell anyone other than the two of them. Me going to the Havenage had caused enough problems. I could imagine the resistance and apprehension the Chasm would cause.

"Erin, discuss it with them. They will be an objective voice," he urged when he asked if it would be enough time to let the others know. The guilt nagged at me, had wrung me dry, but they would be an obstacle I didn't need.

"Then I will be there with you," he suggested.

"Nolan." Fabian's tone held the frigid blast of reason Nolan needed. "Your presence will make Malific suspicious. I know you seek to protect Erin, but what you are suggesting is the opposite of that." Moving to Nolan, Fabian placed his hand on his shoulder. "Stay here. I will honor my word of extending the same protections to your daughter as to others and to you."

"But you won't be of any use when she's in the Chasm. She'll be there alone, with Malific."

"No, Malific will be there *alone, without magic*, with your daughter." Fabian's confidence chased away the lingering doubt as I reminded myself that Malific hadn't been without her magic. Ever. Her very existence, strength, and power was steeped heavily in her magic.

The next day, I left the Havenage with less fanfare than my arrival. The night before during dinner, everyone was informed I would be leaving. Awoken before sunrise by Fabian, he departed with me with a small overnight bag shouldered. I understood why everyone said their goodbyes during dinner. I had only been there a few days, no one had formed an attachment, with the exception of Pascha who had a mild understanding that the extra-dessert train was leaving. The farewells were brief and stilted. Sanaa, who seemed aware of the reason behind my sudden departure, gave me an approving nod.

"You can still change your mind," Nolan said when I stopped by his bedroom to let him know I was leaving. Fabian at my side didn't deter him from his attempt to dissuade me. "No one will fault you for reconsidering this." He looked at Fabian, who made a sound of agreement.

"I'm aware. If I didn't believe it needed to be done, I wouldn't be doing this. Nor would I do it if I weren't confident in my abilities." The latter was optimism and bravado. I wasn't afraid, but it would be naive not to be apprehensive and approach it with the caution it deserved. Malific was a warrior. Magic or not, I was still in for a battle, and that was the reason I needed to do it quickly. It wasn't just because the spell was fresh in my mind and I felt confident in it, but I also didn't want to lose my nerve.

Nolan took my hand. "Be careful." I gave my hand a little tug, coaxing him to release it after he'd held it for so long, I suspected he was giving me time to rethink things.

"I still think I should go with you," he suggested when I turned to leave.

"Nolan," Fabian eased out with strained patience. "You and I discussed this ad nauseum last night. Should I be concerned over your lack of trust in me?"

"Not at all. This has no bearing on trust, but my desire to protect Erin."

A smile spread across Fabian's lips. "Once again, I must caution you to not underestimate your daughter—her history speaks for itself. Find comfort in knowing that I take my accompanying her seriously. I will go to the extent of my abilities, which far exceed yours, to ensure her safety. It is best you stay behind. That will give her one less person to worry about, and once it is done, visit her. Enjoy each other without the looming threat of Malific's interruption."

It took a few moments, but Nolan eventually conceded. Taking my hand once again, he gave it an encouraging squeeze.

Fabian may have lived in the Havenage, but he seemed very familiar with life outside it. After I took him to the parking garage where he kept his car, he gave me his contact information and where he was staying. I made plans to contact him once I'd established a time with Malific. He found humor in me expecting him to use magic for us to contact.

"I want to conserve all my energy. The less magic I perform, the longer I keep the Chasm open for you. Because you will come out of the Chasm." His statement was said

256

with such confidence, I wondered if he had divination abilities.

Once home, I debated whether to let Madison and Cory know of my return and plans. Not wanting them to attempt to talk me out of it, I didn't. When this was over, it would be satisfying to tell them that the Malific situation had been handled. The thought of it made me hum with anticipation, which drowned out the fear. Using the diamond metal Malific had given me, I contacted her. This is it, I breathed, before invoking the spell to call her.

The meeting was brief. I revealed my discoveries and what needed to be done to remove the oath. Malific's eyes held a portentous gleam at the anticipation of being released from it and the wrath she planned to inflict. Unsure of how much she knew of elven magic, I said nothing about the Blose Chasm. I told her we would be entering the Procreso, revealing that the medium would enhance my elven magic and give me the ability to break the binding oath.

"You are indeed resourceful. No wonder Elizabeth fears you." She preened as if the qualities she admired were a result of her gene contribution. One thing Elizabeth had completely accurate: Malific was arrogant and a narcissist.

She left after agreeing to meet at a small park near my home at four in the morning, to minimize the chance of witnesses seeing me open the Procreso. Once she was gone, I notified Fabian of the time and place of our meeting.

CHAPTER 32

*A*live wire of magic and menace was coming off her. Nearly giddy with eagerness, she listened as I reminded her that she would have to stay with me until we got over the threshold.

"I'm your admission," I told her. That wasn't true, but I needed her close. Disable her and get the hell out.

"Of course," she said, as if having to remind her to adhere to rules was absurd. "Do you want to check me for weapons?"

I shook my head. "Truce, remember? You're not going to do anything to me while in there." If I didn't check her for weapons, she wouldn't check me. Fear of leaving anything behind, I kept it simple: stun gun, knife, brass knuckles. Dressing for our meeting was difficult, needing to conceal everything but not dress differently enough to raise suspicion. The cool weather justified the jacket with the thumb loop, and longer sleeves concealed the brass knuckles. Open hem bottom of my leggings concealed the knife sheathed at my leg.

Malific was always dressed as if ready for battle. A sleek fitted long-sleeve shirt, thicker than what she typically wore, and leather pants molded to her body. Furtively, I took in her appearance, taking inventory of possible weapon concealment. Her sword was missing. The boots looked dangerous, but there wasn't anywhere on her where I could readily see a weapon. This was good. Malific relied heavily on her magic, drawing on her speed, strength, and the ability to continue fighting while healing from her magic. Those advantages would be removed.

Goosebumps crawled up my arms when I took her hands in mine. She smirked at my sharp intake of breath. I whispered the incantation, gripping her hand tighter, and we walked through the uninviting dark space. I hoped it didn't warn her off.

It didn't, and once we'd entered the heart of the Blose Chasm, Malific walked past me, taking in the scenery as I observed her from my periphery, watching for any signs that she suspected betrayal.

Unsure of what caused her smile—the beauty of the place or the anticipation of revenge on Elizabeth—I returned it. She attempted to explore more. I clasped her hand and tugged her back.

"This should be far enough."

"You're not curious about this place?" she inquired. "It's beautiful. You should want to get familiar with where you'll spend your days until your death."

The blow to the side of my head came suddenly and with force. Dazed, I released my hold on her and stumbled back. Before I could recover, another hook to my jaw snapped my head back, sending another shock of pain through me. I blocked the ensuing left hook. A well-placed front kick caught her right under her chin, followed by a roundhouse kick that connected with the side of her head. She shuffled back and shook it off, a bemused darkness coursing over her smirk.

"Did you really believe I hadn't heard of the Blose

Chasm?"

My heart dropped to the pit of my stomach.

"Elves are a wealth of untapped spells and abilities. If I couldn't have them as allies, then they were of no use to me. I wanted to ensure they'd not be used against me, either." Despite the anger in her voice, there were traces of begrudging admiration. I'd achieved what she hadn't: an alliance with the elves. The use of their magic against a foe, even if it was her, and the exploitation of it for a wrathful purpose. Oddly, this might be the only time she'd seen me as having any value—a true contemporary.

She charged at me, blocking the blow with my unweaponed hand and striking me on my nose. It didn't break it—I don't think. But the hit blurred my vision. I'd underestimated her, thinking the source of her skills were rooted in her magic where I'd have the advantage. She demonstrated a great deal of fighting skill. It was an over-sight that could cost me dearly.

She wasn't not going to win this. She just couldn't. Drop-ping to my knees, I punched. Using as much force as I could, I punched her in the left kneecap with the brass knuckles. She grunted in pain, my leg swiped her left ankle, and she hit the ground with a thud. Retrieving the taser from my pocket, I aimed it at her. Nothing. Again, nothing. Fuck. Magic didn't work and nor did electrical devices, apparently. I shoved it back in my pocket, making sure not to leave anything behind.

Malific rolled to her feet, moving slower than before, her pain evident as she lunged at me and knocked me to the ground. Her full weight on me and the close proximity prevented me getting enough distance to land more powerful strikes. She was going for my eyes. I was on defense, protecting them. From where I was, I could see the opening of the Chasm, a streetlight from the park where we'd entered.

During the fight, the distance had increased. I pulled my brass-knuckled hand back, risking injury to my face, and punched her hard in her side. A blow powerful enough for her to be dazed by the pain. Shock, incredulity, and disgust manifested on her face as she realized she no longer had her cloak of god magic healing her and chasing away the pain. She was mortal. This was what being human felt like.

Going for the knife, I grabbed it and plunged it into her stomach. I pulled it out, prepared to slash at another vital artery, but she rolled away. Came to her feet faster than expected. Her eyes blazed with fiery anger. Death. She wanted it for me as much as I wanted it for her. Grabbing at her stomach, she looked at the dark blood. She choked out a sound of despair, horror eclipsing her face.

I risked a glance at the opening. It didn't look the same, the light not as bright. The exit was closing. I darted for it, hearing the rushed patter of Malific behind me. *Faster, Erin, faster.* I felt the swipe of her hand trying to go for my jacket. She missed and I ran faster. The weight of a body crashed into me, and I fell forward. We grappled, trying to untangle from each other. Punches swung, nails ripped at skin.

We got to our feet nearly simultaneously. Fury made Malific look insane as she plunged a knife into my stomach. Pain laced through me, so violent and virulent, I couldn't catch breath. My jacket was wet with my blood. She ripped it out. I wailed. She glanced at the opening. I reacted on pure adrenaline and the need to live, hitting her with everything I had in her nose.

The crunch of broken bone shocked her. She stabbed blindly through watering eyes. I hit her again, the blow making my wound ache so much, I thought I'd pass out. She stumbled back and dropped the knife. I grabbed it and stabbed her, but not nearly as deep. Strength was eking out of me. My legs started to buckle. I ran for the exit, not sure what the buckling meant. Was the blood loss too much? My thinking slowed. Everything slowed. It was difficult getting my body to respond to my commands. It wanted to rest. Needed to rest.

"I'm coming," I screamed, but it came out as a crackled whisper. Diminished even more by Malific's promise of ending me in the most painful, torturous manner possible.

"This isn't over," she ground out, pain etched in every word. "I will end you." If given the opportunity, I had no doubt she'd exact all her vows of torture and revenge. She would not get that chance. I pushed my legs harder. My breathing ragged, huffing as the pain became increasingly piercing. If I focused on it, I knew I'd give in to it and pass out.

"I'm coming," I forced out through clenched teeth. It wasn't my imagination; the exit was closing. The edges wavered and shrank. I could hear movement behind me, but I couldn't tell how close and wouldn't risk the time it took to look back. I threw myself through the closing gap, landing on my stomach.

Fabian helped me turn onto my back. "I'm going to try to stop the bleeding, give you some pain relief."

I blinked my eyes rapidly, because nodding seemed too difficult. I could hear spells rushing from his lips, him cursing at their failure, and him explaining that he'd exhausted his magic.

"It's okay, I can do it," I said, my voice weak and raspy. I made an effort, but lifting my hands to my stomach was daunting.

"It's more than soft tissue damage, Erin. It's really…" He trailed off.

Not sure how bad my injuries were, but if Fabian's cursing and his calls to deities were anything to go by, it wasn't good. I could hear the desperation in his voice as he called for an ambulance.

CHAPTER 33

I opened my eyes, groaned as I sat up, and looked around. Hospital room. Madison. She looked tired, her lips set into a firm line. Cory, in the corner of the room, running his hands over the scruffy shadow of his beard. He refused to hold my gaze. Mephisto, leaning against the wall, his appearance disheveled.

"How long have I been here?" I asked Madison.

"Two days. From what I understand, you'd passed out by the time the ambulance arrived. You were stabbed with a Jagdkommando knife, which caused a lot of damage when it was pulled out. The most damage was to your spleen, but it was able to be repaired. You required surgery, not magic." Her eyes flicked to the corner, where Fabian was pressed against the wall, attempting to be inconspicuous, or maybe not be the recipient of a barrage of glares and dirty looks. Nolan's anxious and somber appearance held my attention longer than anyone else as I tried to figure out the subtle dynamics in the room.

"How are you feeling?" Mephisto asked, approaching the bed and placing a hand gently on my stomach.

"Sore. A little pain," I managed the lie. "A little overwhelmed." I'd never been in a hospital and now I was in a room hooked up to monitors, IVs running through my arm, and a tube inside me getting too personal with my lady garage.

"I can help with the pain," he said, and I immediately agreed. He was gentle as he pressed his hand over my stomach. The refreshing tingle of his magic slithering over me and taking away the soreness and pain was welcome.

I was still trying to read Cory and Madison. How angry were they? I immediately regretted not sharing my plans with them. There was definitely going to have to be an apology tour. The nurse entering the room in a flurry of movement was a welcome distraction, especially when she asked everyone to step out. When they returned, Fabian was not with them.

"Who's Fabian?" Madison asked through clenched teeth. "Because the only thing I could get out of anyone was that he was the person who found you after you were attacked."

"My instructor at the Havenage."

"Then why did he stab you?" Cory flicked a glance at Nolan. That explained Nolan's weary demeanor. He'd spent his time trying to defend Fabian. At the mere hint that Fabian was responsible for the injuries, I was sure the room erupted in chaos. Giving him an appreciative mirthless smile, I pulled my attention back to Cory, who was studying the view outside as if it was too captivating to look away from. Despite his best efforts to hide his expression, I couldn't miss the deep-seated frown.

"He didn't stab me. Malific did."

All eyes turned to me. Another wave of sorrow for Nolan went through me for him having to defend Fabian and not having any clear answers of what happened in the Chasm. Neither one of them did.

Through nursing interruptions, a check from the doctor, and nutrition, I managed to tell them everything. Almost everything. I told them I hadn't shared my plans with them because I needed to act fast.

"You had to act so fast that you couldn't send a text, leave a message, or swing by the house to tell me that you were about to do something so reckless and dangerous?" Madison snapped. Then she bit her lips in an effort to keep back whatever else she wanted to say.

I preferred the silence that followed as they processed things. Madison's fists were so tightly closed at her sides, it looked painful. "Nolan told me you were in the hospital," she told me. "So he knew but we didn't."

"Because he was at the Havenage when the plan was discussed."

"Was that by design?" Cory asked.

I shook my head. "Just the way things played out."

Mephisto had remained silent, but my response earned me a disapproving sneer. Maybe I was too fatigued to sound convincing. "Are you tired?' he asked.

Nodding, I hoped they all took the hint. Fighting, a day post-surgery, was too much. The pain had decreased significantly, but there was more than pain. The emptiness I felt while in the Chasm lingered, making me suspect that none of my magic had returned. I couldn't use it to further heal myself.

"Then rest, I'll be back later." He came to the side of the bed, leaned down, and kissed me on the cheek. "Erin, we will be discussing this," he whispered for my ears only. A sentiment I could see on all their faces.

Three days in the hospital. Mephisto, Cory, and Madison continued to visit. My case had been taken from the police and was being handled by the Supernatural Task Force. Which I assumed meant it would not be aggressively investigated and eventually would become a cold case. Nolan visited every day and looked at me as if he couldn't believe I'd made it out.

With the hospitalization, surgery, and visits, I hadn't really had time to fully process what had happened. I'd left Malific wounded, inflicting similar injuries on her that she had on me, which had required surgical intervention. Had she died? When I suggested going back into the Blose Chasm to check, I dropped the topic after Nolan's look of horror.

"Wait until you get some of your magic back, okay?"

My agreement was the only thing that gave him some relief. But I was more than relieved. Malific was gone. One of my problems down. Now I just had to fix the situation with Asial and get the Laes for the Huntsmen. I was feeling more optimistic than I ever thought possible.

A successful surgery, the surgical site nearly healed, and minimal pain, I was acutely aware of the tension that riddled between us. It was more prevalent between me and Madison, who was monosyllabic as she drove me home from the hospital after my four-day stay. The tension was so thick, Cory turned from his position in the passenger seat to give me a reassuring smile. It was a gallant effort. They had every right to be upset. I could only imagine how I'd feel finding out secondhand that they were in the hospital after doing something as dangerous as going to the Blose Chasm with Malific.

At home, I grimaced as I lowered myself to the sofa.

"You have food. I stocked the place yesterday. There are a few easy-fix meals. The surgical site has healed well, so you'll probably only need to change the dressing once if there's drainage." Madison bent down and lifted my shirt to examine the bandages. Seeing that there was just a thin strip of gauze and no discoloration, she silently pulled the gauze away. "It's almost healed. You should be okay. Mephisto said he'll be by later."

I hated how utilitarian and clinical her interaction was with me. Something had been lost in her. We'd had our share of fights, but there was always a trill of philia twinned with our angry words, barbs, and discontent. None of that was present, and I felt its absence.

"I'm sor—"

"No, you're not," she snapped, interrupting me. Standing, she put distance between us that mimicked our emotional distance. "You're never sorry and that's the fucking problem. You're sorry I'm upset. You may even be sorry that you got hurt so badly, but you're damn sure not sorry about what you did."

She lost her effort to keep her voice level and calm. "I had to find out about your hospitalization from Nolan. I got nothing from the lord of the elves—or whoever the hell he is. He wasn't giving a lot of damn information. We were in the dark. All I knew was that you were in the hospital after an attack. And we"—she moved her finger between herself and an unusually quiet Cory who was having a difficult time looking at me—"were left without answers. We didn't know if you would even survive. We had no idea you'd returned from the Havenage. Can you imagine what was going through our minds? Did you even *care*?"

Like Cory, she seemed to be having a difficult time looking at me. Shoving her fingers through the loose curls of her hair, she was drawn into her thoughts.

"You're right," I admitted softly. "I'm not sorry for what I did, but I am sorry that I hurt you both. I needed to do it."

"No, you don't get off that easy. You didn't just *need* to do it. You *needed* to do it without anyone pointing out how stupidly reckless and dangerous it was. And that's you in a nutshell, Erin. You don't give a fuck about anyone. I'm so damn tired of it." Her voice quivered with emotion.

"I give too many fucks. Yeah, I knew it was dangerous and I didn't want to compound a bad situation by having the two people I care most about worrying. It wasn't selfishness. I'm trying to do the best that I can."

The tears I had been fighting back streamed down my face. This was a different fight. I could feel the changes in it. Like the vine of Madison's compassion had broken and I was clinging to it for dear life. The fabric of our relationship felt irreparably damaged.

"Madison, Malific is out of the picture. She can't leave the Blose Chasm and she was in a state I don't think she can survive. Fabian—the man you called the lord of the elves—I don't think he has a title, but he'll help me with my Dareus problem."

"Because you no longer have magic," she pointed out. Perhaps in an effort to curry favor with Madison, Nolan had been more open to divulging information that Fabian wouldn't.

"I don't have my elven magic."

She grumbled something under her breath in French. "Anything can be rationalized. That's exactly what you're doing. I just can't anymore with you, Erin."

Torn between anger, frustration, and sorrow, my words spilled out in an unfiltered croak. "What do you mean you 'just can't'? Family doesn't work that way. I'm *sorry*. How many times do I need to say it?"

"But we're not family, are we?" That was a blow I couldn't recover from. "We're two people whose mothers have an abnormally close relationship. Nolan leaving you with my mother is a technicality. It could have been anyone's door, and that wouldn't make you any more my sister than you are now. You've never treated us like sisters. I've just been the person who fixed things for you. I treated you like an exten-

268

sion of me—like real family. Because that's the way we were raised, and it was what I wanted to do. But it's clearer than ever that this is a one-sided relationship. Things are broken. I don't want this. I don't want yo—"

"Madison."

Cory's sharp interruption only seemed to serve the purpose of keeping her from saying something she'd regret. Nothing could reach her. The most hurtful thing had already been said. Tears glistened in her eyes.

"Things are too broken, Erin. I'm done with it. I'm done with you." She left the apartment without looking back. Just one deep breath before she closed the door behind her.

The tears came too fast for me to brush them away. I knew it. Felt it. Nothing I could say would change this. The finality of it made my chest ache. The ending of a terrible movie where everyone deserved so much better.

"She's just upset and lashing out. There's no way she believes that," Cory said, taking a seat neat to me. I rested my head against his shoulder. His thumb swiped over my cheek, wiping away the tears. They flowed so much he eventually he gave up.

"I should have told you."

He heaved a sigh. "I don't know," he mused. "I would have liked to have known, but I know you needed to do it. If you'd told me you wanted to go into the magicless Thunderdome with a woman responsible for killing a race of people, her own brother, and hundreds of others—I wouldn't have been on board with that. At. All. Madison wouldn't have, either. I get why you didn't tell anyone. I'm only angry because when I got the call from Madison that you were in the hospital and in emergency surgery, I thought I was going to lose you, and it scared the hell out of me. I needed someone to be angry with. I chose Malific and Fabian."

Lifting my head, I wiped my cheeks dry with my shirt. "Why Fabian?"

After several moments, he shrugged. "I don't know. He and M didn't hit it off. M doesn't like him on a feral level. It was probably the way Fabian watched you after surgery, while you slept, and the way he brushed your hair from your face. Mephisto requested that he not ever do that again. It was quite apparent Mephisto was only going to ask once. He said it in the cool, calm voice of a person who doesn't fear anything. It sent a chill up my spine. Even Kai felt the need to get between the two of them. And Fabian couldn't care less. His presence seemed proprietorial. It was like he stayed more as a challenge to Mephisto than to monitor your well-being."

I frowned. "I don't think it's proprietorial. Elves don't like gods because of what Malific did. He's very protective of me only because I'm an elf."

"You're sure about that?"

I wasn't but I didn't want to think about it any longer, or the situation that led to whatever the hell was going on between me and Madison.

"I hate fighting with Madison," I whispered, closing my eyes and resting my head back on Cory's shoulder.

"It'll be fine. She's so angry because of how emotionally connected she is to you. The last few months have been hard on her, too. It's easier for me to step back and not get into all the emotions. But her life dealing with situations that involve you isn't that simple. She loves her position at STF, but you know as well as I do that she often circumvents the rules to help you. When something happens to you—being banished to the demon realm, for example—she's left dealing with the family. A family who for some reason assigned her as your guardian. It's an unfair position to put anyone in. Yet she took it on without complaint and always does what is necessary. I'm not making excuses for her, but I understand her reaction. She's not done with you. She won't ever be done with you. Siblings are an extension of us. You're a part of her."

"But we aren't really sisters," I sniffed. "Realistically, we were just friends raised like sisters. It's not a blood relationship."

"You're right. It's even stronger because you don't have a blood relationship but chose to behave as though you do. She's hurt and she lashed out. You know she didn't mean it. Give her a day or two."

I nodded.

"So, when do you plan to deal with Asial?" Cory asked, neatly changing the subject.

"I don't have magic. Can't summon him. Hopefully some of it will return." Or all of it, when Malific died. "I want to be fully healed before I deal with him. I'll have to figure out what to do with another demon living among us. Worst case, I could keep him neutralized. Fabian might have other options."

At least I hoped he did.

CHAPTER 34

I was under the scrutinizing gaze of Mephisto, who came over after Cory left yesterday. Banal conversations kept us from addressing the twerking elephant in the room.

"I should have told you," I admitted in my curled ball on the couch, unfurling enough to reach for the coffee cup he'd extended. I took notice of the addition on my counter. A new coffee grinder and an upgraded maker similar to the one I'd admired in his home.

Taking a sip from the coffee, I let out an appreciative sigh at the rich, robust taste. Definitely not my brand. The earthy taste with hints of dark chocolate was similar to the coffee he kept at his home and the type I wasn't willing to shell out the money to purchase. Grocery store beans gave me the same caffeine hit.

He took a sip from his coffee without comment.

"It wasn't because I didn't trust you with the information. I wanted the situation over, and I knew you'd want to accompany me."

"I would have wanted to, but I wouldn't have. She'd never

enter with me present. But I would have worried. I don't need protection from worry, Erin. Understand that."

I nodded and shared my experience at the Havenage, my agreement with Fabian not to retaliate against Elizabeth, and what I'd receive in return.

"I don't like Fabian."

"Tell me how you really feel," I teased.

It wasn't jealousy but disdain. Pure and virulent and I couldn't figure out why. "He's motivated to protect the elven line because there are so few of them. His insistence can be off-putting," I offered in explanation, although I wasn't completely sure if that was it.

Mephisto pursed his lips then shook his head. "That's not it. I just don't like him." The frustration of not being able to pinpoint his aversion was clear. "He's very powerful but makes too great an effort to seem innocuous."

"To protect himself. He's trying to save the bloodline. One that was devastated by someone with magic like yours. Do you blame him for not wanting to appear as a threat? Or for you to covet his magic? That's what led to his people being killed," I pointed out, taking another long sip. Maybe the extra expense was worth it for the moment of decadence before starting a day that would be anything but.

Depthless dark eyes were pools of calculation as he considered my explanation. His frown deepened. "I don't think it's to protect himself. He doesn't fear me."

"Do you want him to?"

He shrugged. "I don't need to operate in fear." That poignant reminder of a lion never having to tell anyone he's a lion. A leopard doesn't have to announce that he's a menace, but not knowing that can have devastating results.

"He's possessive of you, and I don't like that," he admitted.

Placing my coffee on the table, I turned to him. "Jealous?"

"Should I be?"

"Jealousy is weird, isn't it? Hard to control, yet many times without merit."

"In other words, I have nothing to worry about." He inched closer, pushing me back on the sofa and settling between my legs. I hissed in pain, and he was away and near the wall, his eyes raking over me and landing on the surgical site. "I hurt you?" he whispered.

"No," I pulled out a pen stuck deep between the cushions. "The pen shanked me."

He chuckled. "The pen shanked me," he said in a poor imitation of my voice. "Undeniably Erin," he whispered before kissing me.

Picking up the Bailer, the magical beacon Mephisto had given me, from the table, I saw that the sigils had been removed. The branding had still been on his arm the night before. Running my fingers along the object, Mephisto's hand covered it and mine, offering an unexpected comfort.

"When did you remove your connection from it?"

"This morning." Relief. It was palpable in him. He apparently experienced the same feelings of any magical being when their magic was suppressed.

"Thank you for doing that for me."

"I'm happy you didn't have to use it." His fingers ran a small circular pattern over my thigh as his lips lifted into a mirthless smile. "Did you take it with you into the Blose Chasm?"

"The goal was to take as few things as possible. It wouldn't have done any good, anyway. Magic doesn't work there. My stun gun didn't even work."

"You went in there, alone, with Malific, counting on Fabian to open the Chasm and your skill against an Archdeity." His tone was tight with both censure and pride.

"I didn't have a lot of choices. Live with the constant fear of her trying to kill me until she gave up or succeeded—my money was on the latter—or do something about it."

He leaned forward, a smirk lifting his lips he before moistened them. "My demigoddess," he breathed against my lips before pressing a kiss to them.

What he perceived as bravery was nothing more than desperation to make it all end. And I was slowly getting there.

Mephisto was reluctant to leave, which gave me a reasonable excuse to avoid the inevitable. I had to talk to Madison. Apologize. And fix things between us. None of that bothered me, nor did I have an aversion to it. I feared her rejection and her refusal to accept my apology. Culling through everything Cory said the day before, I used it as comfort and support. We were an extension of each other. She'd been present all my life; how would I begin to live a Madison-less life? I didn't want to.

Opening the door, I sighed at the massive wolf-shifter at my door. I did not have time for this. "Daniel, move!"

With lazy alertness, he lifted his head, snorted, and dropped his head back to his paws. Groaning a curse, I attempted to step over him, only to have the abnormally large creature stand and nudge me back into the apartment with his face.

Grabbing my phone, I stabbed at the screen to video call Asher. "Move your damn shifter," I demanded as soon as he answered.

Unfazed by my hostility, he bared his teeth in a flash of a smile. "Would it be childish of me to request that you make me?"

Eyes narrowed to slits, my breathing became irregular rasps as I attempted to control my anger. Challenging an Alpha would only compound my problems, and that was the most annoying part about dealing with Asher: that delicate dance of asserting my autonomy without provoking the animal who dwelled so close to the surface and didn't suffer challenges lightly.

"Asher, tell your shifter to leave. I don't need a detail or a sentry."

"An emergency surgery for a stab wound and a four-day hospital stay says differently."

"How did you get my medical records? Are there any laws you believe pertain to you?"

The cant of his head and smirk provided the answer that he pretended to be too modest to say aloud. "You're at your home alone. When you had company they stood down—out of notice. Now that you're by yourself, they will be there to guard you. Their presence needs to be known," he asserted, his tone uncompromising.

"Look, we're friends, right?" I asked.

"Ah, now we're at the emotional coercion part of the debate."

Ignoring him, I continued. "We're friends and I don't want to have to come to your house and punch you in your mint juleps, so call off the detail, now."

His cool look of indifference irritated me more than any response. He shook his head. "I'm hardly concerned about an attack from a woman who was discharged from the hospital just yesterday. I don't know the specifics of what landed you there. You have extended no further courtesy other than a brief response telling me you were okay and that you'd tell me everything later. It's later and I don't have an explanation. Give me one, Erin."

My stubbornness isn't a quality I'm proud of, nor the urge to rebel the moment I'm Asher-ed. Despite his good intentions, Asher's wants would always override anyone's sense of autonomy. It was who he was.

"Erin, I already have one woman who challenges me at every turn. I don't need another." His tone held the same exasperated amusement reserved for his dealings with Ms. Harp.

"How is Evelyn?" I asked.

"Noncompliant and a pain in my ass for no particular reason, as usual. But after her last escape, she promised to do an entire study. Dr. Reyes will return before the full moon next month." He was irritated. I was sure it was from the debts he was accumulating from this. Asher's perceptiveness made my internal debate of whether to bring up my discussion with Ms. Harp moot.

"I know her wishes," he admitted. "They won't be honored."

"Asher..."

"I'm not ignoring them. We will find an alternative to treating her other than shifting. It's something I'm looking into, but the other nonsense bullshit she proposed isn't going to happen. It's just not." His decisiveness left no room for debate and I didn't want to offer one. I wanted her to stay alive. Death couldn't be an alternative treatment.

Some tension eased from me. My discussion with Ms. Harp was one of the latent problems that had anchored me, although I hadn't been aware of until I felt it removed.

"What happened, Erin?"

Not too often had I rendered Asher speechless, but he took several moments to collect his thoughts after I disclosed everything except matters that dealt with Mephisto and the Laes. "So, as you can see, I'm not in any danger. You can tell the horse-wolf to leave."

His mouth twisted before he put down the phone, probably on a stand. Asher relaxed back in his chair, his jaw working. Despite my goals to control it, my irritation flared.

"What is there to think about? I made a request and I expect it to be honored," I fumed. "Move your wolf or I will move him."

A rumble of laughter came from my phone and a snort

from the other direction. A derisive snort from an animal is something a person never gets used to. It's the height of condescension.

"Go ahead, move Daniel. I'd love to see it."

I glared at him.

"I don't want to hurt him."

More laughter just added fuel to the flames of my aggravation.

"It's his eyes, isn't it? More than once, I've been told that they're too soft and unassuming, giving the impression that he's much gentler than he is. Don't let that fool you, Erin."

"Asher." I hated the imploring whine to my voice. Dealing with Asher all these years, I'd learned that he delighted in the battle, taking it as an opportunity to hone his skills of domination. He'd make time for that exercise. He took pride in being indomitable. The very thing that wouldn't allow us to work in a relationship was the very thing I was dealing with right then. Some bouts with Asher felt like an exhausting aerobic activity. "I'll be fine."

After several more moments of consideration his voice raised a few decibels. "Daniel, you can leave."

Be careful, Erin." Asher disconnected the call. By the time I got to my car, Daniel was tugging on his shirt and opening the door of his truck.

CHAPTER 35

*M*y heart pounded erratically when Madison's doorbell went unanswered. Hoping I wasn't being annoying, I started to ring the doorbell again when the door swung open.

"Erin." Clayton slipped past me, an overnight bag hiked on his shoulder. Madison waved at him, and he returned it before turning his attention to me. His reassuring small smile didn't offer the intended comfort because I read too much into it. Was he assuring me that I'd get through the collapse of my and Madison's relationship? That he'd be there for her during the hard times since I'd no longer be in her life? The thought spiraled, and for too long, I stood in the doorway, staring at Madison. Or rather both of us were looking at each other, words lost, in a nebulous state.

"Hi," we said simultaneously.

"I'm sorry," I quickly blurted, offering her the two large bags of Jelly Belly candies. Our comfort food and olive branch since we were children. Taking the bags, she moved aside to let me in.

"I'm the one who should be apologizing," she said, tossing the candy onto the console and pulling me into a hug. "Erin, I

279

shouldn't have said that. No matter how angry I was, it was unacceptable," she sobbed.

"You didn't mean it. I know you didn't." Being with her now, I was sure of it. Yesterday, not so much.

Neither one of us wanting to let go, I was the first to move away but I still kept contact. Something so simple I thought would be lost to me forever. Eventually, she stepped away, grabbed one of the bags of candy, opened it, and took out a handful before offering me some. I took a handful and headed to the living room.

"I still think about the day you were left with us," Madison said, breaking the companionable silence we'd lapsed into. "We literally had a baby left at our doorsteps. And you wailed. And wailed. Nothing my mom or dad could soothe you. You were silent during feedings, would stop crying a little when held, but you were in distress. It was as if you knew the life you were being handed. I wanted you to stop crying—not just because you were loud as hell." She flashed a wry smile brimming with nostalgia.

"My mother had already accepted you as part of the family—she told me I was going to be your sister. I felt it completely. I placed my finger in your hand and for a moment, you did stop crying. I wanted to protect the poor child whose parents had left her. Then it transitioned to more than our parents and their weird relationship. You became the friend I needed to protect. I got the best of any relationship: a friend and a sister. I can't deny that sometimes it's hard having that relationship with you."

"I know. I don't make it easy, do I?" I admitted softly. Our lives had been a rollercoaster but never before had I been so grateful for her to be my partner on the ride.

She shrugged. "It's not a criticism. You were dealt a screwed-up hand, and stumbling and flailing is expected. Sometimes I question whether some of it is self-inflicted. Do you ask for help before it's just short of a place of no return?"

"It's never my intention. I can't be a burden to others. I give you permission not to catch me when I stumble and to let me flail until I get my footing."

"You know I can't do that any more than you could do it for me. *But*, I need to know everything, Erin," she said. "Not the edited version and not the one you think will make me feel less afraid for you. I need to be let in, all the way in."

"I told you everything, just never discussed going to the Blose Chasm for the reasons you said. I knew you all weren't on board with it, but I'd already had the discussion with Nolan. From his response, I knew it would be worse with you all. I just want this whole thing to be over."

There was relief in her sigh when she realized I hadn't held anything back from what I told them in the hospital. "You don't have magic."

"Not so far. The cost was supposed to be just elven magic until…" I trailed off. It seemed morbid to keep discussing the return of my magic being contingent on Malific dying from her injuries.

"You had a transfusion. Could that be the reason?"

I shrugged. The mercurial aspects of magic often couldn't be explained.

"What if it doesn't return and this is what you are now? Just human."

"It's an acceptable sacrifice for a normal life. For us all to have a normal life. I can keep my business and do what I did before. After all, I haven't had access to magic that long."

She frowned. I knew she was worrying if I'd return to my old ways, trying to satiate an unquenchable craving. But it wasn't the same. Before, I'd felt like something was missing, something that I needed to make me whole. I was a walking, functioning, shadow of a person, doing everything I could to fill that void. Things felt different now. Even-keeled. A stasis. I felt complete, even without magic. I wasn't hyperaware of it and the people who possessed it. I wasn't drawn to it like a magnet.

"It's not the same. I don't feel anything. Not even the absence of magic. Before, something was missing. Now, the feeling is idyllic. I can live like this. Cory can provide magic if I ever need it like before."

Searching my face while she chewed on the candy, the tight line of her lips gave way to a smile of relief. "Good. I just want you to be happy, but Fabian will be disappointed."

"Fabian?"

"Yes. I received a visit from the elf lord or whatever. When I asked about his role among the elves, he said there wasn't any other than being your instructor, which I suspect is a complete lie. If there is a hierarchy, he's definitely on top, if not the autocrat."

"He has an important role among the elves, I just never figured out what it was. The elves in the Havenage seem egalitarian. A big family."

Nodding as if pieces of a puzzle were falling into place, she said, "Do you think you're going to be invited to the family? I gathered from his questioning that he was trying to determine how close we were and the likelihood of you moving to the Havenage."

Going over every interaction between the two of us, nothing about any of it had given me that impression. "What do you think of him?" I asked her. Neither Cory nor Mephisto liked Fabian, but they were unreliable narrators; a hidden dislike with a Y chromosome bias.

"He's nice. Polite. Serene. It should have put me at ease, but it made me over cautious, as if it was a mirage of his true personality." She huffed, sinking into the sofa with a grimace. "I'm that person. Ugh. I'm cynical. He genuinely cares about your well-being and I can't help but think he's the devil in disguise."

"Cynicism is needed when dealing with the people we

deal with."

"He seems to really care about your well-being as his 'elven-sister.' I'll hold comment on how weird that moniker is. I wasn't getting *sisterhood* vibes from him."

"Me neither, not without breaking some very appropriate laws. His interest in my welfare is because I'm an elf. It seems that everything he cares about is limited to that. But he's a means to an end."

The end that was coming soon.

"So, Clayton, huh?" I hiked an inquisitive brow. The look he gave her when he left was more than two people having a casual time.

"He was my distraction from admitting I was so terrible to my sister."

"Yeah, he was," I said in the same insinuating voice that Cory often used.

"You hang around with Cory too much," she chastised.

"Yeah, we do."

Her brows drew together. "That one doesn't even make sense," she belted between laughs. A sound that hovered between a cackle and a snort was one of the best sounds I'd ever heard. It melted away any remnants of tension between us. I glanced down at my phone and saw a notification from Fabian.

"Tomorrow. He's coming over to deal with the Asial issue," I said, answering her inquiring look while my fingers swept over the screen asking if he'd found Elizabeth and retrieved the Laes. He responded quickly with: Not yet, but soon.

"Do I need to get a detail for Asial?" she asked.

"No, I'll do until I find a way to manage him. He might surprise us and behave."

My response lacked any air of certainty because there wasn't any. I trusted Dareus more than I trusted Asial. But at least I was no longer bound to the oath.

CHAPTER 36

$\mathcal{F}$abian arrived at my apartment, his gracious smile tightening when he caught sight of Cory. His warm greeting was a contrast to the rigid smile he directed at him.

"My magic hasn't returned. So, Cory's going to summon him," I offered as an excuse opposed to the actual reason: Cory's interest in seeing the magic that made a demon corporeal, which was the reason he gave me in order to hide the other reason, which was that he was apprehensive about Fabian. It wasn't that he didn't trust him, but he was cautious of him.

"He gave you his name, correct?" Fabian asked.

I nodded.

"The witch will not be needed. He will come."

"I don't mind staying. It will be interesting seeing eleven magic in its purest form."

What was intended as flattery missed the mark. Fabian's lips pressed into a tight line as his eyes slowly moved over Cory.

"This is elven matters, and it should remain that way."

"I don't mind Cory staying," I insisted.

"I do." Fabian was leaving no room for debate. But it needed be discussed. Why were the elves so secretive about their abilities and so committed to living in the shadows?

"He can be trusted," I assured him. Fabian stepped closer, his graceful swift movements causing Cory to stiffen at his approach. How protective Cory had become was something I wasn't going to get used to. Perhaps once my life was restored to some semblance of normal, he'd calm some.

"Erin." Fabian's hand rested over mine, giving it an encouraging squeeze. "This is elven matters. I do this not just to honor Nolan, but because you are one of us."

Even with my magic gone and Nolan as my only link to them, he still considered me an elf. It shouldn't have meant so much to me, and I felt naive for feeling that way—but it did. I hadn't realized how much Elizabeth's rejection had affected me. Fabian's inclusion eased it, but it didn't supersede everything that Cory meant to me. Me excluding him and Madison from my plans for Malific nearly ruined our relationship. I wouldn't threaten it again.

"I want him here," I asserted.

"I understand. My help here is no longer needed. Be well." He slipped past me and was at the door before I could offer a rebuttal or plead my case.

"I'll leave," Cory blurted, shooting me a look of disapproval. I had overplayed my hand and nearly lost my chance of satisfying my oath. "Call me later," he said, stepping past Fabian, their eyes connecting in a cool challenge.

"I don't like being threatened," I said. Fabian had positioned himself until he was inches from me.

"In what way did you feel threatened?"

"Taking away assistance that you'd offered, because you didn't get your way. How is that not a threat?"

"My way," he whispered slowly, as if attempting to interpret the meaning. He bit his bottom lip as he studied me. "Do you think my motives are selfish?"

"I don't know what to think."

After a flat-eyed evaluation of me, he said, "I protect the knowledge of our magic, because it puts us in danger. You fall under that protection and *my way* is the belief that we are a collective, blood bound to protect each other. I offer this with no other demand than that you hold these values in the same importance as I do."

"I won't betray my friends for the elves."

His brows furrowed. "Have I asked that of you?"

"No." I was embarrassed by the insinuation.

A bright smile claimed his face. "I never will. I do ask for understanding and acceptance that you are part of the collective and you feel duty-bound to protect our kind. Which is in desperate need since there are so few."

I was reluctant to agree. I suspected my cynicism had warped into nihilism and I was suspicious of everything. The cult language wasn't doing him any favors, either.

He took my hands in his in the same manner he had in the Havenage.

"Can this be important to you as well?"

"I don't want to do anything to hurt the elves," I provided in a variation to his cult-like wording. Internally I made an exception for Elizabeth. She'd escaped my retaliation, but I didn't have any desire to protect her. I was firmly on the team that would do harm to her. My answer must have been acceptable because he moved to the center of my living room, where Cory had already made the demon circle, and walked around it checking for security.

"May I see the contract?" he asked. Making an attempt to call it, I was reminded of my missing magic. Recognizing his mistake, he gave me a weak smile and pulled a retractable pin stick from his pocket. "May I?" he asked, extending his hand. Placing my hand in his, he pricked my finger. He pulled the contract and then slipped the pin stick into his shirt pocket with a smooth flick of his hand before studying the contract.

"I'll summon him," he told me after requesting Asial's summoning name. Seconds after he whispered the summons, Asial appeared in his human form, humming with excitement at the sight of Fabian. If he'd been a dog, his tail would have been frantically wagging.

"Erin." Asial greeted me with very little regard, fixated as he was on the obvious elf, from the pointed ears, sharp features, wizened eyes, and posturing of powerful otherworldly magic. Entwined in his excitement was surprise. He'd probably been resigned to the idea I'd be his host.

Fabian offered a diminutive pleasantry. "Your corporeal body will satisfy this debt, correct?"

Asial bobbed his head, unable to tamp down his excitement, which gave me a renewed sense of pause. Fabian's foot slipped over the line, breaking the circle and releasing Asial. His smoky incorporeal body swirled, in need of a willing host, while Fabian spoke a series of words in his language. Asial slowly became more solid. After several minutes of spell casting, Asial stood before me in human form. He moved around, familiarizing himself with his surroundings, touching things in my apartment, looking out of the window, breathing in the air.

"I must change," Asial said. His shoulders rose and fell. His chest expanded and his breathing became more labored as he prepared for his demon form, which took him several minutes to achieve, much longer than it had in his realm. I'd seen it before, and Fabian looked upon it with boredom. "With practice it will get better," he said to himself before taking more time to transition back to the more palatable human form.

"I'm sure you are aware of Dareus's fate?" Fabian said.

Asial tensed and took several steps back, a dark gust of magic pushing from him. Fabian held his hand up.

"I have no desire for that to be your fate. I can ensure that you are shielded from that by anyone of my kind," he told him. "But I would require an oath from you."

Asial regarded him with suspicion.

"The Black Crest grimoire," Fabian announced. "I'd like you to help me find all copies of them. That is all. As you must know, it is important that we limit all replication of our magic. By doing this, you help your kind as well."

Asial's posture relaxed.

"And for this oath?"

"Immunity from ever being sent back."

"How many copies do you know of?"

"You have more knowledge of this than I do. I'm hoping this will forge an alliance between you and the elves. I don't care what you do here—you will be left to your own devices. Elves will not govern the behavior of demons. I just want to protect our magic."

Fabian had enticed him. Asial didn't want to be subjected to any rules. Elves, who had more influence over him, removing all constraints ensured he would not be inactive. I would have to find a way to monitor him and rein him in. Constantly babysitting a demon wasn't something I wanted, but for now, it would be my job.

Proving my suspicion that this deal had been premeditated, Fabian produced a half-page contract. Asial looked over it, his lips twitching with effort not to show his joy at the turn of events.

"This says that I will make a good faith effort to find all Black Crest grimoires. What if there aren't any?"

"Then you have satisfied your oath. You are aware how contracts are. They are bound to your intentions. If you violate it, you violate the oath."

What a crappy contract. He could just basically ask around occasionally and that would satisfy his oath. Before I could object, Fabian had produced the same pin stick that he'd used on me. Asial, seemingly afraid that Fabian would see the error and the apparent ease of circumventing the contract, quickly extended his finger, allowing Fabian to prick it and sign the oath. Fabian looked at it, then with a flitter of his hand, whisked it away.

Pulses of magic enveloped the room as Fabian moved closer to Asial.

"You are bound in agreement to help me and mine find the remainder of the Black Crest grimoires. With this, do you give me permission to perform the Minesa spell?"

Asial enthusiastically agreed.

Fabian's hand pressed against Asial's chest. Fabian inhaled and spoke the words. A smile of defiance spread over Asial's face as he looked at me. He'd avoided any accountability for any actions and would be given free rein here without fear of repercussions.

Smugness vanished as his eyes widened. The shift happened so quickly and profoundly. A human man, aging before my eyes. Wrinkled, grayish skin sagged from him, his body losing height from the notable curve in his spine. Asial took hollow, gasping breaths before he collapsed to his knees. On my floor wasn't the thirty-something human image that Asial had shown me numerous times, but an unusually aged corpse.

Fabian was too casual about his demon murder. "Your contract has been fulfilled," he said coolly. "Will you be able to get rid of the body?"

Rushing to Asial, I knelt down next to him. "What the fuck, Fabian, what did you do?"

"I satisfied your contract."

"This...this. What the—" Fuck. That was all I had. Clusters and clusters of fucks.

"And the grimoires. How are you going to get the rest? What did you do? Why is he like this?" Asial had died a human death. This was a human man on my floor. A dead human man.

"There are two. One was destroyed and we will eventually obtain the second and destroy it as well."

"And this?" I waved my hand at Asial's soon-to-be-decaying human body.

"Minesa spell." He dismissed it with a wave of his hand.

"Did you even need to see my contract with Asial?" The accusation of his deceit wasn't hidden in my tone.

"No, I just needed your blood. Human fragility is often the peril of most. Your blood mingled with his allowed the spell to age him to death. You didn't kill him or have him killed, therefore never violating the terms of the contract. Old age killed him." The finger prick that he used on me, then on Asial. "I knew what was in the contract from the first showing. Asial needed to agree to the spell. He was proud of the advantage he was getting over you, especially when your expression betrayed your opposition. Not once did he consider that he was putting himself in peril. I'm sure he knew that there weren't enough editions of the grimoire to warrant such a trade. The desire to live unconstrained was too appealing. There was no honesty or virtue in him."

That was a pretty self-aggrandizing speech for someone who just tricked a demon and then killed him.

He'd gotten me out of my oath with Asial, but it had been achieved by deceiving both of us. A hollow thank you was all I could muster. I wanted to see Fabian as the white knight who fixed a bad situation, but something nagged at me. How flawlessly and coldly precise he executed it by playing into Asial's character flaws. There was a tinge of disdain when he spoke of human fragility. A fragility that existed in both me and Nolan.

"I'm happy I was able to help. Has this satisfied my obligation to you?" he asked.

I shook my head, not knowing if this was an oversight but rather another deception. "The Laes. The Huntsmen need it back."

"Of course. And that will satisfy the strife between you and Elizabeth?"

"You'd have to ask her. I'm not the one who tried to get her killed by the Huntsmen, linked her to a psychopath who isn't deterred by pain, or caused her to be imprisoned in the demon realm," I spat back.

The slow roving smile of understanding flitted across his lips. "She has many things to atone for, and she will."

More questions whirled around in my mind, but Fabian didn't stay around long enough for me to sort them and ask. He left with the assurance that he'd notify me the moment he had the Laes.

CHAPTER 37

"He created life." Cory had spewed for the sixth time, looking at the grayish human form I'd covered with a blanket. Madison was still processing everything I told them.

"Technically, he didn't create life. He made him human and did a spell to age him to death," I said.

"Oh, because that is so different. Fuuuuck." Cory was going to have a bald spot if he didn't stop grabbing at his hair.

"It wasn't as easy as you're making it sound. Fabian had to use the same pin stick on Asial that he'd used on me to intermingle our blood and then get Asial to consent to the spell being done. There were boxes that needed to be checked before the spell could be executed." I added, offering me the same comfort I was trying to extend to Cory. This wasn't an easy spell. I needed to believe that.

"Fabian manipulated you both into this," Cory pointed out. His ominous look of concern when he stopped pacing wasn't hard to read. My blood had made a demon human at the helm of elven magic. What would it produce with a vampire?

"I don't think it was human blood that he needed. It was *your* blood. And only the small amount left on the pin. Malific has a unique control over life. I believe you possess similar abilities," Madison speculated.

"You cannot create any vampires with Landon. Find a way to get out of the debt," Cory urged me, Madison's head bobbing in agreement. But what could I offer that would dissuade Landon?

As Cory occupied himself with getting rid of the body with a spell, Madison sat in the kitchen nook, paper in hand, cataloging elves' magical abilities while I replayed everything that had transpired between me and Fabian. When he asked me to agree to protect the elves, was it a verbal or a magical contract? No magic passed between us; I was sure of that.

"Can other elves shift into animals?" Madison asked, breaking into my thoughts.

"No, just me, and technically I can only shift into *one* animal."

The twisted moue of irritation and prompt return to her paper made it clear that wasn't important. After moments of deliberation with her paper, looking at the empty space where the humanized demon had been, Madison frowned. "I want to paint him as this monster, but I can't," she admitted. "Is it something we wouldn't have done, if we had the knowledge? We spent days trying to figure out a way to nullify the contract. He was successful at it."

"Murder—The Success Story, available on Hulu," Cory mumbled. We were in the grayest of areas, a place we'd been before, but Cory couldn't navigate out of it this time. It was rooted in his suspicions and dislike of Fabian.

"Cory," I entreated.

"I know," he said with a sigh. "I'm just frustrated. These reveals about other magical beings are getting more horrifying. I know you said Fabian denied any connection between the elves and demons, but there has to be. And this seems wrong. Like using a familial link to cause harm. It's ridiculous but it's how I feel."

I agreed with him. And was navigating around the internal debate of whether Fabian had been truthful with me so far. "He hasn't lied to me," I said. It was true. "He omitted information, manipulated the situation, but he didn't lie to me."

"Be careful around him, okay?"

I gave Cory a reassuring smile.

"He's going to ask you to go to the Havenage," Madison asserted without any hint of doubt. Rarely was she that sure of anything. "What will be your answer?"

"No." The answer didn't require much consideration. I belonged here, where my life—despite being magicless—had the potential to be normal. "If my magic doesn't return, things might not be so bad." I turned to Cory. "It's my magic that draws Landon. You think he won't notice things are different with me? Inviting me to the Havenage when I don't have magic would be of no benefit to them. I hope Malific is dead, but she can't be released or harm me if she's not. The elves are the only ones who can open the Blose Chasm—and we don't have to worry about them ever doing it." One of the few things I could be absolutely positive about was that the elves wouldn't open the Chasm.

Concern drained from Cory's and Madison's faces as they chose to see the benefits of my new situation. Armed with a fresh perspective and different life, I felt optimistic about my future. Hell, I was even looking forward to a magicless existence.

A smile curled Madison's lips and a glint lit in her eyes. "And if you're looking for more changes, we're still looking for employees for the archives department."

The job didn't appeal to me the first time she offered it and it didn't appeal to me now.

CHAPTER 38

"*P*roblem, Clay?" I finally asked. It was the third time I'd caught him scrutinizing me while I ate the omelet Isley had prepared for brunch. Of the five days I'd been at Mephisto's, Clayton had joined us for three meals, and today had brought Madison with him.

He shook his head and smirked. "Just musing over the pretentious opulence of some lifestyles," he said, sending an accusatory gaze in Mephisto's direction.

His teasing was limited with Madison present because she was quick to point out the hypocrisy in his judgment, which she had done when he made a snide remark about Mephisto's car in the driveway. Madison responded by pointing out the extravagance of an in-home theatre, home gym, and a luxury shower with a rock wall. "It was like showering in a cave," she told me a few days ago. She also mentioned his collection of motorcycles and the wall-size aquarium in his living room. Upon further investigation, one that Madison refused to terminate at his request, she discovered that Mephisto didn't own a plane.

Unable to give him a pass on his hypocrisy, Madison had

her counter-remarks in the chamber in response to Clayton's teasing of Mephisto's *lifestyle*.

"Yes, please do go on. Did those musings venture into your mind earlier in my pool, or while joining us for brunch?" Mephisto volleyed back with a taunting grin.

It was comforting to see their banter return to where it once existed.

Clayton shrugged. "It comes and goes."

"Oftentimes at your convenience."

"Coming at an inconvenient time would do nothing to help my ridicule, now would it?"

Mephisto dismissed his response with a shake of his head.

Again I caught Clayton's inquiring gaze on me and a silent exchange between him and Mephisto. It didn't seem to bother Madison, or she'd missed the signs that they were doing it.

"Stop it! If it's concerning me, I want to know."

After a few moments of consideration, Clayton said, "How are you doing, Erin?" A simple but potent question, gilded with concern.

He'd managed to keep it from showing on his face, but it was replete in his voice. Since the situation with Fabian and Asial, I had settled into my new norm, life without magic. Mephisto was convinced that my magic would return, but he believed Fabian knew it would take longer than he'd informed me but was reluctant to tell me in case I wouldn't go through with the plan. I wasn't sure of that. I was convinced it was an unexpected situation. With all Fabian's interest and pronouncements, I was still a part-caste and only of use to them if I had elven magic. After a series of debates, we agreed to disagree.

"Fine, I really am." An assurance that garnered more scrutiny and sheer fascination. Whatever tension Madison held, relaxed, a smile spreading and reaching her eyes after studying me for a few minutes. It wasn't a lie.

Most of my life I had lived without magic, and my complex relationship with it was woven into the fabric of my being. Living with magic both elven and god, and finding peace without it, was something I didn't realize would be such a radical thing for them. I was an oddity to be dissected and studied. At the root of it was how most magic wielders responded when their magic was temporarily restricted. The most refined, even-keeled person became a rabid animal, clawing and rampaging against the restriction if it lasted too long.

Nodding in acceptance, he and Mephisto exchanged a look. I wasn't sure what it meant, but the stifled camaraderie between me and Clayton had changed. I suspected it had a lot to do with my sacrifice. I understood why. Unintentionally, I remained an obstacle to them returning to the Veil. I was reaping benefits from their sacrifices while not viewed as making any of my own. It was a flawed perception but colored by their single-minded desire to go home.

There was a tacit acceptance that life would be managed differently now. We'd have to succeed where Fabian had failed and find Elizabeth or an alternative path to them getting back to the Veil. Despite my acceptance of being magicless, I would have to live in a perpetual state of the unknown when it came to my magic. Was Malific dead? Nothing was definite. Was she dead and Fabian was wrong? Or was she clinging to life and once it ended, my magic would return?

From his desk, Mephisto had stopped with the furtive glances he'd been giving me for the past hour as I sat on the opposite side of the room, curled up on the modish, utilitarian sofa that was more comfortable than it looked, sorting through my emails for potential jobs in an attempt to revitalize my suffering business.

"You don't intend to give yourself any rest before returning to work?" he asked.

"I did rest. I've been here five days on a staycation, and I had another four-day stay where I was brought food and uniformed people made sure I didn't die."

He frowned. "Erin, just choose a place and we can go for a few days. Get out of the city and relax."

It wasn't about relaxing but giving me a distraction. He saw past my façade of indifference. A magicless existence didn't bother me, but I was aware how much my life had changed. Whether I accepted it or not, it was different. Malific may not be a direct threat, but Elizabeth was. Being a realist, if the magic she was using eluded Fabian, I wasn't confident in our ability to find her. What chance did I have working around whatever obfuscation or cloaking spell was keeping her hidden?

And my relationship with the elves was in limbo. Mephisto's persistence about handling the Landon situation meant it had moved to the top of the list. We had a meeting scheduled later in the week when I planned to put the cards on the table—tell him everything, or a very hopeless version of it. He would see that he wouldn't be creating a new version of vampire, just the same run-of-the-mill, unimpressive, bland vampire that every vampire created. That would discourage him more than anything. Finding more joy in that prospect than I should have, the notification on my phone startled me.

Fabian. He wanted to surrender the Laes.

Mephisto appeared to have difficulty removing the hopeful skepticism from his expression. Looking away from me, he inhaled a deep breath. "That's promising."

It wasn't just promising. It was the end of a fifty-odd-year search. The end of banishment. A return to his old life. I settled into the joy of it, ignoring the bittersweet sadness that accompanied it.

Even through his reticence, he notified Kai, Simeon, Clay, and Benton about Fabian's visit and the return of the Laes.

Fabian arrived at Mephisto's later than expected, entering the home with reserved hostility that morphed into unabashed censure. Fabian's behavior was unexpected and unsettling. He hadn't seemed to have had a problem meeting me at Mephisto's, but clearly he had, or maybe it was dealing with Mephisto again and the obvious enmity that existed between them.

"You all do seem to have quite an interest in us," Fabian said. His statement provided the reason for his hostility. I wasn't able to determine if he had a problem with Mephisto, or a problem with me being with Mephisto. Did he believe that our relationship was contingent on my magic—elven magic—and its disappearance would have meant the end of it?

"Not you all, just her."

Fabian frowned. "A distinction without a difference. A god interested in an elf, how expected."

Mephisto's languid look of apathy traveled over Fabian, illustrating that his thoughts and opinions were unimportant. Fabian put noticeable effort into the appearance of it not bothering him.

"Has your magic returned?" Fabian asked me.

"Not yet."

"It will. And when it does, know that you are welcomed at the Havenage for further education."

"You have Elizabeth?" I wanted confirmation, although it was doubtful that the Laes would be in his possession if she wasn't.

"She is with us." Easing closer to me, he added, "It is important that you know Elizabeth is not your enemy. We all share the goal of protecting the elves. One you claim to share as well." Whether we shared a goal or not, I hoped that she hadn't just been sanctioned but imprisoned. Or at the very least, confined to the Havenage where she could no longer be a threat to me.

"Elizabeth made me her enemy, I had no say in it," I reminded him.

Frowning, he sighed, using the time to gather his words. The consideration was apparent in the dark depths of his eyes that withdrew into thought. "Erin the person wasn't who she considered an enemy. It was what you represented. Malific's daughter. I believe that animus is no more."

He handed Mephisto an oddly shaped aqua-colored object that looked similar to a misshapen trefoil. Inspection of the markings on the bottom edge of it sent a flash of anger over Mephisto. He barreled into Fabian and hoisted him in the air, Fabian's feet searching for purchase. Gurgling sounds came from him as Mephisto's fingers pressed into his windpipe.

"Do you think I don't know what a mortem spell is? Who dies if we destroy this?" Fury reverberated in his voice. "Is this linked to Erin?" Mephisto growled.

Fabian's life was dependent on the right answer. The muscles of Mephisto's arms were becoming tauter as he pressed harder. When an answer didn't come, he eased his hold enough to allow him to speak.

"She's an elf, I'd never hurt her," Fabian rasped out.

"Then who?"

His eyes dropped to Mephisto's arm, signaling he wouldn't speak until released. A request Mephisto didn't seem amenable to honoring.

"Let him go, Mephisto," I urged, sidling up next to him.

Releasing him, Fabian fell to the floor into a crouched position.

"You must know, I am committed to keeping Erin alive."

Fabian's attention shifted to me. "Remember when you asked if there was a connection between the demons and elves?"

Apprehensive, my head barely moved into the nod.

"There isn't, but there is one between the fae and elves. I don't care about them, but you do." He whispered a spell, the markings from the mortem spell on the Laes quickly becoming obscured by other interlocking symbols. The ones I could make out reminded me of symbols of the fae courts.

Flashing in my thoughts was Madison, his visit with her, and how he had manipulated Asial into agreeing to a spell that killed him. It all converged into something that needed to be sort out. My mind raced. The pounding of my heart matched the images that ran through my mind as I went over everything she told me about his visit.

"Explain," I demanded, my nails pressing into the palms of my balled fists.

"We can influence their magic and manipulate it to our advantage. May I?" Fabian requested. Mephisto handed him the Laes. "It is a mortem spell." His fingers raked along the symbols at the bottom. Mephisto's expression didn't reveal his lack of understanding and I would have missed the tick in his jaw if I hadn't been watching him so intensely. We both knew something was wrong, but not what.

Fabian swallowed up the minute distance left between us. He whispered another spell, and the symbols repeated atop of the other.

"Erin, please know my actions are altruistic, even if you do not agree with my methods. Malific is cruel, bloodthirsty, and unreasonable, but no one can accuse her of not having a vision. It was the wrong one. Elves can't be allied with gods, nor should we live under your rule." He directed a warranted watchful eye in Mephisto's direction.

"I don't believe you should be under our rule, either," Mephisto challenged.

"A sentiment we share. One of very few. I believe free

movement through the Veil shouldn't exist. You will have your world, and we'll have ours." Fabian moved to Mephisto. His long fingers swept over the bottom of the Laes then he handed it back to Mephisto. The markings glowed, and another matching string of markings covered the Laes. Mephisto's expression showed the effort it took not to use the Laes to bludgeon Fabian.

"What are the markings on the Laes, Erin?" Fabian asked.

Inching closer, I looked at them.

"Do you remember the plant spell?"

I nodded, pulling together the threads of information he was doling out at an infuriating rate. Elizabeth wanted the Huntsmen gone and never to return. The plant spell: using one species to affect another. The pieces weren't forming well enough to make sense. How could destruction of the Laes affect the fae?

Fabian addressed us both, but I garnered all his focus. "The mortem spell is for the fae. To stop it, the Laes must be destroyed. It will also release the Huntsmen from their imprisonment. Once they pass through, it will be closed."

"Then I guess I won't destroy the Laes," Mephisto challenged.

Fabian's brow rose. "You will. A relationship with a woman whose sister's death is at your hand would be impossible. We both know that. You're on the clock."

Duplicate markings twined around the Laes. "I wouldn't let the spell be completed if I were you and if you truly care about Erin." He wouldn't explicitly say that once the spell covered the Laes, it would be completed, but I knew. The illuminated sigils continued to wrap around the Laes at a consistent tick. Time was limited.

My mouth dried. Breathing came in short shallow bursts. I wasn't getting enough oxygen to stay lucid for long.

"An elven spell that involves life or death must be agreed upon. That's why you needed Asial's consent," I blurted.

There was no way Madison would agree to such a thing. "No fae in their right mind would agree to this damn thing. No trickery could get them to."

"Elizabeth is a part-caste. Elf and..."

He waited for me to answer. But I couldn't bear to say it aloud. "Elizabeth would never agree to it. If the Laes isn't destroyed, then she'll die, too."

"She *would* agree to such a thing because she knows that you would not sacrifice Madison's life for revenge against her. We all know that." His face grew grim. "Sacrifices need to be made, Erin. Elizabeth's surrender came at a cost and this is it. The Huntsmen must leave. As I said before, Elizabeth is a wealth of information and untapped spells. She's the one who learned how to close the Veil. Once they are gone, I will close it for good."

Out of my periphery, I could see Mephisto calculating the situation. Malice lingered behind his intent. Would ending Fabian stop a spell that had already been set in motion?

"Fabian, please, give us more time. Halt the spell," I pleaded in a reedy voice that I didn't even recognize. It came from the depths of my desperation.

Fabian's eyes slipped from me to Mephisto. And when it returned to me, there was a dark cast of disdain. "Time is the one thing I refuse to give them." Then he moved his finger between me and Mephisto. "To this." His response was laced with ridicule.

Another line of sigils wrapped around the Laes before I felt the surge. Something I hadn't felt in over a week, the thrum of otherness that had dwelled in me. Magic overwhelmed me and interwove with the anger that brewed. The sphere hit Fabian's chest. Shock rendered him unable to respond fast enough before crashing into the wall. He covered himself with a protective wall and I rushed to bring it down. It wavered but never fell. I kept trying to disable it but without success.

"Erin, you're still a part-caste. An *impressive* part-caste and a threat to others with inferior magic. But not mine."

Deception. Fabian had proven to be a master at it.

As if he'd read my thoughts, he said, "Not deception… motivation. You are talented. You needed to know it. Feel confident in it. I cultivated that in you. What would I have proven by defeating your efforts before they were fully realized?"

"You're no better than Elizabeth," I hissed.

"Perhaps. The magic you have now is because of Elizabeth. She is the ally you will always need. One willing to do the distasteful. You put things in motion, but it was Elizabeth who finished it."

"Malific's dead," I whispered. Elizabeth got to do what she wanted all along: kill Malific. Something she'd never have achieved if I hadn't left her nearly dead.

Fabian glanced at the Laes and offered a mirthless smile. "Tick, tick, tick. There isn't much time left," he told us. "He needs to leave before the spell is complete or be responsible for the death of the fae until the Laes is destroyed. Choose now: the life of your sister or a life with Mephisto."

I couldn't look back at Mephisto. He knew what the decision would be. The pressure of his hands against my back before turning me to face him made tears well in my eyes. I refused to let them spill in front of Fabian. He wouldn't get any satisfaction from this.

"Now." He wasn't talking to me, just letting me in on a conversation that he'd shared with the others. Magic and emotions thickened the air. Kai, Simeon, Clay, and Benton entered. The Huntsmen glared at the man sequestered from them by his field of magic. The very thing saving his life— and what I desperately wished I could break.

Mephisto traced his fingers along my jaw. Then he kissed me. A long, tender kiss. It was all him. An experience I had for too short a time but would miss immensely. Slipping my hands into his, we clasped them tight.

He looked in the Huntsmen and Benton's direction. "We have to go," he told them. There was some commotion in the background behind me. The sound of fingers on phones. Were they executing contingency plans? I had no idea. My glare seared into Fabian as Mephisto coaxed me to release his hands. The effort it took to let go was exhausting.

Mephisto hugged me and placed a kiss on my temple. Then, pressing his lips to my ear, he whispered, "There's no fucking way we end like this. I will be back." The assertion was made with the conviction of a promise. One he'd never break. It emboldened me enough to put some space between us. Losing any grace of movement, I lumbered back a few feet from Mephisto.

At the sound of breaking glass and a victorious look of satisfaction on Fabian's face, I closed my eyes, breaking my promise as one obstinate tear escaped. When I opened them, Fabian had released the field and was inches away from me.

"This was for the good of our kind. A new beginning. You will soon realize I'm not the enemy. This was done for the betterment of us all. You'll see," he promised.

Worry glazed over his features as he studied me. All the emotions from the betrayal, Fabian's concession to Elizabeth along with their alliance, the threat on Madison's life, and sending Mephisto away culminated into a virulent fury and thirst for revenge. And I couldn't keep the emotions from showing.

Face to face with Fabian, I snarled. "Perhaps you believe you're not my enemy, but I'm sure as hell yours. If you thought Malific was a terror—you have no idea what her daughter's going to be like."

MESSAGE TO THE READER

Thank you for choosing *Hellcrossed* from the many titles available to you. My goal is to create an engaging world, compelling characters, and an interesting experience for you. I hope I've accomplished that. Reviews are very important to authors and help other readers discover our books. Please take a moment to leave a review. I'd love to know your thoughts about the book.

For notifications about new releases, *exclusive* contests and giveaways, and cover reveals, please sign up for my mailing list at McKenzieHunter.com.

CPSIA information can be obtained
at www.ICGtesting.com
Printed in the USA
BVHW050115080223
658118BV00012B/314

9 781946 457226